I0523046

PRAISE FOR LARA BERNHARDT

From the very first book, Kimberly Wantland demonstrates she is someone who recognizes that both the spirits and the living are haunted.

— RICK LUDWIG, AUTHOR OF *THE MAUI MYSTERY SERIES*

Keep these stories coming!

— AMAZON REVIEWER

Each book in this series just gets better and better!

— AMAZON REVIEWER

Lara Bernhardt is a jewel of a writer.

— AMAZON REVIEWER

HALLOWEEN IN HANNIBAL

The Wantland Files Book 4

LARA BERNHARDT

Halloween in Hannibal

Copyright © 2021 by Lara Bernhardt

Print and eBook editions published by Admission Press

All rights reserved.

This is a work of fiction. Names, characters, organizations, places, events, and incidents are either products of the author's imagination or are used fictitiously. Any resemblance to actual persons, living or dead, or actual events is purely coincidental.

No part of this book may be reproduced in any form or by any electronic or mechanical means, including information storage and retrieval systems, without written permission from the author, except for the use of brief quotations in a book review.

Cover design by BEAUTeBOOK

LARA BERNHARDT

HALLOWEEN IN HANNIBAL

THE WANTLAND FILES

ADMISSION PRESS

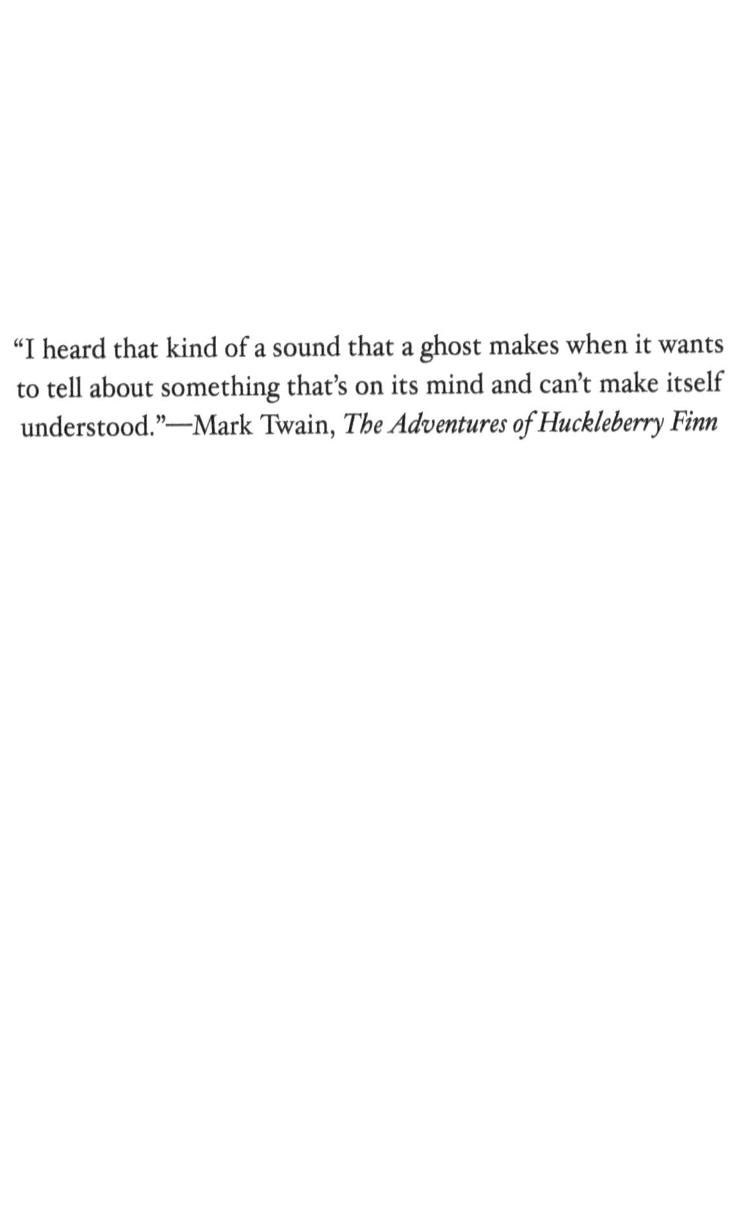

"I heard that kind of a sound that a ghost makes when it wants to tell about something that's on its mind and can't make itself understood."—Mark Twain, *The Adventures of Huckleberry Finn*

KAYLA WATCHED her boyfriend pick the lock, shivering and sweating in the heat and humidity of a sweltering Hannibal summer. Crickets chirped in the distance. For the thousandth time she imagined footsteps, sure they were about to be discovered.

"This is a terrible idea, Cory. Let's just go home."

"I thought you wanted to see a ghost. You said you wouldn't be scared."

Typical Cory, taking her words out of context and twisting the meaning. "Not what I said and you know it."

Cory grunted as the metal picks slipped from the lock. "Damn it!" He glowered at her and retrieved his tools. "Yes, you did. I'm doing this for you."

"I said that if your aunt was cool with it, I'd love a tour of the building. And that I didn't think I'd be scared of a ghost if we happened to see one. I never suggested you break in. Where'd you learn to pick locks anyway?" This was the sort of thing it seemed she ought to know about her boyfriend.

He squinted, angling the tiny picks back into place. "You-Tube video."

"Seriously? And you had lockpicks laying around your house?"

"Nah. Ordered 'em off Amazon."

"Of course you did. Now that we've established I never requested a B and E, can we please—"

A click from the lock lit Cory's face. "Got it!" He turned the knob and opened the door.

Somewhere in the hallway, a security alarm beeped, demanding the code.

"Oh my God, Cory! They have an alarm!"

"Yep." He sauntered to the glowing panel, opened it, and tapped buttons. The beeping stopped.

Cory held his arms wide, expecting applause, praise, hugs—or maybe all of the above. "Who's awesome?"

"How did you know that code? Did you steal it?" She could not get in trouble. *Could not*. Her parents would—

"Nope. My aunt let me work here a couple summers ago and gave me the code."

"And it's still the same?"

"You kidding? They're old. They don't change their passwords."

"We're still breaking and entering. We're here without permission."

"My aunt won't press charges. Even if we somehow get caught. Which we won't." He held out a hand. "And night is the best time to catch a glimpse of a ghost. Right? Wouldn't that be awesome? Our 'What I Did During the Summer' essays will blow everyone away."

That would be super cool. And who would ever know? "You promise I'll be home by midnight? I can't get in trouble. My parents would ground me so fast—"

He placed a hand over his heart and bowed deeply. "Your sainted curfew shall be hallowed as always."

"Hey! Just because your dad lets you—"

"Come on!" He grabbed her hand and yanked. "You're wasting valuable time."

She'd crossed the threshold. They were doing this. Nerves bubbled over into giggles.

"What's funny?" Cory asked.

"I dunno. It is kind of thrilling."

He lit up, clearly delighted he'd won her over. "Heck, yeah. What first? The stage? Props? Costumes?"

She squeezed his hand. "Show me everything."

He led her through the hallway, winding from the back entrance toward the front of the building. The flashlight from his cellphone illuminated the path, playing off old wood paneling and floors. The building smelled old, but not musty or dirty. A chill ran down her spine.

In the lobby, she could see the huge doors leading from the street entrance, plus the doors into what she knew was the actual church, where services had been held. She'd like to see that too, but Cory went straight to the stairs.

"The theatre is in the basement," he said.

"You told me before."

She picked her way carefully down the worn carpeting of the stairway. Outside the soft, limited glow of the phone flashlight, she couldn't see much of anything. The thought of being alone in complete darkness sent a shiver running down her spine. She squeezed Cory's hand.

Inside the auditorium, he led her to a row of center seats and flopped down. He patted the one beside him. "Best seats in the house."

"I thought we were going to look around," she said, though the idea of wandering through a costume shop and construction area in the dark sounded less fun and creepier the longer they remained.

"We will. Let's sit for a bit."

"I'd rather be on stage than in the audience."

"Come on. Sit."

She threw her hands up in surrender and did as he suggested. He stretched and fake-yawned and the next thing she knew his arm was around her. "What are you doing?"

"Just getting comfortable." He turned off his cellphone flashlight and pocketed the device.

She heard a noise from the stage. "What was that?"

"I didn't hear anything. Relax."

"I'm sure I heard something."

"No one else is here. Maybe it was the building creaking."

"Cory, it's really dark in here. Can you maybe turn on a light?"

"I dunno. I kinda like the dark." He leaned close and kissed her.

She forgot about the sound and kissed him back. Her parents didn't like her to date and had only recently, and reluctantly, allowed Cory to take her out unchaperoned. Kissing was still new—and he was good at it. He wrapped both arms around her, leaning into the kiss. She opened her mouth, a fluttering excitement skipping through her stomach.

But then his hands started to roam and grope. She didn't know if she was ready for that. Kissing was one thing, but he seemed to be pushing for more tonight. She broke off the kiss and pushed him away.

"What?" he panted. "What's wrong?"

"What are you doing?"

"Enjoying being alone. How often do we manage to be completely alone? No one to interfere?"

He leaned into her again, and she once again got swept away in his delicious mouth on hers. He had a point. Maybe they could find a quiet corner in the costume shop and—

Out of the corner of her eye, she saw a figure looming over them, a dark solid mass against the grayness around them. She leapt to her feet.

Cory fell forward before he caught himself. "Okay, jeez! Just say no. You don't have to—"

"I saw someone!" She breathed heavily, trying to calm her racing heartbeat.

"What? You're so jumpy. There's no one here."

She strained her eyes, staring at the spot she'd seen the dark figure a moment ago. She thrust her hand into her purse for her phone. Whatever Cory thought about the dark being awesome, she wanted a light. A rustling sound from the stage sent her spinning around.

A face ducked behind the curtain.

"Cory! Oh my God! Someone is in here!"

"Again? After you insisted you wouldn't be scared—"

She finally got her shaking hands to hold her phone and punched the button to turn on the light. She shone it on the curtains just in time to see them shimmy back into place.

"What the hell?" Cory jumped to his feet. "Hey! You're not supposed to be in here! Come out or I'm calling the cops!"

She tugged his sleeve and crouched on the floor behind the bank of chairs in front of them and whispered, "We're not supposed to be here either! You can't call anyone. Then we'd have to explain why *we're* here!"

"I can't leave some random guy in my aunt's theatre. What if he jacks the place up? She's already having financial problems."

"Let's get out of here. In the morning you can make some excuse to your aunt to come check on the place."

"Nah. Might be a hobo or something. I'm gonna go see."

She reached to grab him, but he shook her off. "You can't leave me here alone!"

"Come with me then."

"No way."

"Whatevs." He trotted down the aisle and stomped up the steps to the stage.

She watched his phone flashlight bob along in the darkness, dimly illuminating his form as he thrust his head through the curtains.

She held her breath.

Cory turned. "He's not here anymore. I'll check the back-stage area. You go upstairs and see if he ran up there to hide."

"Are you crazy? We can't split up! Don't you watch horror movies?"

She could hear the eyeroll in his tone. "This is not a horror movie. Probably just some drunk guy who wandered in and passed out."

"Wandered into a locked building?"

If Cory heard, he didn't answer. She crouched to the floor again, trying as hard as she could to be invisible and silent. Her thumping heart and rasping gasps made that impossible.

She took deep, controlled breaths and tried to reassure herself. *Everything will be fine.* They wouldn't be hacked to pieces by an axe murderer. That sort of thing didn't happen in real life.

A shadow fell over her.

She gasped and jerked her head up.

A draped figure stood directly in front of her. How? She hadn't heard any footsteps.

She crab-crawled backward, blinking and willing her brain to stop imagining things.

But the figure remained.

She turned and scrambled to her feet. "Cory! Cory, help me!"

She ran and didn't look back. She'd seen enough movies to know you don't look back. If you did, you either tripped and fell and the axe murderer got you or you ran smack into the axe murderer who somehow got in front of you when you looked away.

Okay. Okay, where were the doors? It was dark and she hadn't paid attention when they came in. And where was Cory?

She heard a noise and spun around. No dark figure. Where had it gone?

"Shit. Shit shit shit." She closed her eyes and pressed her fingers to her temples. *Don't panic. Think.* They came down the stairs into a lobby. Yes! She needed to get back to the lobby.

Feeling better, she turned, sure of the way out.

And ran right into a body.

She screamed and flailed her arms, pummeling with her fists.

"What the hell, Kayla?" Cory grabbed her arms.

Momentary relief gave way to fury. "Where have you been?"

"Looking for the hobo, duh. I can't find anyone. Did you?"

"Someone was here. Didn't you hear me yell for you?"

"You saw the hobo? In here? Why didn't you tell me?"

"I screamed for you. Where were you?"

Cory flipped on his cellphone flashlight, cutting a hazy beam through the darkness.

The curtain fluttered again.

"What the hell? I just checked back there."

"Cory, don't. Let's just go!" Tears pricked at her eyes. This wasn't fun. She wanted out.

Ignoring the stairs, Cory hopped onto the stage. Before he could right himself and investigate, the curtains parted.

A man stood there, grinning.

"What the—" Cory scrambled backwards so fast, he toppled off the edge of the stage, plunging them into darkness.

"*Where's my spotlight?*" A man's voice—not Cory's—echoed eerily through the theatre, a hollow sound that made her shudder.

The building alarm went off, angry screech piercing the dead quiet of the night.

She heard footsteps pounding. "Cory? Cory!"

She sat down on the floor, tucked her knees against her chest, and rocked back and forth. Cory had left her. Left her with the axe murderer! How could he? At least she thought he had. The shriek of the alarm filled her ears, drowning out potential breathing or footsteps.

Scared to move, too terrified to breathe, she fumbled for her cellphone. Maybe Cory was still here. Maybe he'd hurt himself when he fell. But then, what footsteps had she heard pounding up the aisle toward the lobby?

She wiped her sleeve across her forehead, mopping up the

sweat dripping from her temples. Taking a deep breath, she flipped on the flashlight. Careful to avoid illuminating the stage area, she shone the beam over the rest of the room—the banks of seats, the aisles. Nothing. Slowly she dragged the light to the stage edge. Nothing. She lifted it to the curtains. Nothing.

She bent forward, relieved, determined to catch her breath. Cory—that jerk! He'd ditched her and run for safety, leaving her alone. Her parents were right, he was bad news.

Scowling, she turned toward the aisle, formulating exactly what she'd say to Cory once she found him.

Her flashlight revealed the hem of a dark cloak. Her light went out.

"*Where's my spotlight?*" The question reverberated around the pitch-black room, echoing alongside her screams, drowned out by the sirens. A hand clamped down on her shoulder.

CHAPTER ONE

KIMBERLY WANTLAND PEERED over her sunglasses at the ramshackle building Sterling Wakefield cruised past in his i8. She glanced at her phone, where her map app confirmed she had arrived. "This is definitely it."

Sterling slowed to a crawl. "Doesn't look too spooky in the light of day."

She had to agree. "Old. Crumbling. Apparently an historic site, nearly condemned and demolished."

"Not sure it shouldn't be."

"I think the new owner would disagree. Well, newish owner. The woman who saved it."

He pulled into the parking lot. Several news vans sat waiting, replete with stylishly dressed reporters clutching microphones and less well-dressed camera operators, all waiting to pounce for the next story. A crowd of curious onlookers had gathered as well. Sterling's i8 set them off. Necks craned. Fingers pointed. They recognized his unique vehicle and knew the celebs sat inside. As the crowd buzzed, the reporters smoothed hair and outfits, lifted microphones, and started toward the car, their camera operators hoisting equipment to shoulders.

"Ready to go inside?" he asked.

A dull headache throbbed at her temples as she reached for the handle. "I have to be ready."

He grabbed her other hand and lifted it to his lips for a quick reminder that at least she didn't have to face the crowds alone anymore. "Sit still. I'll get your door. And remember, big smile!"

They'd been on the road together for weeks, creeping toward Hannibal as they reviewed and prepped previous investigation footage, responded to media requests for interviews and fan interaction, and tried to rest up a bit—and yet she still hadn't adapted to Sterling's determination to open doors for her, wedge himself between her and their over-exuberant fans (easier with female fans, naturally), bring her coffee in the morning, order on her behalf. She asked herself why she hesitated to accept these little gestures of kindness, why she continued to doubt the sincerity and watched for signs of ulterior motives.

Perhaps because she had been independent and self-sufficient for so long, she found it difficult to let anyone truly close, to let go of that tight grip on her life. She'd been taking care of herself since she was ten, ever since her mom fell down suddenly and inexplicably in the kitchen and never got back up. Heck, she'd stepped up and helped take care of her dad after that horrific, life-altering day. Later relationships always seemed to involve guys who wanted her to take care of them, one way or another. She found life easier without that sort of complication. Making all the decisions, functioning alone, calling all the shots— controlling and juggling everything in her life was difficult enough without adding a relationship.

And yet, she met Sterling's gaze and saw nothing but kindness and concern in the depths of those dark brown eyes, like always. He melted her heart. Every time. Melted the inner voice demanding she was a grown-ass woman, fully capable of taking care of herself. True, she acknowledged, and she'd proven it nearly her entire life. But, oh, it felt so good to know someone had her back. Did that make her weak?

Sterling shot her his characteristic grin—the one that sent

her stomach quivering and shivers of excitement jolting from her abdomen through the tips of her fingers—and popped his door open. Still smiling, he waved to the crowd, seemingly unperturbed by their raucous presence.

"Somebody see a ghost?" he asked, resulting in delighted laughter from the group. They flocked to him, a jumbled cacophony of delighted squeals, shouted questions, and pleas for selfies.

She marveled at his ability to take it all in stride. He swung from left to right, leaning in to flash his dazzling smile for one selfie after another, while managing to send back a response to every question lobbed at him.

He's mine, she thought, and went all squishy and warm. Funny, she didn't feel jealous anymore of the adoring female fans flocking to him, pressing in close, looking at him like they wanted to gobble him up with a spoon. Not even the one with the super low-cut blouse, thrusting her chest forward as she lifted her phone aloft for a picture of them together. Nope, not a bit. He was hers and hers alone and he made it clear daily. The woman threw her arms around Sterling and squeezed.

Okay, that's enough of that, lady. Kimberly grabbed for the door handle.

But of course Sterling extricated himself beautifully, before she could even get out of the car. She had to laugh at herself. Apparently the only thing she abhorred more than crowds of people were women hanging on her man. If someone had told her a year ago that she would be willingly launching herself into a noisy crowd to take her place next to Sterling Wakefield, she would have told them they were out of their mind.

Sterling held up his hands. "Okay, okay. You're scaring my partner. Everyone, take a step back and quiet down. I'll bet we can convince her to join us if you calm down."

Sheesh! What was she? An animal in the zoo, hiding under a rock?

A few shouts of "We love you, Kimberly!" erupted before a

general hush fell. No doubt about it—Sterling could handle a crowd. He had these fans and reporters wrapped around his little finger. He even convinced them to be quiet for her. And who could resist being praised like that? When he opened the door for her, the smile on her face was genuine, not forced for the benefit of the cameras.

Sterling looped an arm around her waist, pulled her close, and somehow maneuvered to keep the fans close enough to interact but far enough away she didn't feel threatened. No matter how the bodies around them ebbed and flowed, he angled himself between them and her. She waved and allowed photos—she even chatted with a few of them. Normally the most detested and most draining part of the job, hobnobbing and fan interaction didn't seem so bad with Sterling basically Velcroed to her hip.

She turned to him and caught his profile as he chatted with a young boy. Her chest swelled with delight and pride at his kindness even as she reined in the deep urges his features stirred in her—the cut of his cheekbones, the slant of his nose, and his eyes, those eyes that always caused her heart to stutter a bit. For all her belief in the paranormal and the influence of forces we couldn't begin to imagine much less understand, she could not fathom how this man made such a deep impact on her. The universe had dumped him in her lap.

Sterling pulled a quarter from behind the boy's ear. The boy's mouth dropped open, then he hid his face in his mother's stomach. The woman laughed and encouraged her son, "Go on, take it!"

In that moment, Kimberly couldn't understand or identify what she felt. Something overcame her, unlike anything she'd experienced before, possibly ever. She took mental check—nothing hurt, she could breathe fine, she wasn't stressed, her chakras all seemed aligned and balanced, nothing flared out of control—

And then she realized that lack of problem was it. That's

what seemed off. She felt . . . good. She was happy and balanced, a feeling apparently so foreign to her it had nearly set off a panic attack.

Sterling noticed her looking at him and did a double take when he saw the look on her face. "What?"

She shook her head. Not the time or the place.

"Kimberly!" A woman near her elbow held out a photograph, apparently printed from the internet. "Would you sign this? Please?"

She did, and then offered to take a photo with the woman as well. She almost . . . enjoyed the encounter. The woman's delight and excitement rolled off of her in waves, impacting Kimberly's energy, feeding into it. She'd always fought so hard to hold people at a distance. She wasn't about to hug the lady or anything—too much energy could overload her and send everything haywire. But this she could live with. Sterling made it tolerable.

She couldn't wait to get him back to the hotel room later and thank him appropriately.

And though he adamantly refused to consider her belief that he was in fact a sensitive in his own right, he looked at her quizzically the moment her orange chakra flared with desire, her heart chakra spinning with adoration. "You're in a good mood."

"I am." She rested a hand on his back and pushed some of the overflow of positive energy into his spinal column, knowing it would send his nervous system buzzing.

He gasped. "Oh, you—"

She grinned.

He leaned down, pressing his cheek against hers, his lips brushing her ear, and whispered, "Just remember, payback is hell. Wait until I get you alone tonight."

She met his intense gaze, stomach quivering in anticipation. "I was just thinking the same thing."

His eyebrows shot up so fast she giggled, and he turned, staring wistfully at his car. His orange chakra pulsed and throbbed, and she knew he was debating skipping the interview and driving her straight back to their room.

The door to the building opened and Michael, her director and show runner, appeared. He spotted them and waved them inside.

"Sorry, everyone," Sterling said. "Work calls. Be sure to like us on Facebook and follow us on Twitter. And tag us in those pics! I want to see some Insta-stories on the Gram."

As they went inside, Michael pecked her on the cheek and clapped Sterling on the shoulder. "What did we do without you? Look at her! She's positively glowing after working a crowd? Now I've seen everything!"

"Oh, come on!" she told him. "Not like you've never seen me happy before."

Michael raised one eyebrow. "Not like this. And I'm not complaining. Let's go. They're waiting for us in the auditorium."

CHAPTER TWO

KIMBERLY NEARLY WALKED STRAIGHT into thick cobwebs several times as she followed Michael through the building. A giant spider clung to one, huge unblinking eyes staring at her, red legs clinging to the web. Ick. Even fake spiders made her skin crawl. Not as badly as scorpions but bad enough.

They passed an open coffin, an empty cauldron, more bats than she could count, and at least three complete skeletons.

She jumped when they rounded a corner and ran smack into a body hanging from a noose.

"Sorry, Kimmy," Michael said when she squealed. "Should've warned you."

"You think?"

Sterling rested a hand low on her back and muttered, "I hate Halloween."

She felt his red chakra flair in response to his frustration, survival and anger impulses piqued. His attitude made perfect sense. He'd shared how he'd been deceived and terrorized by teenagers as a ten-year-old trick-or-treater. Add to that his personal beliefs that paranormal activity didn't exist—beliefs he had recently begun to question and even doubt as a result of working with her—and his fear of being duped in any way, and it was no wonder he harbored negative feelings for the holiday. People dressed up, disguising themselves, often in fantastical, supernatural costumes, for a holiday originally intended to fool spirits and ward them off.

In the dim light, the way he walked a bit more hesitantly and stayed close by her, she could see the ten-year-old boy, alert and on guard. Yep. Halloween ticked off all of Sterling's boxes, landing it squarely on his crap list. She ran a hand along his back and tried to reassure him. "It's okay. All of this truly is fake. Nothing to worry about."

He glanced at her like, *Come on.* "I know that."

He knew it mentally, but she could feel his deep-seated discontent.

They walked down a set of stairs, through a lobby, and into the auditorium, festooned with strings of orange and black lights. When they entered the room, a woman broke away from the small group clustered on the stage.

"Hi! I'm Jillian." The woman thrust out a hand.

"The theatre owner?" Kimberly asked. "Nice to meet you. I'm—"

"Kimberly Wantland. Of course. And Sterling." The woman shook his hand as well.

She cringed. Of course Jillian knew them. She'd invited them. Obviously she knew exactly who they were. Still, just once, she'd like for someone to give her a blank stare and shake their head in confusion, no idea who she was. Sometimes, as much as she loved her show and appreciated all the good things it brought to her life, she longed for her days of anonymity.

"You went all out for Halloween," Sterling remarked. "A little surprising, considering you're concerned about a ghost infestation."

"Ha! Infestation!" Jillian's huge laugh filled the entire hall. "Once the news broke about the kids' experience here, the entire town became fixated on the possibility of encountering a real ghost. We decided to capitalize on our fifteen minutes of fame. In addition to our play this month, we're operating a haunted house."

Kimberly wrinkled her brow at Jillian's "spooky" voice and hand gestures that accompanied "haunted house."

"Let's get started, shall we?" Michael suggested, gesturing to the group gathered on stage.

Sterling held her hand as they scurried up the stairs to the circle of chairs arranged stage center. She, Sterling, and Michael took empty seats, then smiled and nodded at each person as Jillian introduced them. The members of the repertory group brought back memories of her college days and the little bit of community theatre she'd participated in. Ian, Debbie, Candace, Nate, and Marie all raised their hands in greeting when introduced.

Two teens in the group looked as though they'd rather be anywhere else, particularly the girl, introduced as Kayla. If she remembered the general briefing correctly, the teens actually reported this disturbance—and she recalled something about the police being called.

"You two saw the ghost?" Sterling asked, pointing to Kayla and Cory.

Jillian laughed, a light happy sound that caught Kimberly off guard. She was accustomed to tears and hand-wringing and unbridled fear of the dead. She sensed nothing like that from Jillian. Interesting.

"What can you tell us about your experiences?" she asked, watching Jillian closely.

Jillian gestured to the young adults. "My nephew apparently brought his girlfriend—"

"I am not his girlfriend!" Kayla crossed her arms and slumped in her chair.

"You were when we came," Cory said.

"Yeah, well, you left me in here with an axe murderer and a ghost. Just left me behind and ran off to save yourself!"

"Axe murderer?" Kimberly asked. She would definitely

remember if someone had mentioned an axe murderer during the investigation briefing.

"I thought you were right behind me!" Cory said, throwing his hands up in the air.

"Oh, sure! And you didn't hear me screaming for you. Sure."

Jillian shook her head and gave Kimberly a knowing look.

"I don't remember hearing anything about an axe murderer," Kimberly said. "Maybe you can walk us through your experiences that night?"

Cory spoke up. "Am I going to get in trouble again? I already got grounded for a month. And dumped by my girlfriend. After I brought her to see the theatre like she wanted."

Kayla leaned forward. "I wanted to come during the day! I never asked you to break in! I said—"

Kimberly held up her hands. "No one will get in trouble. We want to help your aunt figure out what's going on here. Something happened that night that seems to have sparked an ongoing disturbance."

One of the others in the group, Debbie she thought, finally spoke up. "Not to be disagreeable, but most of us have experienced inexplicable things in this building before now. We haven't felt threatened by them necessarily. But mostly our reports have been dismissed."

Jillian's laugh cut through the room again. "I agree some of us are more convinced than others that we have a haunting here. However, the kids saw some things that made it difficult to completely disregard."

Kimberly turned back to the kids. Getting details out of this group was like pulling teeth. "Such as? Can you guys tell me what happened?"

Kayla chewed her cheek and rolled her eyes but eventually clicked her tongue and spoke. "Okay, so he told me we could come see the theatre. And I'm like really into theatre, right? So I was really excited. But then he picked me up late in the day and the next thing I know he's using these little tools to break in and I never asked for that."

"Okay, we get it," Cory huffed. "I'm a total jerk."

Sterling puffed out a breath. "It's all good. We were all kids once. Can we move this along? Cuz I haven't had dinner yet and we've got a long night ahead of us."

Kayla cast a side-long glance at Sterling, and Kimberly did not miss the slight flush that crept up her cheeks when he smiled at her encouragingly. She understood exactly how the girl felt.

"So we snuck into the auditorium and we were just sitting here and we weren't doing anything at all." She cut another glance at Sterling. "And then I saw something. And Cory was convinced it was a hobo or something so he went to check it out."

"Well, I couldn't leave some guy in here jacking things up. My aunt has enough problems here."

Enough problems? Kimberly made a mental note to have Elise look into what that meant. Jillian had led them to believe this was a recent development and hadn't mentioned other problems.

"But like I couldn't find anything anywhere," Cory continued. "I never found a hobo and I didn't find anything that looked like someone had been camped out here or broken in."

Kayla jumped back in. "Meanwhile whoever it was came after me here in the auditorium."

"No one was here," Cory said.

"Something came after me!" Kayla insisted, leaning forward to scowl at Cory. "And the alarm went off, so don't dismiss me like that."

"The alarm?"

"The security alarm," Kayla said. "It didn't go off when Cory broke in cuz he knew the code to deactivate it."

"But it went off later?" Sterling asked. "Interesting."

"Can you describe what you saw?" Kimberly asked.

"We didn't turn any lights on so it was super dark in here. All

I could really see was like a shadow. A great big shadow coming closer to me. And I kept thinking about that guy who got his head chopped off by an axe murderer. That wasn't very far from here! I was afraid they were coming after me!"

Kimberly blinked, tensed, and looked at Michael. "There's an axe murderer in Hannibal? Why haven't we heard about this?"

Michael held his hands out in a huge shrug. "Hasn't been anything in the news."

Jillian's light laugh broke the tension in the room again. "She's talking about ancient history. The old Stillwell murder, never fully solved. I'm sure Annabel Stillwell was not here menacing you with an axe, Kayla. Her old mansion is blocks from here."

Kimberly startled at the mention of her middle name but couldn't dwell on it as Kayla continued.

"Well, you weren't here! You don't know how scary it was. And then we saw some guy up on the stage saying, 'Where's my spotlight?' and it was crazy creepy!"

Jillian nodded. "And that is why I can't completely disregard their experiences. One of our troupe members used to say that. And there's no way these kids could have known that."

Kimberly looked over all the members sitting in the circle. "Who?"

"Donald. He isn't with us anymore," Jillian said.

"He, uh, died," one of the women said. "Right here on the stage."

Now that changed things. "And this is recent?"

"About a year ago," Jillian confirmed. "He was an older gentleman, a little high-strung—"

Debbie scoffed. "That's an understatement. High-strung? I don't know why you kept that guy around."

"Oh, come on," Jillian said. "He wasn't that difficult. And he was a good actor. You have to give him that."

Kimberly thought back to some of the actors she'd known back when she was involved in theatre. She'd met some characters herself, particularly in community theatre. Always more shy than outgoing, she remembered one table read for a small character part she'd been cast in—a loud and rambunctious granny. One of the louder, more flamboyant cast members approached her during the break, eyed her wearily, and said, "You'll be playing Granny? I'll be glad to work with you. You don't seem the right type." Taken aback by his shameless mansplaining, she couldn't even think of a response. But she blew him—and everyone else in the cast—away when her turn to read came. She knew what she was doing. Of course, he never apologized for being out of line. He guffawed loudly after her scene and said something along the lines of, "Now I see why the director cast you!"

She'd met plenty of real-life characters in her experience back then, not to mention during her work investigating paranormal disturbances. But Debbie looked more than simply irked by Donald's behavior.

One of the other women joined the discussion. "At least he wasn't fixated on your name. He went by Donny and since I'm Marie, he called us the Osmonds and always referenced bits I didn't know. And then acted shocked I didn't know what he was talking about. Every time."

The cast seemed to be hinting at things Jillian preferred not to share. Kimberly made eye contact with the women. "What can you guys tell us about him? It will help with my investigation to have some working knowledge and details."

Debbie answered first. "The man was a self-absorbed prick. I believe Kayla completely because every one of us heard him bellow, "Where's my spotlight?" a million times. He could never hit his mark and expected everyone else to change their blocking and adapt to wherever he wandered on stage. Including the lighting techs."

Marie nodded. "Jillian is correct that he would deliver during the performance. Give him a funny part and he'd always have the audience rolling. Of course, the rest of us were busting our butts working around him, but the audience never knew that."

"Okay, sure, he always delivered," Debbie said. "Even if he was a bit of a hack. But the six weeks of rehearsals leading up to performances? He was insufferable. Made the rest of us miserable."

"He'd been in some commercial years ago or so he claimed. Who knows if it's even true. But he used it to elevate himself above the rest of us 'players,' referencing his professional experience we didn't have." Marie's face twisted into a scowl, as though she smelled something disgusting.

Ian swiped at his brow and shuffled his feet. "You guys. I mean, I don't think you should speak ill of the dead. You have to admit it was awful when he collapsed on stage."

"Once we realized he'd actually collapsed and wasn't just screwing around like always, hamming it up for attention, sure."

Ian shook his head and smiled at Michael. "I did my best. I'm trained in CPR, but he was gone by the time he hit the ground."

Ian was cute, Kimberly couldn't help but notice. Not rustic and drop-dead gorgeous like Sterling, but cute and endearing in a nerdy sort of way.

Jillian's laugh pierced the air yet again, high-pitched and harsh. "You know actors. Everything is a crisis or a scandal. We artists can't help it that we feel things so much more acutely."

Did she though? Kimberly didn't get the feeling that Jillian was particularly upset by any of this. Suspicion crept into her thoughts, clouding the sensory input from the psychic energy in the room. "You're convinced Donald is the one causing the disturbances then?"

"He must be," Jillian said. "The kids' experiences prove that, doesn't it?"

Sterling cleared his throat but said nothing.

For once, she wished Sterling would speak up and call this woman out. Her team back home always vetted her cases, but something about this seemed off. She wanted out. Anxiety built to the point her flight instinct kicked in. She stood and held out a hand. "We will see what we can find."

Michael stood as well, looking flustered. "I guess we're finished for now. Thank you. We will start setting up for tonight and let you know."

Ian lingered longest, hesitating a moment before he thrust a hand toward Michael. "Nice to meet you. Do you . . . do you have dinner plans? I could suggest someplace to eat."

Michael's face lit up. "I'd love some recommendations."

"I know the best little pizza place not far from here."

"Kimmy? Pizza okay for dinner?"

Pizza. Why did they eat so much pizza on the road? She looked at Sterling.

"I'm down with pizza. Sure."

Ian beamed. "Great! It's called Brick Oven Pizza and it's near all the touristy things you might want to do while you're here, but it isn't a tourist trap. It's just genuinely good food near all the historic spots."

She watched Jillian as the group broke up and went their separate ways, certain the woman wasn't telling them the entire story.

CHAPTER THREE

Brick Oven Pizza turned out to be an excellent suggestion. Quaint and quiet, near the busy, popular downtown destinations, but far enough away it wasn't packed, the crew settled at several tables in the back corner, away from the front door and windows where they might be easily spotted.

Sterling could obviously tell something bothered her. She noticed the glances and the slight furrow of his brow. He raised an eyebrow, but she shook her head. Right now, she didn't have enough information to even begin formulating an idea about this investigation. She would focus on dinner and then later could discuss the case when they were alone.

A little shiver raced through her at that thought.

Sterling pulled a chair out for her, leaning close to whisper, "What's up? Just hungry or is something wrong?"

She smiled up at him as she took her seat, a gentle glow warming her chest at his concern. "I'm okay."

He gave her a look that indicated he knew that wasn't entirely true. He read her so well. He'd only been in her life a few months, and yet, their bond had grown and strengthened, the connection she felt with him bordering on electric.

She always had people fussing over her, wanting to get close to her, needing help from her. This new addition to her life, someone watching out for her, wasn't bad at all. Sterling's attention counterbalanced the draining effects of constantly being pulled at. He recharged her battery, and in a way no one she'd ever known had done. Not even Rosie, her best friend, who had for years been her stalwart support, keeping her emotional state in balance, her chakras aligned, and her psychic energy fully charged offered the type of connection she felt with Sterling. What was it about him?

Sterling took the seat next to her, grabbed her hand and squeezed, pulling her hand into his lap. Michael and Rosie joined them, of course. Typically, they talked about the current case over dinner. But the young man who'd suggested they eat at Brick Oven, Ian, hovered over their table. She could tell he wanted an invitation to join them, even though the table was intended for four diners.

Unwilling to risk a post on social media about what a cold, unfeeling hag she was, she gestured to the open end of the table. "Won't you pull up a chair and join us?"

Ian lit up. "You sure?" He dragged a chair from an empty table and sat before anyone could answer.

Sterling squeezed her hand again and tugged at her, as if trying to pull her closer. He brought his lips to her ear and whispered, "Everyone wants to be close to you."

Knowing the types of comments he received on any picture of himself he posted to social media, she was well aware that if either of them had a massive line of fans hoping to get close, it was Sterling. Still, his belief he had reason to be jealous amused her. She didn't mind his protective nature to guard and shield her.

Rosie was uncharacteristically silent, she noticed. She stared across the table, trying to get an idea what might be going on, but Rosie hunched over her phone, brow furrowed, deeply engrossed in something.

A horn blew, startling her so badly she jumped.

"What the hell?" Rosie yelled. "I nearly dropped my phone!"

Ian laughed. "You'll acclimate. I promise. The paddleboats cruise up and down the river and blow their horns pretty regularly. You guys should totally take a river cruise while you're here!"

"We'll try to work that in," Kimberly promised.

"I don't do boats," Rosie said, returning to her phone.

Ian swung his attention to Michael. "You'll come on the river cruise, won't you? I mean, you gotta. You simply cannot come to Hannibal, Missouri, hometown of Mark Twain, and not experience some history."

"I'm sure Elise will make sure we soak up some history," she assured Ian while glancing at Rosie. *What so distracted her stylist?* "And Rosie will come too if we decide to go on a riverboat."

"Don't do boats," Rosie repeated.

The waiter arrived at their table. "Everyone decided? Ready to order?"

Sterling lifted a finger and drew the waiter's attention. "My girl needs the healthiest salad you have, dressing on the side. And the two of us will split a veggie pizza, extra marinara."

He knew exactly what she'd order. No one had ever been so attentive, so determined to ensure her satisfaction. Though at first she'd assumed his motives related to job security, he'd proven again and again that her happiness meant something to him, that he genuinely wanted her to be as comfortable as possible at all times. And she found, she wanted the same for him.

She tried to reciprocate. "What about you? Don't you want pepperoni? Do you want to get two pizzas and we can both have our favorite?"

"Nah." He patted his stomach. "I've noticed the difference, eating healthier with you. I feel better. Besides, I can't get fat and disgusting and give some super-buff guy the opportunity to steal you away."

She nearly spit-sprayed water everywhere. "Oh, sure." That

was so not her. Yes, she found Sterling attractive physically. Okay, he was hot. Totally hot. But the way he looked at her, the strong connection she felt with him, and his desire to put her needs ahead of his own, combined with an intriguing fascination that he harbored latent psychic sensitivity—those were the things that had eventually won her over and convinced her to give a relationship a try. And though the relationship was still new, so far she had no regrets.

He gave her the look that completely melted her, and she caught herself leaning forward, eyes on his lips. He lifted an eyebrow and cocked his head, silently asking if she really wanted to do this. She leaned back and took a deep breath. And another drink of ice water. No public displays of affection had been her idea, one of the relationship guidelines she'd established. For the good of the show, but mostly because she didn't like people butting into her personal business. As a celebrity, keeping some things to herself, away from the prying eyes of the public, was important. She needed a personal life separate from her public life. The fact that anyone wanted to know her personal business still boggled her mind. Why did anyone care?

"Can we finish ordering here or what?" Rosie had finally lifted her eyes from her phone. And Kimberly saw a look in them that she'd never seen there before.

The others each gave the waiter their orders and he scurried away.

Sterling waved his hand behind her ear and held a piece of chocolate in front of her. "Your dessert. For later."

She grinned and accepted it, wishing they'd gone back to the hotel alone and ordered room service. If the hotel even offered that. "That's the first magic trick you ever showed me."

"I remember." His eyes practically glowed.

"Are they always like this?" Ian asked, having finally dragged his attention away from Michael.

"Always," Rosie said, a note of displeasure in her voice.

What in the world?

"It's disgusting," Michael confirmed

"I don't know," Ian said. "It's kinda cute."

Kimberly looked back and forth between her two best friends, incredulous. These two had carped at her for years to open herself up and consider a serious relationship. Now that she'd finally let someone in, they were . . . what? Annoyed? Irritated? She recovered her voice. "You were the ones who kept telling me to get along with him."

Michael shrugged. "Your constant bickering was annoying. This is disgusting."

Weary of this conversation topic, she steered it elsewhere. "How long have you been with the Hannibal Players, Ian?"

"A few years now. I joined right after college. Not much you can do in Missouri with a theatre degree. Especially in a tourist town like Hannibal. Well, aside from, say, impersonating Mark Twain or something along those lines."

Michael nodded. "LA, Chicago, or New York. That's what Kimmy and I had drilled into our heads during our college years."

Ian brightened. "You guys are theatre majors? You knew each other in college?"

"Yes and yes," Kimberly answered, accepting her salad from the waiter.

"Well, you guys get it then. It's impossible to just pack up and relocate with nothing—no money, no place to stay, no contacts or leads. I should've gone to medical school like my dad wanted."

"It's never too late," Sterling said, snitching a bite of salad. He shook his head. "I'm even starting to like salad, God help me."

"Like I could even pass the MCAT," Ian said. "Plus I don't have any of the prereqs. Who am I kidding? I'd be miserable as a doctor. But I went up to New York for a few auditions and nothing. I didn't even make call-backs."

"I wish I had some advice for you," Michael said. "I didn't go that route. I got lucky—knew someone with an extraordinary gift she turned into a show. I'm just along for the ride."

He always downplayed his vital role. She and Michael had been complete partners, financing her little side paranormal project, just the two of them. "So not true. Don't listen to him. He worked as hard as I did, every step of the way."

He waved away the praise. "That was back before we got picked up for a show. Anyway, my focus was always directing and producing. Not as much performance. So I'm afraid I don't know what to tell you."

"I . . . I'm really interested in paranormal activity," Ian said. "I don't suppose you'd allow me to tag along and watch?" Ian aimed his question at Michael, not her.

But Michael looked to her, one eyebrow up, corners of his mouth turned down. She knew him well. This look meant he was okay with it but would wait for her to accept or decline.

She in turn turned to Sterling. "Would you be okay with that?"

His crooked little grin let her know he was delighted to be consulted. "I am if you are."

"I have no problem with that." She smiled at Ian, but he was waiting for Michael to confirm.

"You're in," Michael told him. "We will start around dusk."

"You guys, this is the best thing to happen to me since . . . since I can remember."

Though his "you guys" presumably was intended for everyone at the table, Ian only had eyes for Michael.

Sterling leaned close again, his cheek pressed to hers, lips against her ear. "And I thought this guy wanted to have dinner with *you*."

She ducked her head to hide a smile. It wasn't only in her mind. Sterling saw it too.

Ian's hands punctuated his words, confirming the excitement in his voice. "I promise not to get in the way. In fact, I can be helpful. I've been there and know a little bit about where the others have experienced weird things."

"Don't suppose you're a hardened skeptic?" Sterling asked.

"No. True believer. Sorry."

"We have plenty of those on staff. We need more skeptics to balance things out."

"Not on this show," she teased him, elbowing him in the side.

"That's only your opinion," he said. He dug fingers into her side, knowing how ticklish she was there.

She squealed. "Sterling! Stop that!"

Their pizzas arrived.

"Thank goodness," Rosie muttered. "Just in time."

She kept waiting for Rosie to break into her wide smile and admit she was only joking, that she was thrilled to finally see her happy. But she went back to her phone. This attitude was so unlike her. She would have to find out what was going on. But later. When they were alone. "Ian, tell me about your experiences with the theatre group. What kind of disturbances have you guys noticed?"

Ian nodded and finished the bite of pizza in his mouth before he spoke. "Nothing huge, if you only look at my experiences. Props out of place, lights blinking on and off when no one is near the switches. The types of things you'd explain away and not think about again. But after the kids heard Donny demanding a spotlight, I realized he's been here all along, trying to get our attention."

She glanced at Sterling, who raised an eyebrow but continued eating. "You try the pizza yet? It's great."

She hadn't but followed up with Ian regardless. "What about the others in the group? You mentioned their experiences."

"Oh, yeah. They definitely spoke out about strange things happening. Marie specifically. She kept saying the old fart stuck around just to keep antagonizing her. But Deborah and Nate eventually admitted to some strange things happening to them too. Jillian always laughed it off and wouldn't take them seriously."

And yet Jillian called her show to bring them in to investigate. She filed that away with her suspicion the woman wasn't being fully honest with them.

"Strange things, odd things, odd experiences," Sterling said. "Can you give me specific examples? What did the others report?"

Ian shrugged. "I don't remember their specific complaints. I didn't pay close attention, plus they were talking about it, like, pretty much right after he died. I guess back then I was more like you, Sterling. Thought they were seeing what they wanted to see."

If he didn't believe them at first but changed his mind, that meant something had happened to him, something inexplicable enough to turn him into a believer.

"How long ago did the others start reporting experiences?" Michael asked, beating her to it.

"About a year ago, I want to say." Ian closed his eyes and bobbed his head, presumably checking his memory. "Yeah. About a year ago."

She took mental note. Roughly when Donny passed. "And when were your personal experiences?"

"I think just before the kids set off the building alarm and triggered the media circus. I'd been pretty weirded out already but that convinced me I really did experience paranormal activity."

Sterling nodded, pulled a small notebook and pen from his pocket, and began to write. "About how long before the kids reported their experience did you notice these occurrences?"

She cocked her head and leaned sideways, trying to see what he wrote. His tone didn't carry a trace of snark. What was he up to?

"Hmmm." Ian chewed thoughtfully. "Probably the weekend

before. We were super busy. Final performances of *Noises Off* finished our summer season that year—"

"Ha! I love that play!" she said. "Remember, Michael? I played Brooke our sophomore year! Spring semester, wasn't it?"

"Yes. That's right."

"And you played Lloyd!" She laughed, remembering. "You were incredible! Your face when you dumped the 'sardines' on that other guy's head."

Sterling made a face. "Sardines?"

"Prop sardines, but yeah. He was so funny!"

"What about you?" Michael said. "That one line, 'Bag! Bag, bag!' You had the audience roaring every show."

"I only pulled it off cuz the character is such a ditz," she said. "I just had to walk around the stage with wide eyes, sound British, and be clueless."

"I'm sure being in lingerie for several scenes didn't hurt," Ian said.

"You were on stage in lingerie?" Sterling asked. "Did you guys get pictures of this? A ditzy Kimberly wearing lingerie in public?"

"It was a costume! You make it sound like I went grocery shopping in my underwear."

"Kimmy was amazing," Michael repeated.

"If you guys have done the play," Ian said, "then you know what a massive undertaking that was. Huge set, tons of props, timing critical. And a big cast! We had to use people from the community. I don't know what Jillian was thinking. Donald always wanted to do that play. Thought he'd be a perfect Selsdon. Why she opted for that one after he was gone . . ."

Sterling wrote something else. "And that's when you had the prop issues?"

"Yes. What a nightmare. Since I actually have a theatre degree and some real training, I help with everything. I mean everything. Set construction. Lighting. Props. I even sew costumes."

"You were basically the character Tim Allgood, but in real life."

"True! I was so ready to be done by the time we hit tech week. And that's when weird things started happening."

Sterling wrote something else in his little notebook. "You had issues with the props?"

"Yes. Props, lighting, costumes. Things kept disappearing and then showing up in the most random places. Crazy."

"But people could have simply moved things around, right?" Sterling asked.

"I mean, we did have people from the community in the cast, but we put the fear of God in them about touching props or anything that they didn't use in the play. I don't think anyone did."

"What do you mean they showed up in odd places?" she asked. "In the wrong place on the prop table?"

"No! Not on the prop table at all. Weird places like out in the audience or across the room. And then I didn't even want to be in the building alone. It's never bothered me before, but one night I was the last one there and I heard talking. It weirded me out cuz I knew everyone else had left. I called out to see who was there. Everything went silent and then I heard someone say hello. But I walked through the entire building and no one was in it. And no one could have left the building without passing me."

Sterling scribbled in his notebook again. She had to get a look at that notebook.

"And then of course Jillian started holding auditions for *Blithe Spirit* so we could start rehearsing that show after we struck *Noises Off*."

"Aren't you doing *Blithe Spirit* now?"

"It's our Halloween show every year. You know, like *A Christmas Carol* is a standard Christmas show. We always do *Blithe Spirit*. Not the same this year though. Donny always played Charles. Always. It's weird running the show without him."

"What a logistical nightmare for you, trying to manage *Noises Off* alone. I remember how tough that was to pull off with a full crew of indentured students. How did you juggle it all?"

"I'm still trying to remember. It's all a blur. I was so ready for a break. And then Jillian had the bright idea to host a haunted house." Ian bit into another slice and shook his head.

"That's not your responsibility though," Sterling said.

"It is if we want to keep the place. We all pitch in—playing characters, selling tickets. We decorated the place. Anything to help. I'd hate for Jillian to lose the building."

"And that's a possibility?"

"Something is going on," Ian said. "She saved the building from demolition. But I don't know all the details. It's an historic site, but something is wrong. I just have a feeling."

Another mental note, something else to follow up on. She felt more certain than ever that Jillian wasn't giving her all the facts. According to Ian, the woman had laughed off reports of paranormal disturbances from the other members of her group. And yet had asked the *Wantland* crew to come resolve a haunting she didn't truly believe in? She'd never arrived at an investigation and had the person offer her the culprit on a silver platter. *Here you go—here's who's haunting my building. Take care of it. Voila.* Something about this situation gave her a bad vibe.

CHAPTER FOUR

KIMBERLY AND STERLING stood in the auditorium while the crew performed sound checks and loaded fresh batteries into all the cameras for the walkthrough. They also distributed camp lanterns that could be adjusted to let specific amounts of light through. These could be opened or closed as well as draped with diffusing cloths in order to mimic ambient light they would normally have in an investigation. This basement space had no windows to the outside world and could be dangerously dark without some addition of dim light.

Kimberly sipped calming tea and attempted to clear her mind of all distractions. Anything that affected her psyche and depleted her energy would not be helpful now. Her energy felt low, though she couldn't imagine why that would be. She closed her eyes and breathed deeply, in and out. *Focus. Put aside everything but the investigation.*

Rosie had applied makeup and styled their hair, but only seemed to be going through the motions. And she hadn't yet joined them in the theatre.

"How can I help?" Sterling asked.

Not long ago, his interruption would have twanged her every nerve. Now she understood his offer of help as genuine. Funny how things could change so radically when you got to know someone better. Where once his voice had grated, now it sent a shiver of delight throughout her body.

She opened her eyes. "I'm okay."

He lifted a skeptical eyebrow. "You seem a bit restless. And Rosie seemed off to me. I'm not sure she gave you her undivided attention."

More convinced than ever that he had sensitive proclivities, she agreed. "You're absolutely spot on. She's upset about something for sure. You still deny your psychic abilities?"

He threw his head back and laughed. "I'm merely relying on keen observation. Nothing psychic about it. You ever watch the show *Psych?*"

"I did! Really enjoyed it. Dulé Hill is hot."

"Well, there you go. I'm the James Roday character."

"You can tell I'm restless though."

"Sure. Because I'm giving you my undivided attention. You're pacing, clutching your quartz, repeatedly glancing at the door. You're worried about Rosie. That's knocking you off kilter. And if you believe your rainbow is out of whack, then your belief will cause you to feel off. Causation, not correlation. And I don't need to be psychic to 'feel' that."

She grinned at his description of her chakras—her rainbow— and the memory of explaining chakras to him sent a warm flush blooming over her cheeks. She'd simplified the idea of the seven energy centers for him, describing how they spin and glow at various points along the spine when activated and how they can become "clogged" by emotional distress. That moment had been a turning point for them, one that began thawing an initially icy relationship.

He was correct that Rosie normally acted as her stabilizing touchstone. Her stylist not only made sure she looked great on camera but also ensured her psychic abilities remained honed and functional at full capacity.

"However you sussed it out, you're correct. Rosie only

perfunctorily charged up my energy. I'm not as relaxed as I should be. She seemed distracted. I don't know. I thought she could talk to me about anything."

He lifted her hand and massaged it, turning tiny circles in her palm with his thumb. He exerted exactly the right amount of pressure in just the right spots. "Does this help?"

She closed her eyes, reveling in the warm, gentle motions. While his touch tapped an emotional well she didn't particularly want resonating at the moment, peaceful bliss coursed along her nerves, suffusing every fiber of her being.

He moved slowly up her arm, both hands squeezing while his thumbs continued applying gentle pressure, releasing stress and anxiety.

Michael's voice startled her. "Is this some new kind of fore-play? Or can we maybe get started?"

Embarrassed, she opened her eyes. And discovered Rosie standing just inside the auditorium door. She waved, hoping perhaps her stylist felt better. But Rosie only scowled. Great. Just what she didn't need.

"Where shall we start?" she asked Michael.

"Here in the auditorium? And then branch out from here?"

"Sure."

Stan, her senior camera operator, and TJ, her younger, newer addition to the team, moved into place. She pulled Sterling close. The cameras focused on her. Just as she was about to start the investigation introduction, Rosie dashed into the frame with powder. Finally, some normal behavior.

Rosie patted her down first, then Sterling. "I see you're using the pressure points I taught you," she said as she brushed powder on his face. The undercurrent of irritation in her voice wasn't lost on her. Or apparently on Sterling either.

"Yeah. Why did you think I wanted to learn them? To use, obviously."

Sterling had asked Rosie to teach him pressure points? "You're learning reflexology? For me?"

He shrugged like it was no big deal, but it meant a lot to her. A lot. "Figured it couldn't hurt to have a backup person. Besides, I like making you feel good."

"Oh, puke," Rosie said. "Listen, I'm her trained healer, okay? I'll take care of her."

After Rosie stalked away, Sterling lifted his hands to his temples, as if using psychic abilities. "My powers of observation definitely picked up on an undercurrent of jealousy there."

"Yes. She's an emotional wreck. I'll talk to her." She faced the cameras and waited as Michael counted them in. Three . . . two . . . one. "The Old Catholic Church, saved from demolition and transformed into a community theatre, has a long history and changed ownership multiple times. Is it currently haunted by a former actor, who died here on the stage, possibly lonely and seeking interaction from former friends? Or is it something more sinister left behind from the building's hundred-year history and provoked to irritation? We're here to find out. Stay with us as we investigate this Halloween haunting in Hannibal, tonight on *The Wantland Files*."

She grabbed Sterling's hand and pulled him close, leaning up to whisper in his ear. "You'll watch for anything that seems off, right?"

"Of course I will. That's what I do. What do you mean, off?"

"I don't know. Something feels strange about this."

"I'm the skeptic, remember?" He nudged her with an elbow.

"I know. And I can't pinpoint exactly what's triggering all my red flags. But I think Jillian is hiding something."

"No problem. I'm always glad to help my girl."

His girl. She was still adapting to that, but she liked the sound of it. Despite her doubts, her job was to figure out what was happening here. And she could not deny the children were genuinely shaken and had clearly experienced something they could not explain. A building as old as this one would be expected to have some lingering spirits roaming the rooms.

Nothing unusual there. But something seemed to have triggered a recent outbreak of manifestations. What?

She took a deep breath and wrapped her hand around the quartz crystal on her necklace. Focusing all her energy, she opened her psychic senses, inviting connection to the other plane of existence. Connection required tuning in to just the right frequency, honing her senses, partially blocking out her immediate surroundings, and touching the other side. Sterling's chakras resonated nearby, pulling at her to distraction. Rosie's unsettled frustration blazed all the way across the room. This wouldn't work. Distractions interfered. She took another deep breath and forced all her thoughts and concerns to the deepest recesses. Only a quiet mind could hear the frequency she listened for.

The usual static greeted her as she turned her dial along the spiritual plane, a living satellite searching for signs of life in a foreign landscape. Unusual, but she picked up on nothing. Again, she noted the sensation that her energy felt low. Dare she go so far as to say it felt weak? Not a fan of wasting time, she opened her eyes and shrugged at the crew.

"Let's try the stage," Ian suggested.

Her entire crew whipped around, shushing the young man.

"Dude!" TJ said. "Don't interrupt her during the walk-through. We're only here to observe and record. She'll go where the spirits lead her."

Ian's eyes widened. "I am so sorry. I only meant to—"

"It's okay," she assured him. "The stage is a good idea. The kids talked about seeing someone peeping out from behind the curtain. Let's see if the spirit feels like making an appearance today."

She climbed onto the stage and stood in the exact spot Kayla had reported seeing a face peer around the curtain. Nostalgia washed over her. Remembering the thrill of performing on stage brought a smile to her face while a deep pang of remorse squeezed her heart. Oh, she missed acting. Yes, she worked in front of the camera for her show—and knew many envied her that vocation—but the rustle and murmur of a live audience, laughter, applause—nothing matched it.

But nothing, no one, bumped against her psyche. She knew something had terrified the kids. Sure a presence haunted the space, she decided to push a little.

"Donald? Donny? Are you here in the theatre?" She listened carefully, reaching out with her sixth sense for anything unusual. She heard whispers and opened her eyes. "Okay, I really need quiet."

After a beat of silence, Michael said, "No one said anything, sweetie."

"I heard whispering."

"It wasn't us."

She listened again. Faint whispers seemed to drift down from the ceiling. "I hear something. I can't make out words, but I hear at least one voice. Whispering. Sterling, you don't hear that?"

"I don't hear voices," he confirmed. "Anyone else but you, I'd be highly concerned about hearing them."

"This sounds like the perfect time to try out the new device," Elise said.

"Break it out," Michael said. "Let's introduce it to the viewers."

Stan and TJ moved in and focused the cameras on Elise while she unpacked the newest piece of equipment that Michael wanted to try.

"What is this?" Sterling asked.

Kimberly frowned at the equipment as Elise extracted it. "Oh, it's a new gadget Michael saw and got excited about."

"But what is it?"

"This is the Audioxx," Elise said, holding out the black metal box in her hands. "It senses environmental changes in the room and translates them into words we can understand."

"What?" Sterling asked.

Even in the darkness with shadows skewing everyone's

features, Kimberly knew exactly the face he made, could see his mouth curl sideways into a smirk, his nose crinkle, his eyebrow shoot up. "It operates basically on the same principal as EMF recordings, where we capture voice phenomena. This thing is supposed to produce actual words though."

"Supposed to?"

"Kimmy wants to keep doing things the old-fashioned way," Michael said. "She doesn't trust the machine to interpret properly."

He turned to her. "Really? You don't believe this will work?"

"I'll believe it when I see it."

"I really am rubbing off on you."

"I know I can understand spirits when I connect with them. But this thing? How will we learn anything substantial from it?"

"Okay, well. It's a start." He rubbed her back. "You're skeptical of the new device and want to see results. That's my girl."

Elise flipped on the Audioxx, and the crew fell silent again as they all watched it buzz and crackle softly. She reached out, hand clasped about her quartz, and listened intently.

Faint mumbling, as if quiet recitation, the same string of sounds repeated in the same tone and cadence, reached her. But no matter how she strained and concentrated, no words formed. To her complete satisfaction, the Audioxx continued to produce nothing but white noise.

"I hear it again. It sounds like it's coming from the balcony or the ceiling. Above us somewhere. How do we get to the balcony?"

"I can show you the stairs," Ian volunteered. "But there's also a small apartment up there."

"An apartment? Really? In a church?"

"I'm not sure why it was originally built, but I know Donald lived in it when he first moved to Hannibal."

Bingo. "Donald lived here in the old church?"

"Yes, but I don't know why Jillian let him move in here."

Another question to add to the growing list for Jillian. But if

Donald had lived there, he could have left psychic energy behind, his spiritual footprint as it were. For that matter, if Donald's soul didn't cross over and he didn't realize he had died, he could still be wandering the building, lost and confused. Returning to a familiar place, an apartment he once lived in, would make complete sense. However, feeling comfortable in the space, falling into old routines, could solidify his belief he hadn't died. And a soul unconvinced of its body's death could be a most stubborn spirit. She'd cross that bridge when she came to it.

"I know how to get to the apartment!" Ian said. "There's a secret passage, but I know how to get to it."

"A secret passage?"

Stan and TJ fell into step behind Ian, TJ proudly wearing night vision goggles. Ian ran his hands along the wooden wall, knocking at the boards every few feet. "One of these panels is actually a door—"

A click and a squeak, and the wall opened to reveal a short hallway and stairs.

"Absolutely fascinating," she said, and started for the steps.

"Oh, hell no!" Sterling switched on a flashlight, illuminating cobwebs and dust motes in the blinding beam.

"Sterling!" She turned away and covered her eyes.

"Dude! Now none of us can see!" TJ yelled.

"Aside from dancing white spots," Michael agreed. "Be mindful of pupils and retinas, Sterling. No sudden bursts of light without warning."

"I'm not letting Kimberly in there without verifying it's safe." His tone held no note of apology.

Stan sighed and spoke as if explaining to a child. "But now anything we might have captured on camera will be washed out."

"And probably scared away," Michael said. "Trust us to use our tools to clear her way."

"Sure. Cuz that's just as good. Even she doesn't believe in that talk-box nonsense." She could hear his eyeroll, even in her currently blinded state.

"That's not exactly what I said," she reminded him.

"Seriously, dude, do you think I wear these night vision goggles cuz of how cool they make me look?" TJ asked.

"Nope. Never once thought that," Sterling answered.

TJ punched Sterling's shoulder. "Smart-ass. As soon as I can see again, I'll go first and check for safety and for paranormal activity."

"Can I have a pair?" Ian asked. "I'll help."

She didn't mind Ian tagging along. And showing them the secret passageway had been helpful. But letting him operate equipment with no training seemed like a bad idea. "I don't think we have another—"

"Here," Michael said. "Have mine. I can't stand them."

Okay. Apparently they were doing this. Whatever. If Michael wanted to take him under his wing, that was his call.

"It's clear," TJ said.

"And I know the stairs are good," Ian said. "Donny used this not that long ago."

"Watch for the hobo the kids were convinced they saw in here," Sterling muttered.

Kimberly followed TJ and Ian into the dark passageway. Old wood and dust filled her nostrils. She placed a foot onto the first step of the staircase. It creaked under her weight but seemed sturdy enough as she continued to climb. A slight tingle brushed over her skin. The higher she climbed, the more her skin prickled until the hairs on her arms stood on end.

"I'm getting something," she whispered. "No direct connection. No voices. But definitely something residual here."

The rest of the crew crowded along behind her. Elise's Audioxx hummed quietly but produced no words.

"I'm not getting anything on the FLIR," TJ said.

"K2 normal. EMF readings ambient," Michael said.

The stairs opened into a small apartment space. The sparsely furnished room seethed of loneliness, a desolate bite to the space that nipped at her sixth sense. But she detected something else as well, peace and calm and a general sense of comfort mixed with a dollop of anxiety. So many layers, stacked one atop the other. Like an archeologist, she would need to dig down, sift through them, and tease out which residual emotional relic belonged to the spirit they hoped to connect with.

Something or someone brushed against her. A hesitant attempt to interact? She checked her arm to ensure she hadn't simply walked into a spiderweb but found nothing. "Is someone with us? Would someone like to talk to me?"

The Audioxx crackled, but otherwise nothing.

Residual emotions and decades-old thoughts swirled around her. At least one of the spirits producing these remnants wanted to connect with her. She pushed a little harder. "Who is here with us?"

The murmuring started again, whispered words that eluded comprehension.

"I can hear you, but I don't know what you're saying." Frustration clouded her emotions.

"Kimmy, talk to us," Michael said. "What's happening?"

"You can't hear that? At all?" She twirled, attempting to determine the source, hoping to move closer and perhaps discern what was being said.

"Nominal temperature drop on the Thermoscan with KII registering a corresponding EMF elevation. Very slight. Nothing to get excited about. I wouldn't even mention it, but you seem to be picking up something."

Temperature drops and spikes in electromagnetic frequencies often accompanied spiritual manifestations. Spirits could influence the physical world around them as they drew warmth and energy to power apparitions.

The whispers grew stronger when she moved away from the door and farther into the room, until she stood in the corner. The volume intensified as if someone whispered directly into her ear. A shiver ran down her spine.

"Elise, bring the recorder here, right next to me. Maybe we

can capture EVP." Electronic voice phenomenon sometimes presented on audio recordings, even when undetectable by the average human ear.

"Will do," Elise said. "And maybe the Audioxx will pick up something."

"Doesn't hurt to try, I suppose," she said, though she doubted the equipment could pick up anything her own senses could not.

Sterling pressed against her. "I'll listen, too."

A thrill shot through her, not only due to his physical presence, but also at the thought he wanted to attempt to harness the latent sixth sense she fervently believed he possessed. Not to mention the excitement the thought of investigating with a true psychic partner rather than a skeptic sent pulsing through her. He'd seen a ghost at their last investigation with her help. Maybe someday, with some training, he could manage without her assistance. Then again, as terrified as he'd been by the manifestation, she wasn't certain he could handle regularly seeing the spirits who remained in this realm.

"Anything?" she asked.

"No whispers," he said. "You still hear it?"

"Yes. Definitely."

"Maybe you could give me a boost?"

She hesitated, concerned her low energy should be conserved. Particularly since she couldn't explain why it felt so low. Sharing her psychic energy with him would further deplete her own abilities until she had the chance to recharge. That would leave her less available to connect herself. On the other hand, he'd never asked her to share her energy before, and he sounded so eager. How could she say no?

Curling one hand across the back of his neck, she massaged gently, relaxing his muscles and creeping as close to his indigo crown chakra as she dared. Overloading would be bad. He groaned slightly at her touch, a sound entirely too similar to intimate noises he moaned in bed. She quickly tamped down the flare of energy in her lower groin as her orange chakra spun and resonated in response to Sterling. Oof. Maybe this wasn't such a great idea. Partially depleted and completely distracted, she would never be able to connect. Oh, well. The first night rarely resulted in the best pieces to the puzzle anyway.

She tapped her psychic energy and pushed some of it down her arm, out the tips of her fingers, and toward his spine to fuel his chakras and power his own abilities.

He sucked in a breath and slammed his eyes closed. For a moment he stood absolutely still, as if paralyzed.

Maybe she'd overloaded him, despite her best efforts. How did one gauge this sort of thing anyway? It wasn't as if she'd been trained in how to appropriately siphon off her energy to share with others. "Are you okay?"

"I hear it," he murmured. "I hear the whispering."

Her heart skipped a beat. She had never in her life shared moments like this with anyone else and found herself even more drawn to Sterling. Sharing with him on such an intimate level piqued her curiosity and roused her interest in a way no man ever had.

His lips began to move in sync with the mumbled words she heard but could not understand.

"Wait a minute. You understand?"

"Hail Mary, full of grace . . ." he intoned, loudly and more forcefully. "Oh, yes. I'd recognize these prayers anywhere. She's saying a rosary."

"You're sure it's a woman? I had that impression too but wasn't certain."

"Definitely. A nun who once lived here."

"I . . . how do you know that?"

"I can just tell," he said. "It's the strangest sensation in the world. And you feel this all the time?"

"Well, not constantly, but off and on, yes. I think you're connecting better than I am with this one, though."

"Must be a Catholic thing," he joked.

Incredible. Who knew Sterling's Catholic upbringing would

one day help with a paranormal investigation? Then again, who expected Sterling to help with an investigation in any way ever? She should have been able to sense at least a little bit of what Sterling described. She grabbed her quartz and reached out beyond herself.

And detected nothing. Her low energy sputtered. She could not blame this on Rosie. She'd never felt her tank so empty before. Why would that be? A flare of panic lit her system.

The Audioxx crackled and produced a robotic word. Or part of a word.

—ave

"The Audioxx! She said something!" Elise forgot to keep her voice down in the excitement of the new equipment functioning.

But what did it say?" Kimberly asked. "I couldn't understand that."

"It sounded like 'wave' to me," Elise said.

"I thought it said 'save,'" TJ said.

"We hear you but still can't understand you," Kimberly said. "Can you tell us again?"

—ave

"No improvement," she said. "I still didn't understand."

"We don't know what you're trying to tell us," Sterling said.

Help

That they understood loud and clear.

She saw Sterling's face light up at the response. She had never been more turned on in her life.

CHAPTER FIVE

At footage review the next morning, Kimberly sipped coffee while waiting for her crew to discern anything useful. She exchanged sneaky glances with Sterling, always met with a sly smile. She ought to be completely and painfully exhausted, and yet she fairly burst with energy. She wanted to sit beside Sterling and snuggle up to him, but this was work and that seemed entirely inappropriate. Circling the room left her feeling aimless, restless. What was wrong with her? She could run a marathon if one happened by. She glanced again at Sterling and caught him staring at her, his gaze intense yet soft and warm, with an undercurrent of what looked like adoration. She spun away, her skin buzzing, longing for his touch. That look. It sent electricity coursing through her, setting her on fire.

He tipped his head at the empty seat beside him and she slid into it, heart hammering. She knew she was a mess yet was helpless to resist his draw.

Someone played footage from the connection Sterling made with the nun. Every head in the room swiveled to face her, inquisitive looks pinning her to the seat.

"What?"

Michael cleared his throat. "You could have given us a heads-up, Kimmy."

"Heads-up? About what?"

TJ answered. "I mean, you literally said that none of us should say anything about Sterling seeing a ghost at the Stone Lion Inn. You insisted the show format had to stay the same, with one believer and one skeptic."

"Nothing has changed. So what's with the looks?" Everyone in the room stared at her as if she'd just told them Santa Claus wasn't real.

"But last night . . ." Michael pressed his lips together and seemed to struggle to get the words out. "You didn't even warn me."

"Warn you about what? I don't know what you're upset about."

"That you and Sterling had your own plan. I mean, you want to shake things up, fine. I've always supported you, haven't I? Not trusting me hurts, sweetie."

"Not trusting—With what? I am so confused."

TJ crossed his arms. "You literally told us—"

"Hey, kid," Sterling said. "You are literally saying literally when it's literally unnecessary because simply repeating what Kimberly said literally implies she literally said it."

TJ whirled on him. "You were in on it with her! You don't get to say anything."

The pieces clicked. "Are you all upset because Sterling had an experience?"

Michael struck his stubborn pose. "Not that he had an *experience*." His air quotes around the word caught her off guard. If he was resorting to air quotes, he was really upset. "That you two kept it to yourself and didn't share with us. We were all blindsided and didn't know how to react to this. Was the thing at the Stone Lion Inn one big set-up for this new twist? Have you two been plotting this all this time? We're supposed to be a team here—"

"Hold up! Plotting? We didn't plan anything," she insisted, looking to Sterling for confirmation.

"Really, guys, I'm as baffled as anyone else. She does this thing where she touches me and—"

"Eww." TJ scowled. "Do not want to hear this."

"Puke," Rosie said from the corner where she sat alone.

How could they all turn on her like this? "Stop! You're all twisting this into something it isn't. We've discovered I can share my psychic energy with Sterling and when I do he can tap into his own sixth sense. We should be looking at the recordings and trying to figure out exactly how that's happening."

"No one is more surprised than I am," Sterling said. "I don't get it and I didn't want to believe it at first, but I can't deny something happens. I will still be watching for other explanations during investigations while we try to sort this out. But meanwhile, looks like I can also confirm what Kimberly sees in her visions. Or hears, as was the case last night."

"You're suddenly psychic too?" TJ asked. He turned to her. "How can you let him do this? Just let him hijack the entire show? You both insisted on maintaining the psychic versus skeptic aspect."

Hijack the show? She liked the idea of a psychic partner. They could be like the well-known paranormal investigators Ed and Lorraine Warren, made famous in films. *Amityville Horror* and *The Conjuring* movies were all based on their casework. The couple had founded the oldest ghost hunting group in New England and had even been involved in a trial.

So what if she and Sterling started out as Mulder and Scully? She liked this better, with Sterling starting to acknowledge maybe there was something there. Come to think of it, Ed wasn't even clairvoyant like Lorraine. He was a demonologist but not a clairvoyant himself. He believed in Lorraine and supported her. Maybe she'd never have a psychic partner, as she'd sometimes fantasized about. But she could work with a fascinated and interested partner.

Sterling held up his hands. "I'm not trying to radically change anything. We can edit out anything that involves me contributing to her psychic phenomenon. Frankly, it would be better that way. I'm not ready to go so far as to say that I'm psychic, and the viewers would probably balk at that strong of a deviation."

"Look, I'm just here to record," Stan said. "I don't want to rock the boat. But what's the point of these supposed experiences you're having if we're not going to use them some way for the show?"

"That's what I'm telling you," Sterling said. "This isn't some fake scenario. It's happening. I don't understand it. I'm not convinced of anything yet. And for that matter, Kimberly has voiced some skepticism about this investigation to me that—"

Michael's head jerked up and he spun to face her. "What? First I've heard of this. When did you intend to share with the rest of your team?"

"You're taking this out of context! I mentioned it in passing—"

"Mmm-hmm. And do you have to be sleeping with someone for them to tap into your psychic energy? Because we've been best friends for over a decade and you've never shared with me."

"Michael!" Heat flushed her cheeks. "That is entirely inappropriate."

She swept her gaze around the room. Rosie, Michael, and TJ all glowered at her while Stan and Elise stared intently at their screens. Ian dropped his head and looked away. Her crew had never behaved this way. Never. And over what? Sterling. After every one of them had pulled for him to join the show. Well, not TJ. And then pushed her to get hannvolved with him. Okay, also not TJ. He was behaving normally. But the rest of them . . . And Rosie was the worst of all.

"Let's talk about team," she said. "Why exactly would I come running to share anything at all with people who are currently giving me the cold shoulder? And for what? Because I'm happy?

First you all criticized me for not wanting Sterling on the show, now you're irritated that he is and we're working well together? The show is doing better in ratings than ever and yet I feel like I can't win no matter what I do. How is the team supporting me?"

"We've always supported you, sweetie," Michael said, all the anger gone. "I'd just like to be kept in the loop. We all would."

"No one kept you intentionally out of anything."

Stan pulled off his headphones. "If everyone could stop bickering and focus on the actual investigation, I have something I'd like you to see."

"Excellent. Thank you." Finally, something to shift gears away from the current conversation. "What did you find?"

As they all gathered around his monitor, Sterling pressed close behind her, resting a hand on her hip. "You okay?" he breathed softly in her ear, so only she could hear.

She nodded, his morning scruff rough against her cheek. The others in her crew left some distance, and a distinct chill sent a shiver down her spine. Stupid sixth sense. Times like this she wished she could switch it off. Maybe she shouldn't train Sterling. He had no idea what he asked for. She shivered again, frigid though the room around her had not changed temperature.

Stan clicked "Play" and images from last night moved across the monitor. The audio crackled from the speakers.

"Dude! Now none of us can see!"

"Aside from dancing white spots. Be mindful of pupils and retinas, Sterling. No sudden bursts of light without warning."

"I'm not letting Kimberly in there without verifying it's safe."

"But now anything we might have captured on camera will be washed out."

"And probably scared away."

On Stan's monitor, a face peered around the corner before ducking back into the stairway.

Sterling stiffened. "See? Someone was hiding in there!"

"Really?" Stan asked. "You think a man was hiding in that tiny space the entire time we were all crammed in there? Where?

And he breathed silently? Or held his breath the entire time? Didn't once rustle or shift? Come on."

"I admit that would be highly difficult, but—"

"Besides, look at this." Stan switched to a second monitor. "Look at the footage from the FLIR."

A blue figure leaned around the corner before disappearing into the stairwell.

"That proves someone was hiding there," Sterling repeated.

"The image isn't red, dude," TJ said, "which means it wasn't a living being. Blue means cold, endothermic, needing to draw heat from the environment."

"And we couldn't see the figure in real time because *someone* flipped on a flashlight and blinded us all."

"Yes, and this confirms my concerns. Why is everyone being so weird?"

"Why are *you* being so weird?" TJ asked. "Last night you supposedly connected with a spirit, today you're refusing to acknowledge what we all know is a spirit on the recordings."

"We don't know that. We see a humanoid shape. Nothing about that indicates a ghost."

"It's blue!" TJ looked ready to tear his hair out. "Look!" He picked up the FLIR and turned it on the people in the room. "See that? See the images? Every one of us is showing up in red because we're alive and producing heat."

"I understand that, but there could be another reason for the image showing up as a shadow—"

"No, there isn't! Ms. Wantland, tell him. We've been doing this for years, and we know."

Sterling shook his head. "I'm just saying there could be a rational explanation—"

"Yes! There was a spirit. That's the explanation. Pick a side! You either believe or you don't."

"I'm not on any side except the truth," Sterling said. "And you've all been accusing me of 'switching sides' but I never said that. Did I hear someone praying last night? Yes. Can I explain it? No."

"Yeah, well, after your big connection last night, I think you have to turn in your skeptic card."

"I always said that if I experienced something I couldn't explain, then I would acknowledge it. And I did. But that doesn't mean I'm going to turn into a gullible fool and start believing anything and everything."

"This is so straightforward. It just doesn't get any simpler. It's right here. Red images are caused by living beings. See how the chairs and inanimate objects—"

TJ gasped and bobbled the camera, nearly dropping it.

"What? What is it?" Kimberly asked.

He turned the camera to show her. A dark hooded figure stood behind Michael.

CHAPTER SIX

KIMBERLY SAT with Rosie and Elise in her trailer, still shaken from the daytime manifestation of the cloaked apparition. No one had been more freaked out than Michael, as it appeared to be creeping closer to him before it disappeared. No amount of assurance could assuage his belief that the thing had been stalking him. The only good to come from the discovery was that it shocked them all out of their funks and back to normal. Mostly.

Rosie distributed calming tea and sat with them. She still seemed a bit distant, but no downright hostility rolled off her. "What did you really feel when that ghost was after Michael? A menacing sense of foreboding? The need for revenge? Murderous rage?"

She couldn't help but smile at Rosie's horror-movie assessment. If only anything was ever that simple and straightforward, her job would be so much easier. "No, nothing like that. Nothing specific at all."

"Wait, you were serious? I thought you only told Michael that to calm him down. No one freaks out like Michael does. How has he stayed in this business all this time?"

"I wish I'd felt something. Anything. Knowing is always

better than not knowing. Honestly I'm a bit freaked out that I felt nothing. How did that thing creep up on us and I didn't feel so much as a twinge?" She didn't admit to her concern about low energy just yet. She'd see how tonight went. Maybe everything would be back to normal.

Rosie pulled down the corners of her mouth. "There was a lot of animosity filling the atmosphere. I'm sure that distracted you. Plus I didn't charge you up as well as maybe I should've. Not that we expected you to need to be fully charged."

She sipped her tea. "True. No reason to be fully charged at footage review normally."

"Kayla mentioned a dark figure," Elise said, flipping pages of her notebook. "But we didn't capture any good EVP last night. Really hoped we'd get to hear the guy asking for his spotlight."

"Would have been nice," she agreed. "But the face we saw wasn't hooded. And Kayla definitely thought the figure she saw was hooded."

Elise flipped back a page. "She mentioned seeing a face peering around the curtain on stage though."

She pressed her fingers to her temples and rubbed. "So really we have no idea who or what we're looking for. And it sounds like we have at least two spirits wandering the building. And I can't shake the feeling Jillian is keeping something from me. Nothing about this is going to be easy."

Elise flipped pages in her notebook and took a deep breath. "I have something to share with you, if we can take a break from the investigation for a moment."

"Share with me?" she asked. A break sounded good. And if Elise had something important about—

The door swung open, and Sterling joined them. "Well, the guys are all completely freaked out, but I think we managed to calm Michael down a little bit."

She took a deep breath at the sight of him, glad to see him. His presence brought calm. "I've told you there are spirits around us all the time, like fish swimming in a pond. It's odd to see one in the middle of the day though. Did you convince Michael it was simply there and not out to get him? Or a harbinger of terrible calamity befalling him?"

"Excellent use of the word harbinger, but no. I was making things worse by telling him it was most likely nothing but a shadow."

"But you said you managed to—"

"'We' meaning Stan and TJ. I helped by leaving. I seem to make everyone angry no matter what I do. I experience something strange and they're mad that I'm not a skeptic. I express skepticism and they're mad that I don't believe them." His brow furrowed and she felt his confusion and concern.

She opened her mouth to comfort him and let him know she felt exactly the same, but before she got any words out, her cell phone rang. The ringtone belonged to Angela, the woman who housesat her home in Albuquerque while she was gone the majority of the year. She held up a finger and took the call.

"Hey, Angela! Everything okay?"

"Hi, Kimberly. I thought it was time to reach out to you. The last few nights I've been waking to footsteps in the attic. On top of that, I have some pics I'd like to text you. Is this a good time?"

"Yes, definitely. Please do. I'm glad you're keeping me in the loop."

"I'll call back if things get any stranger."

"Absolutely. I'll talk to you later."

She hung up and caught Rosie watching her intently. "Angela. She heard footsteps in the attic, which has never happened before. She's going to text some pictures too."

Something tugged at the back of her mind, wanting attention but eluding her grasp.

"I know that look," Rosie said. "What is it?"

She shook her head, not even sure herself yet. Her phone sounded eerie footsteps, her text notification alert. Opening the first text, she discovered a photo of Angela taking a snap of herself in front of a mirror. An orb hovered behind her, blue and elongated. A simple light reflection? Or a spirit encroaching on her space?

Sterling peeped over her shoulder. "The camera flash reflected in the mirror? What am I missing?"

"She said her flash was off. So what's reflecting? It could be an orb. A spirit manifesting."

"Or it could be light from the window."

Elise pressed close and stared at the photo. "No. Look at the shadows in the room. They don't support Angela being backlit. See how they're cast from above? Light from the window isn't the answer. Ms. Wantland, I was trying to tell you—"

"Speaking of window . . ." She brought up the second picture, showing a crack rising from the corner of one pane of glass.

Sterling took the phone and examined it. "Easy. Older house. Showing signs of wear. Needs to be replaced. No paranormal activity yet."

"Wait a minute," Rosie said. "Window? It isn't . . ."

She took the phone back from Sterling and turned it so Rosie could see.

Rosie's hands lifted to her face and she shook her head. "No way. Your bedroom?"

She nodded. "Bedroom window."

"Guys, this is no big deal," Sterling said.

"She renovated the house when she bought it," Rosie told him. "Replaced all the windows when she discovered a crack in her old bedroom window."

Sterling seemed to consider. "Well, it could be a structural defect then."

"The windows are still under warranty, less than a year old. Isn't this the third window to break? In exactly the same place?" Rosie looked quite pleased to deliver the information.

"This is the third, yes. The first replacement, the company concluded installation error and sent their best, most experienced men. The second window they suggested structural issues but couldn't find any."

"I mean, it's a nice house," Rosie said. "Not a dump. I've been there so I know."

Her stylist appeared to be reveling in knowing more about her than Sterling did. Rosie's improved mood buoyed her own, as always. Moods and attitudes and the environment around her always impacted her own emotional state. But Rosie, her best friend, influenced her more than anyone else. Sterling had gained the power to affect her too, but that was an entirely different emotional range.

"Rosie is exactly right. This is the third window now to crack in the exact same place in the exact same room. Angela says she heard the sound when it happened, and that it was preceded by a noise in the attic and a gust of cold air that blew through the house."

"House noise and air movement are not signs of supernatural beings," Sterling said. "Sorry, guys, but this is easily explained."

"Not when there was nothing in the attic, the windows are all closed, and the fans are all off." Rosie's eyes glinted as she sparred with Sterling.

"We weren't there. We don't know any of that."

"Angela is there. She knows. And Kimberly trusts her."

"No offense but Angela will be inclined to send whatever she thinks will make Kimberly happy. Of course she's going to send a paranormal investigator indications of spooky activity."

"Spooky?" Rosie scoffed. "What are we, five?"

The something in the back of her mind tried to surface but the bickering, no matter how good-natured, distracted her.

"Ms. Wantland," Elise said, "I know you have a lot on your mind, but I think you'll want to hear this."

She held her hands up to quiet Rosie and Sterling. "Oh, yes. You wanted to tell me something."

"I think I've found the house in New Orleans where your mother lived as a child."

Forgetting all about the activity in the house she had grown up in, she turned to Elise, heart hammering. "You're sure? You found record of her?"

"Pretty sure." Elise glanced around the space at all the eyes on her and pushed her glasses up her nose. "Since we learned your mother's birth name from Gloria in Guthrie, and that she possibly lived in New Orleans, I went looking for her. Took some time, but I weeded it down, and I think I've found her. And your grandparents. And the house she grew up in, not far from the French Quarter. In fact, I think your grandparents moved back there from Guthrie after she and your dad got married and moved away from Oklahoma."

All basic, normal information average people knew about their ancestry, but which had been hidden from her for some reason. Why? Why didn't her dad ever share any of this with her? She'd had no idea when she led her team to Guthrie, Oklahoma for an investigation that her father had grown up there. That his family had deep roots there. That he'd met her mother there after her parents had picked up and relocated from New Orleans.

Guthrie, Oklahoma back then, tiny and remote, could have been the type of place someone might go to hide.

And then, according to Gloria, her parents had fled suddenly, and no one ever heard from them again.

Almost as if they'd run. Run to hide.

But from what? And why hadn't they ever shared any of this? Not once had they traveled to New Orleans to visit family on a holiday. Or Guthrie either. They'd never told her their parents, her grandparents, were deceased, but she'd assumed. They'd lived, just the three of them, in Albuquerque, never venturing far, with nothing but vague references to an aunt on her father's side and her daughter, Kimberly's cousin, Dolly. Hazy references to a falling out explained her father's estrangement from his sister.

And yet she'd barely blinked, much less questioned the veracity of the will, when her father left her childhood home to his sister rather than her. By that time, she'd become alienated from her father and for all she knew he'd reconciled with his sister in his final days—

She gulped hard and closed her eyes, fighting to control the emotional swell. She'd had no idea when his health took a turn for the worse. He hadn't reached out, made no attempt to reconnect and perhaps find a peace of sorts before the end. Not even when he'd been dying could he set aside his shame and embarrassment and find it in his heart to forgive her. She was certain he blamed her for her mother's death. She'd been home and had not saved Mom. Dad never got over that, never forgave her. Now she'd go to her own grave carrying the enormous weight of guilt, shackled in her afterlife.

And she'd seen enough spirits to know first-hand what a hollow, miserable sort of existence they had. Weighed down by guilt, tied to the earth long after they'd passed from it. Wandering in search of redemption and forgiveness, slowly decaying rather than passing to the next plane.

She shuddered. If only people knew what grudges and hard feelings could inflict on the objects of their emotional war—to the point the spirit that remained could not rest in peace, much less move on from this world. She worried she'd seen a glimpse of her future.

A hand rested on her shoulder, Sterling's long fingers curling over her. "You okay?"

She nodded and drew in a deep breath. She had no choice but to be okay. The time for words was gone, the chance for forgiveness washed away by the constant ebb and flow of time, like a sandcastle destroyed by the tide.

"If you're truly okay, I'd like to go examine the Audioxx before we use it again tonight."

Elise's head snapped up. "What do you mean, 'examine'?"

"I'm going to take it apart and see what exactly prompts it to 'talk.'"

"Take it apart? That's expensive equipment."

"I can reassemble it."

"What if you take it apart and can't reassemble it? We already told you it detects and interprets EVP, like we sometimes hear after the fact during footage review. But if we can hear attempts to communicate in real time, we can act on it then rather than later and decrease the investigation time."

"But what exactly triggers it? What's the mechanism? What is it interpreting as attempts to communicate? All of us talked throughout the night and nothing. Not a peep out of the box. Then it randomly squawked out noise and everyone attempted to discern a word from the staticky sound."

"We don't have EVP on our digital recordings when they happen—only after the fact. How do you explain that?"

Sterling grimaced and sucked in a breath. "That there's no voice at all? Simply background noise misconstrued into something it isn't."

Elise pointed her pen at him. "You heard a voice last night."

"I did. And I can't explain it. But maybe if I can figure out what the Audioxx picks up on, I can start to understand what triggers Kimberly to hear things."

Kimberly's turn to grimace. "Oof. We're back to I 'hear things'? You think I have a chip planted in my head?"

He frowned. "Of course not. I didn't say that. I just need—"

"Need to understand. Need physics to rationalize for you. Go ahead, Elise. You'll want to ensure he doesn't inadvertently ruin the Audioxx in his examination."

Sterling clutched his chest. "Your lack of faith wounds me. I'll have you know I've taken apart and repaired watches, small appliances. I'm good with tools."

"Nonetheless, Elise will feel better this way."

Elise pushed her glasses up her nose. "I planned to go look at land records in New Orleans, family trees, yearbook records. But maybe I should go with Sterling instead."

"I appreciate that, but the current investigation should take precedence over my personal research. I feel guilty about you devoting so much time to it."

"Okay, I'll go with him. But as to the family history, look at it this way—the more information we have before we investigate your house in Albuquerque, the better prepared we'll be."

She raised her eyebrows. "Good point. Thanks for all you do, Elise. And Sterling?"

He turned, his shock of dark hair falling into his eyes.

"Don't break the equipment. I don't want to get in trouble."

CHAPTER SEVEN

LEFT ALONE WITH ROSIE, Kimberly took a deep breath and grasped her quartz, hoping to discern what bothered her friend.

"Uh-uh. Don't read my spectrum."

She dropped her hand. "Okay, well, I'm sorry I wanted to see how you're feeling."

"You could just ask me."

"Hard to have a conversation when you're avoiding me and won't talk."

Rosie sighed. "Fair enough."

Kimberly patted the chair Sterling had vacated. "Come on. Sit. What's up?"

"I don't wanna talk about it," Rosie said, but dropped into the seat anyway.

"I think we need to talk about it."

Rosie shook her head. "No. It's stupid. I just need to get over it."

"We all have stupid feelings sometimes. They still bother us, stupid or not." She turned to the array of essential oils, picking up a few before settling on one. "Lemongrass? Will that help?"

"Would you believe I secretly hate that one? It reminds me of bug spray."

"But you put up with it for me."

Rosie shrugged. "Sometimes you need it. Helps with clarity."

She lifted another bottle. "Patchouli?"

Rosie took the bottle and replaced it in the lineup. "I don't need essential oils. I need . . ."

"Go ahead. What is it?"

"You'll be mad."

"I won't. You can talk to me."

"I miss when it was just the two of us."

"That's what you're upset about? Why would that make me mad? I miss that too."

"No, you don't! You have Sterling now."

"True. And while I enjoy that new element, it comes with new anxiety. I worry things will sour between us and we won't be able to salvage the show. I'm scared my viewers will hate this season, with the addition of him in every episode. Maybe they'll accept him better if the believers win over the skeptic a little bit —convert him, so to speak. Or maybe like you they'll miss the good old days. Conversely, any *SpookBusters* viewers who follow him over will be turned off if we lure him to the dark side. Things have definitely gotten very complicated."

"Wow. I didn't realize. I thought you were just happy to have him here."

"I am happy. Cautiously. Hesitantly. But I'm also scared."

"But he's here with you. All the time. I wish . . ."

"Lorenzo?"

"I miss him so much, girl." Rosie's voice broke and tears collected in her eyes.

She pulled her friend into a hug. "It'll be okay."

"I don't know what's wrong with me. Maybe my biological clock is ticking. Maybe something is simply fundamentally wrong with me. I mean, look at you—you never needed a guy. Maybe I'm just not meant to be alone."

She leaned back, frowning. "And you think I am?"

Rosie dabbed at her eyes. "You always seemed fine. Always listened to me prattle on about my latest fling."

"Just because I stayed calm and listened to your massive train wrecks—"

"Hey!"

She cocked an eyebrow and folded her arms. "Really? You want to go there?"

Rosie held her arms out in a come-at-me-bro pose. "I admit I've struggled with relationships."

She sucked her upper lip and nodded. "Mmm-hmm. So when you walked in on Marcus or Mario of whatever that guy's name was—"

"Marcus, but he goes by Mario."

"—in your own apartment, three different times, with the exact same girl, that wasn't a major fail? We're categorizing that as relationship trouble?"

Rosie blew out a huge breath. "Okay, I gave him way too many chances. I concede your point on that one. But—"

"And Joseph, the sweet little born-again Christian who wouldn't actually have sex with you—"

"Oh, gawd!" Rosie covered her face.

"—but got caught and arrested in a 'massage parlor'—"

"Stop!"

"Or Angel, the nurse who claimed he accepted a temporary month-long position in California, professed his undying love, then ghosted you, never to be seen or heard from again? You waited months for him to answer you. Months."

"I need to be loved! I'm not a strong, independent woman like you."

"We all need to be loved. That's universal. The two of us just approach things differently."

"I just—I don't know. Everything is so different now."

"True. Lorenzo is thoughtful, attentive, treats you well. He seems ready to commit if you want that."

"I don't know what I want. Maybe I don't want that. I don't like this long-distance thing."

"Look, don't rush into a decision, either way. You're out of sorts because this is so unlike anything you've experienced before. Don't dump him because he's nice to you, and you don't know how to handle nice."

"It will fall apart. I know it will. Better to be the one to end it. And before I get even more attached."

"Things don't always fall apart. Maybe this will be the one that doesn't. If you want that."

Rosie shook her head. "I'm supposed to be the relationship expert."

"That's the other problem. You're used to me being single. Now I'm not. We're both navigating new relationships, making time for other people."

"I don't like it."

"It's different, and different can be unsettling, even if it's a good different. But nothing stays the same forever. We'll figure it out."

Rosie hugged her. "Thanks, girl. I keep fighting the urge to call home. But I also keep thinking, I want my mom. How ridiculous is that?"

Kimberly glanced away. How often did she long to be able to call her mom, wish she could visit and share and discuss issues? Every day. "Not ridiculous at all."

"I'm so sorry, girl! That was thoughtless of me."

"Don't be silly. Sure, I miss my mom, but that doesn't mean you can't mention yours. And you should call her. Call while you can."

"I know she will guilt-trip me though. And want to know when I'll come visit. And if I mention Lorenzo, she'll get excited and start talking about settling down and finding a real job."

She laughed. "This job pays more than anything we could find back home. She'd rather you were waiting tables or answering phones?"

"I know. She's too much like your dad was, never happy with us driving around chasing ghosts. And I don't even chase ghosts. I put on your makeup and fix your hair."

"I'm homesick too. And ready for a break from having to travel all year. But you should call her anyway."

Rosie stared at her hands. "She says I should open a salon there in Albuquerque."

This was new. And if she wasn't mistaken, she heard interest in Rosie's voice. "Do you want to open a salon back home? Is this something that would make you happy?"

"That's probably what I'd be doing if I hadn't met you. Except I don't know if I would have been able to open my own place. I mean, I love being here with you and doing the show. Don't get me wrong. What an incredible opportunity and I get to work with my best friend. But lately Mom is really pushing for me to think about it. I think I might enjoy having my own place, and now I can afford to do it. But Lorenzo is in Eureka Springs and Mom and Dad are in Albuquerque. How do I choose?"

"You don't have to choose today. See what happens with Lorenzo and cross that bridge if you come to it. But call your mom."

"I will, I will. She and Dad are so excited we'll be filming the season finale right there in Albuquerque."

"I am too. For several reasons."

Rosie grabbed her hand. "We'll find your mom. Seems like Angela has reported a lot of activity in the house lately."

"Activity does seem to be increasing. I wonder why. And I wish I was there now while it's happening."

Rosie tapped her lips with a finger. "Angela mentioned footsteps in the attic. Has she heard those before?"

"No, not that she's mentioned."

"We kept hearing footsteps in the attic in Guthrie. Could it be related?"

The idea that had been pulling at the back of her mind clicked into place. "That's it! That's what was bothering me. The footsteps in the attic. The spirit plaguing the Johnsons stomped around their attic, and he mentioned my mother. How could he possibly have known about her?"

"We sort of forgot that connection, didn't we?"

"I thought maybe I heard Mom too, when I fought him for Faith, after he stole her away."

"While you were in the Nightshade?"

Kimberly shivered as she thought about the Nightshade, the strange plane of existence where spirits dwelt when their bodies expired but their spirits didn't successfully translocate to the next world. "Right. Sometimes I think I smell her perfume, lavender and freesia. Sometimes I hear her saying my name. But I can't ever connect. She always seems just out of range. Maybe she doesn't want to connect. Maybe she's upset because I didn't help her the day she died."

"I can't believe she's upset with you. Maybe she can't connect. What do you know for sure about the Nightshade?"

"For sure? Almost nothing. Only bits and pieces and my best guesses." Most people were unaware the Nightshade existed. Even most psychics never saw the realm. How could she know about it with no one to teach her?

"What was it like? When you were there?"

The decision to enter the Nightshade during their previous investigation had been a last resort to rescue a young teen dragged there by a vengeful spirit. The strange, distorted land-scape, fractured and static, wasn't meant for still-living beings with bodies. "It was kind of like I got pulled into an old film, only that's not quite right. It wasn't sepia-toned, but varying shades of blues and grays, like a dull, washed-out version of the real world. But time and space are fluid."

"What, like a Dali painting?"

"No, not that distorted. It isn't that surreal. Except it kind of is. This isn't making any sense, I know. It's difficult to describe."

Rosie sipped her tea, squinting as she thought. "Can spirits move from place to place in the Nightshade?"

"I don't know. In my experience, spirits remain bound to the place where the body perished or to an object important to them in life. But does that mean it's impossible for them to travel? I thought so. Maybe not."

"Maybe they only think they're stuck. Or maybe they don't think at all. What if it just doesn't occur to them to try to move?"

"That could be the case. Especially for the spirits who don't realize they're no longer living. They're so busy trying to hold onto what they know, they don't move on. And the next chapter might be so much better."

"That's so sad."

Was her mother doomed to such an existence? Wandering an empty house, searching for her husband and young daughter, wondering why they left her all alone? She shuddered at the frightening loneliness of it all and her heart ached for her mother. But if her mom remained trapped in her old house, why did Kimberly sometimes detect her presence when she brushed against the Nightshade?

"What if they don't move through the Nightshade but can send messages through it?" she asked Rosie.

"Could anyone but you even receive the messages?"

She shook her head. "I simply don't know. Other psychics exist of course but would anyone be listening for messages from the other side besides frauds and con men relaying invented messages from beyond?"

"Do you think the spirits can communicate with each other through the Nightshade? Could there be a connection between your mother and a spirit in Guthrie? Maybe she was trying to get a message to you through another spirit?"

"An excellent question. And with so little to guide us, I have no idea."

"Do you think there's a connection to the footsteps in the attic? Or was it complete coincidence?"

"Without more information, who knows. I know what Sterling would say," she said as the door opened, and Sterling and Elise came back in.

"What would I say?" Sterling asked. "About what?"

"Don't worry about it. Did you already figure out the Adioxx?"

"No. I need some different tools to get into it. I'll find a store. Or order from Amazon."

"I'm free to get back to research," Elise said, snatching up her notepad and pencil and adjusting her glasses.

"Oh, hey," Sterling said. "Ian told me about a ghost tour that runs through town most evenings. I'll book tickets for us, if you'd like to go."

"You'll go on a ghost tour with me?" Was he hoping to explore his own abilities? Or simply looking for ways to make her happy? Either way, she loved it. She glanced at Rosie, worried this would set her back off.

Rosie smiled. "That would be a lot of fun. We can hear some history and learn some of the local lore."

Sterling nodded at her. "That's what I was thinking. I'll book an entire tour for the crew. Our own private look at Hannibal."

Kimberly breathed a sigh of relief to see her best friend back to normal. "That sounds great." She'd never thought to take a ghost tour during an investigation. She was all ghosts, all the time. Sterling brought a new element to the show.

"One more thing. Michael said I should warn you that we will have to work around the haunted house on weeknights and the play on weekends. Monday is their only dark day."

She blinked. "Last night was the only night we will be in the building without other people? And no one told me before we arrived? How is that possible? Not acceptable. I need to talk to Michael right now."

Rosie reached for the calming lavender oil. "Now, don't get worked up—"

Sterling slapped his forehead. "Actually, one more thing. He also said Hoffmeier wants us to sponsor a Trunk or Treat for any local children who want to participate. He thinks it will grab a lot of attention and also get some good footage for the episode. Make it extra Halloween by having the cast dress up and hand out candy."

"Dress up and hand out candy? Hard pass. I'm here to do a job, not goof off dressing up." She jumped to her feet. "Michael didn't even ask me! Where is he? I need to talk to him right now and get him to shut this down."

"No can do, Khemosabe. He and Ian snuck off to get lunch together. Alone. Destination unknown. It's almost like he knew you wouldn't like any of this information and decided to let me be the bad guy."

"I didn't agree to this! He knows I don't like publicity stunts—"

"Oh, come on, girl," Rosie said. "Handing out candy to kids? You can't say no to that. Dressing up and decorating cars will be fun."

Elise lifted a hand. "And how cool would it be if you and Sterling dress up as the Stillwells?"

"The what?"

"The who!" Elise grinned. "I'm sure we'll learn about them on the tour."

"We're all here with you," Sterling said.

She narrowed her eyes. "Sure. Until you get spooked in the haunted house and bail on me."

"Come on. How bad can it be?"

"Did you really just ask that? Have you never learned what happens when you tempt the universe like that?"

CHAPTER EIGHT

THE STROBING black light disoriented Kimberly as ghouls and gremlins jerked around the lobby of the Old Catholic church, seeming to move in fits and starts. She watched Sterling grimace, duck, and jump in the jarring dim light as shadows, real and imagined, startled him. Cobwebs draped every surface.

They all turned a corner, where a skeleton shrieked at them beside a bubbling cauldron, stirred by a cackling witch, who reached out and grabbed Sterling by the wrist.

"Hello, my pretty. Want to stay for dinner?" The witch lifted her giant wooden spoon and offered a taste of foaming sludge to him.

He leaned away and Kimberly saw his jaw tighten. She hurried forward and stepped between them, holding up a hand to the witch. "We're still stuffed from dinner."

She grabbed Sterling's hand and pulled him away, noting both Stan and TJ recorded. He moved ahead of her again, leading the way down the hall toward the stairs to the auditorium. She sighed. His male desire to protect her had stopped being cute and was beginning to annoy her a bit.

A giant spider fell directly in front of him and bounced on its bungie-cord web.

He spun around and closed his eyes. "I freaking hate this!"

She heard TJ laugh and hoped Sterling hadn't. At least TJ didn't say anything.

"You broke the cardinal rule and asked how bad it could be. The universe heard you and accepted the challenge."

"The universe can bite my—"

"Sterling!"

Out of the corner of her eye, she saw a Grim Reaper—a figure she'd presumed animatronic—come to life and creep toward Sterling, who had already passed by and would never see him coming.

She waved her hands frantically until she caught the actor's attention, then pointed to Sterling and shook her head furiously like, *This one is off limits.*

The Grim Reaper paused and appeared to mull it over before continuing to creep after Sterling, one bony hand reaching out to grab him.

How dare he ignore her! Struggling to remain silent lest the exchange tip off Sterling, she pointed at the stubborn actor, shook her fist, and drew her finger across her neck. *Try it and die, pal.*

The Grim Reaper nodded and reversed course, retreating backwards to his starting position where he froze, waiting for his next victim. And her camera operators probably happily caught every bit of that. Hopefully Sterling wouldn't see it.

His survival, or root, chakra, spun madly in his pelvis, triggering all his danger alarms and sending adrenaline coursing through his veins.

"Let me go ahead of you," she suggested for what felt like the eight thousandth time. "I can run interference."

He shook his head, determined to take the lead. But she felt, like no one else could, and understood, like no one else could, how difficult this was for him. He wanted to face down his childhood demon and slay the dragon once and for all. But while her childhood demon was, she suspected, an actual demon, Sterling's came in the form of obnoxious teenagers who tormented his ten-year-old self at a Halloween haunted house. He'd shared the incident with her in Eureka Springs. That was his darkest secret and his defining moment, when skeptic Sterling had been born, determined never to be duped or caught off guard again.

"Why couldn't we just come do our thing later tonight, after the haunted house is over?"

"Because they don't close it down until midnight if people are still inside. That's too many hours to sacrifice. But, hey, it's only three nights and then they switch over to the stage play."

"Great. Only three nights of torture. And then how will we investigate when we can't get into the auditorium?"

"Maybe we will solve it before then. You never know."

She caught sight of Ian wrapped up as a mummy. He waved her over.

"I'll come help as soon as I can get out of my costume! And no one is allowed in the theatre itself. We can't risk someone damaging the set or stealing props."

"See, Sterling?" TJ teased. "We only need to make it to the auditorium and then you'll be safe."

"You're a riot." Sterling rolled his eyes.

"Jillian told me we could ignore the warning signs and go right in," Michael said.

Kimberly frowned. "When did you see her? Is she here? I want to talk to her."

"Just in passing. She left about the time I got here."

"Why do I feel like she's deliberately avoiding me?"

Michael shrugged. "I don't know. Inexplicable paranoia?"

She shook her head and turned to Sterling. "You're right. These guys are a riot."

When they reached the stairs leading down to the basement theatre, a skull and crossbones greeted them, the sign proclaiming "Abandon all hope, ye who enter here."

They stepped over and around the red velvet ropes hung between gold poles to discourage passage. Crime scene tape, plastered all over the doors that opened from the theatre lobby to the auditorium, further declared DO NOT ENTER. A nun stood beside one set of doors, an old-fashioned habit that obscured the actor's face. Kimberly expected Sterling to crack a joke about nuns, but he didn't. Probably still too worked up over the haunted house.

As if to underscore her point, distant shrieks from above carried down the staircase.

The nun lifted a finger to indicate quiet as Kimberly and her crew ignored the crime scene tape and opened the auditorium doors. She nodded at the actor. Best not to make noise and attract the haunted house participants who shouldn't be in this part of the building. She was glad someone would be watching the doors, so she needn't sacrifice one of her crew to keep watch.

Kimberly had been around actors enough to know most theatres were considered haunted. Nearly everyone could share at least one inexplicable experience. Those stories, combined with speculation and theories about who exactly the resident ghost might have been while living, combined to add an element of intrigue and infamy to many locations. In fact, back in her acting days, she couldn't remember a single theatre she'd performed in that didn't purportedly harbor at least one lingering resident spirit. Were artistic souls more likely to remain behind after the demise of the physical body? Or were artists more open to experiences with the supernatural and less likely to rationalize it away?

"Back to the apartment?" Michael asked. "What are you thinking?"

She considered. They did encounter a spirit in the apartment. But she wasn't convinced that one had any bearing on this case. "I think tonight we fan out and get a more general feel for the location. I don't think the apartment holds the key. I'll try to encourage a connection with other spirits rather than the same one. At least as much as I can with the building crawling with people."

"We did feel something in the apartment though," Sterling said.

"We did. I'm just not convinced that one is our relevant resident spirit. Besides the interference of living beings during this investigation, we're also going to have to contend with other spirits who may be hanging around."

"What makes you so sure the ghost I heard last night isn't the one?" Sterling asked.

"A recently deceased spirit makes the most sense, based on the teenagers' accounts and the information we have so far. It would seem to indicate an actor. And don't discount Jillian's beliefs. As weird as it is to show up to an investigation and have someone tell me they know who the ghost is, the evidence does seem to be pointing to Donny."

Sterling scratched his neck. "I'd kind of like to go back to the apartment and see what happens."

She fought to suppress a smile. He was like a child with a new toy, fascinated by his brush with the paranormal and eager to try again. "You could go ask the nun in the lobby if it was her up there, saying her prayers before bed," she teased.

Sterling frowned. "Nun in the lobby?"

"Yeah. Standing by the door when we walked in. Just kidding. Obviously it wasn't her."

"There wasn't a nun. What are you talking about?"

"She was right by the door." She hiked a thumb over her shoulder. "Told us to be quiet."

He eyed her as if expecting a punchline. "The lobby was empty."

She turned to Michael for confirmation. "You saw a nun, didn't you? In the lobby?"

Michael shook his head.

"No one else saw the nun?"

Everyone in the group shook their heads and looked at her as if expecting she might be playing a Halloween prank. They'd worked with her long enough to know better.

"You must have seen a ghost!" TJ said.

"I don't think so. I didn't get any vibes from her."

"Come on. We'll go look," Michael said, draping an arm around her.

They traipsed back to the lobby.

Empty.

"She looked so real." She looked to Michael. Was she losing her touch? "Why didn't I realize she was a ghost? I truly believed she was a person. She indicated we should be quiet."

Rosie rested a hand on her shoulder. "We didn't charge you up before we started. I'm sure that's it." Rosie had charged her up though, as she always did, with massage and essential oils to clear her chakras and Reiki to rejuvenate her reserves. Her friend was covering for her.

Michael gestured to Rosie. "There you go. And if the nun was simply a loop, just doing what she always did and admonishing people to be quiet when they came inside, she probably wasn't giving off much energy. Right?"

"Maybe." That sounded like a pathetic excuse, though. An excuse to cover her mistake. She saw the looks of sympathy on all their faces. This wasn't like her. "I'm sorry, guys."

"None of us noticed it either," Stan said.

"But I'm supposed to be in tune and show you where to focus. We missed an excellent opportunity and it's on me."

Sterling curled an arm around her waist. "The nun isn't even the focus of the investigation. You said so yourself. Don't beat yourself up."

"I suppose that's true." Warmth suffused her, then gratitude for his support. Not long ago he would have completely dismissed the discussion as pointless nonsense.

"And hey," he said, "that may be who I heard praying last night, so maybe I'll get lucky and connect with her again tonight."

She didn't have the heart to discourage him. "Good point. Maybe she can tell you're Catholic. You go ahead and check out the apartment again. The rest of us can fan out and search for evidence Donny is still around, lingering in the afterlife. We need to either verify he's here or rule him out. Once I make a connection, hopefully he will share what he wants. Which I still think would be easier if Jillian would talk to me more in depth. I still feel like she's hiding something."

Sterling smirked and shook his head a bit.

"What?"

"Nothing."

"Go ahead and say it. You want to say something about my insistence on using the word 'evidence,' don't you?"

"No, I'm laughing at myself actually. Because that's exactly what I'm doing. I want to go back and look for evidence to support what I experienced last night. To see if it's reproduceable. I'm starting to doubt myself. Wondering if I imagined it."

"You didn't imagine it. But go ahead." Unfortunately, she knew he wouldn't be able to reproduce the experience without her help. Or highly doubted it at least. If he could, that would prove her theory he did, in fact, harbor psychic abilities he tried to deny. Perhaps this interaction was opening him to the idea and could trigger the suppressed gift. She held out hope her show would morph into an investigative psychic team instead of psychic versus skeptic. She enjoyed a cooperative, agreeable atmosphere more than an antagonistic, argumentative one.

But for now, no matter what happened, she couldn't afford to slip up again. Everyone was depending on her to get to the bottom of this. She needed to find Donny.

CHAPTER NINE

SHE WATCHED Sterling veer off toward the secret door, noting a sense of loss. How quickly she'd grown accustomed to his presence, to the point that not having him at her side left her feeling out of sorts.

"Ms. Wantland? Where should we go?" TJ asked.

She shook off the melancholy and refocused. She couldn't afford to let her emotions influence her energy right now. Besides, she was being silly. She'd operated without Sterling for a lot of years. "Stan, can you please accompany Sterling? If anything happens in the apartment, don't miss it."

"Wouldn't dream of it," Stan said and followed Sterling. She knew better than to pair Sterling with TJ. Though they got along much better lately than they had initially, sometimes their teasing still got out of hand and they got on each other's nerves.

"Elise, can you sit here in the auditorium where Kayla sat and conduct an EVP? I'd like to see if you can entice the ghost into interacting, like the kids did."

"Sure. With any luck the Audioxx will pick it up and translate for us."

She eyed the equipment. "It didn't last night. All it did was confuse everyone. Make sure you keep your old-school digital recorder on too."

"Of course. And I'll take copious notes." Elise lifted her pen and waggled it.

"Good. Michael, you head backstage and check out the green room, costume shop, scene shop—"

"The building isn't that big, but I'll explore what they have."

"And I'll focus on the stage itself. Maybe our deceased thespian will make an appearance and perform for us tonight."

Screams and squeals from above, ear-piercingly high-pitched but muffled by distance and walls, resounded through the space, followed by shrieks of laughter.

"Seriously?" she heard Sterling bellow. "They're laughing? Who thinks this is funny? What sick souls enjoy this?"

"Everyone who came to the haunted house, Sterling," Michael yelled in return. He shook his head and looked back at her.

A subdued chuckle drifted from the stage.

The hair on her arms lifted, an electric sizzle vibrated across her skin. Apparently, an actual soul enjoyed this exchange.

She whipped her head to the stage, scrutinizing the empty space. The curtains rustled as though someone dragged a hand across the heavy red drapes.

"TJ?"

"Yes, Ms. Wantland?"

"Camera and night vision on the curtains, please."

"Yes, ma'am!" He sucked in a breath. "They're shimmying!"

Not her imagination. "You stay with me. Keep the camera on the curtain for now, please."

"Yes, ma'am!"

She tiptoed up the steps. When she reached the stage, a faint whisper tickled her ear. "I hear something. I think it's coming from the stage."

Leaning forward, ready to retreat if necessary, she rested one hand on the curtain edge, where the drapes met in the center.

She pulled it back, revealing the dark stage—but no person, no leering ghoulish face.

Nothing.

The whispers stopped. But then she swore she heard mumbling offstage, from the wing to her left. "TJ? Do you hear a voice? Stage right?"

"No. Nothing."

She turned and crept toward the noise. Her ears strained as she followed the muffled sound, but though the soft murmuring continued, she could not discern any words. Wrapping her hand around her quartz crystal, she sent out a beacon and invited connection, hoping her sixth sense might assist in interpreting the voice.

"What is it?" TJ asked.

She held up a hand to quiet him and leaned forward. She could almost make out the words. If she could understand what the spirit said, she could figure out what it wanted. Was it Donny? Jillian seemed so certain. But how could she know that? Did she know something that she kept to herself? She felt certain the woman was not being forthcoming. Why? If Jillian truly believed Donny haunted the building and wanted him gone, why hide anything?

She motioned TJ closer. "I hear whispering. Let's see if we can capture it on the recording."

But no sooner had she reached the wing, where she'd felt certain the whispering emanated from, than it seemed farther away, no longer in the wing at all. "Dang it. Now I don't hear it."

"I never heard anything," TJ said. "Sorry."

She turned slowly, ears pricked so taut they almost hurt. "Anything on the cameras?"

"Nothing."

An echo bounced down the hallway, a quiet male voice teasing her, as if delivering the punchline to a joke told at her expense.

"There. I hear it again, but now it sounds like it's coming from the hallway."

Dim, diffuse light and glow tape guided her way down the black, darkened hallway. TJ, his night vision goggles on and camera up, crackled with anxiety. She felt it rolling off of him in waves.

"Something feels off—"

She shushed him, intent on the whispering drawing her forward. No spirit would be this vocal unless he had something critical to communicate to the living. And yet, something kept him from clearly communicating his message. The continued string of sounds resembled actual words yet understanding eluded her. And this did not strike her as a mumbled prayer, as they'd heard last night. Not a feedback loop, with the spirit repeating words spoken in life. This felt specific to her, an actual attempt at interaction.

"What are you trying to tell me?"

"You want me to get Elise on the walkie and have her bring the Audioxx?" TJ asked.

"If I can't understand the spirit, I don't think the Audioxx will either."

"But that's why we got the equipment. To fill in the gaps. Maybe it would be more sensitive and understand the words."

She was the sensitive. What she needed was quiet. Not a crackling box.

The hallway turned sharply right and opened into what she presumed was the green room. Chairs and an old sofa lined the walls in the dark, empty space. An abandoned water bottle sat at the foot of one of the chairs.

"Anything on the FLIR?" she asked TJ. "Anything at all?"

"I'm not getting a thing. Maybe we should call for backup."

Another door led out of the green room. The voice seemed to be on the other side of that door, so she motioned to TJ to follow and opened it.

Goosebumps broke out along her arms and a shiver ran down her spine.

What are you trying to tell me?

On the other side of the door, they discovered the dressing room. The makeshift space held makeup stations and mirrors and rolling racks of hangers and costumes. It also currently held Michael.

"Well, hello," he said. "I thought you were going to stay on the stage."

"She's hearing voices," TJ said.

She sighed. "Really? Again with the hearing voices? Can we not find a better way to say that?"

"What are they saying?" Michael asked.

"I think it's only one voice, but that's the problem. I can't tell what he's saying."

"It seems to be luring her this way," TJ said.

"Luring? I don't like the sound of that. Kimmy?"

"I don't know. I think the spirit wants to tell me something. It doesn't feel malevolent."

Michael stared at the KII in his hand. "I have noted a few sudden drops in temperature. Wasn't sure what to make of it. Perhaps the spirit is trying to communicate but you're the only one who can hear it."

"Then why be so elusive?" TJ asked. He stared around the room, then addressed the spirit. "Just say what you need to say."

A sound off to their right caused all of them to whip their heads in that direction, instantly silent.

After a moment of quiet, TJ ventured to speak. "You guys heard that, right?"

"Yes. And right after you urged communication," she said. "Anything on the KII?"

"Slight uptick," Michael said. "Nothing crazy."

"No visuals on the camera, but I'll keep looking," TJ said.

While they swept the room with cameras and thermometers,

hoping to glean some tidbit of information, she noticed a small office in the direction they'd heard the noise. Certain she heard someone talking in there, she wrapped her hand around her quartz and followed the elusive voice. *Come on. Talk to me. I can help you.*

The door squeaked when she pushed it open. The tiny room, possibly a closet that had been renovated into a workspace, held a desk and phone. She ran her hands over the desk, eager for a glimmer of insight. The whispering continued—and distracted her as she strained to understand the individual words in the steady stream of incoherent utterings.

Hushed voices drowned out the ghostly murmurs she tried so hard to interpret. And then the crackling of the Audioxx washed the space in ambient white noise. TJ, Michael, and Elise all stood in the doorway of the little office.

She spun to face them. "I'm trying to listen. The additional noise hinders the process."

Elise held out the box. "But Michael and TJ said you need some help. That you can't understand the spirit."

And after she missed that the nun in the lobby was a ghost, they no longer trusted her to come through on this. Were they right to doubt her? Was she having an off day? Or was something else at play here and impacting her abilities?

"I haven't understood him yet, but—"

The box buzzed and hummed, twisting and distorting the sounds around them into a strident semblance of a woman's voice.

"I haven't understood him . . ."

The electronic voice, hollow and false, seemed to mimic her, poking fun at her inability to understood.

She gritted her teeth. "I'll get it. If everyone will be quiet and—"

"I'll get it . . . be quiet . . ."

The inanimate object could not admonish her. It simply didn't have the capacity. And yet, hearing her words repeated back to her, the metal box mimicking her, she couldn't help but want to take the thing and drop kick it across the room.

But the whispering started again. She raised a hand to quiet them, closed her eyes to focus, and turned her head, desperate to understand. *Come on, they're all watching me.*

While she struggled, the Audioxx buzzed. Then the electronic voice emanated from it again. In the midst of inarticulate static and crackling, one word came through loud and clear.

"*Pay.*"

They all stared at each other, eyebrows raised.

"Someone will pay?" Elise asked.

"*Pay.*"

Elise looked up from the LED screen that displayed the words as the box translated, beaming. "That was pretty clear. Who will pay?"

"*Jillian.*"

Kimberly looked at Michael. "Still think Jillian isn't keeping things from us?"

CHAPTER TEN

KIMBERLY GULPED coffee during footage review while TJ played the clip of the Audioxx vocalization over and over for the people who hadn't been present the night before. Stan leaned forward, head cocked, listening closely.

Her head throbbed. Two days in and the exhaustion already took its toll. Sterling, seated beside her, ran a hand across her back—a gesture she found wonderfully relaxing despite the lack of sleep. She noted the heavy dark circles under his eyes. This job was not for the weak.

They had continued their investigation into the wee hours of the morning. By the time they arrived back at the hotel, exhaustion overwhelmed them all. Sterling had allowed her to ready for bed first, then seemed to debate whether or not to suggest they share a bed, or each take one of the two in this double room. Fatigue and the pull of sleep won the debate. She worried Sterling would be annoyed or irritated that she didn't fall into his arms, unable to resist. But he'd fallen asleep moments after his head hit the pillow.

Her show, her livelihood, took so much of her life, she didn't think she could manage a relationship too. Until Sterling came along. He never complained, never criticized her for being too busy. He hadn't once implied she didn't give him enough time. Of course, the relationship was still new, but so far, she'd been surprised.

She looked around the auditorium from the stage, where they had set up card tables temporarily for footage review. Once the play resumed, they could easily fold them up and clear them from the space.

Michael looked around the room. "Feedback? What are you guys thinking?"

Stan leaned back and shrugged. "We got absolutely nothing in the apartment. Nothing. Not a rustle, not so much as a creaking floorboard.

"So the whispering spirit trying to interact with me was our active spirit last night."

"And presumably a different manifestation than the one we encountered in the apartment the first night, but it's difficult to know for sure. Male? Female? The Audioxx doesn't really offer any insight into that."

"Which is of course one of the major flaws with that equipment. I can assure you I heard a male voice. And I am also certain it's not the same voice Sterling and I heard the night before. These are two distinct manifestations."

"When do you not have two ghosts?" Sterling asked. "Every episode I've been on, you discover a second ghost impacting the case."

"This is such an old building, I wouldn't be surprised if we encounter additional spirits as we continue with the investigation. But I'm not sure the nun has any bearing on this case. As Michael pointed out last night, she seems to simply be going through the motions of her daily activities from when she was alive—saying her prayers, welcoming people into the sanctuary and reminding them to be quiet."

"As long as she doesn't bring out a ruler and crack our knuckles to get us to go to confession, I don't care what she does," Sterling said.

"Yikes," TJ said.

"I don't think they do that anymore," Kimberly said, wondering if he was being silly or speaking from experience. "Michael, I thought you were going to ask Jillian to join us today. Is she coming later?"

"No, she said something about a meeting this morning that she couldn't cancel last second."

"That's very frustrating. You would think after we came all this way to help her, she would be a bit more accommodating."

"She did say she'd try to meet up with us early tonight."

Sterling frowned. "I don't think we can make it back early tonight. In fact, we might be a little later. Remember I've booked us all for a ghost tour tonight. I think Kimberly will enjoy that. Plus, we will get some history of the town too."

"Guess you'll miss the haunted house," TJ teased.

"What a shame." Sterling rolled his eyes.

"Why does Jillian expect us to work around her schedule?" she asked. "She knew we were coming. Why schedule an important meeting during our investigation? Who does that?"

"Maybe she forgot," Rosie suggested. "I know sometimes I'll have two things planned and remember them both, but it doesn't hit me they're the same day until I'm trying to juggle both."

"I'm sure it's something like that," Michael said. "Let's not make assumptions."

"I think this spirit is trying to tell me something but is having trouble getting the message across. If Jillian can add something, anything at all, it would be useful."

"We will be sure to fully charge you up tonight," Rosie said. "And you need to stay very relaxed and not let your emotions get the better of you. So don't worry about Jillian. We can deal with it."

"If she would contribute to the investigation, maybe give me something to start with, I could make progress faster. Right now, I have no idea. Nothing."

"Why do you think Jillian can help?" Ian asked.

"She let him live here in the apartment. She seems most likely to know something about him, at least a little bit. I can't believe she let a random stranger live here. Was there something going on between them?"

Rosie's eyebrows rose. "Like what? What could have been going on between them?"

She thought back to the interview with the troupe of actors. "I'm not sure. No one mentioned anything or gave any indication. No raised eyebrows, no shared glances. If something was going on, how did they keep it from everyone?"

Rosie's eyebrows lifted higher. "Going on? Do you think they were having an affair?"

She recognized Rosie's ready-for-gossip face.

All heads turned toward Ian, who squirmed a bit at the sudden attention. "I don't know about that. You guys didn't know him. He was so arrogant and sure of himself. And a lot older than her. Plus he looked older than he was, like life had been really hard on him."

"Wouldn't be the first time a woman went for an older guy," Rosie said.

Ian nodded. "They did seem to know each other. At least some. I had the vague impression maybe they'd been friends a long time ago or something like that."

"What makes you say that?" Kimberly asked.

"He kind of bossed her around."

Not what she expected. "How so?"

"He was pushy. Always wanted his way. Never compromised. If she disagreed with something, he'd complain and pester and badger her until she gave in and gave him his way."

"Doesn't sound like much of a friend."

"But does sound like a boyfriend," Rosie said. "Maybe they were in a relationship but kept it quiet."

Ian shuddered. "Ick. I hope not. I can't begin to imagine her with him." He wrinkled his nose. "I didn't get that vibe. He commented a few times on her appearance, how good she looked, that sort of thing. But still . . ."

"Sounds like he had something on her. Why else would she put up with that?"

"The Audioxx clearly stated, 'Jillian must pay,'" TJ said. "We have to be dealing with someone who knows her."

"Whoa, whoa, whoa." Sterling raised a hand. "When did that happen? The device produced a sound you interpreted as 'pay' and a sound you interpreted as 'Jillian.' Don't layer on intent that isn't there."

TJ scowled. "What do you think it means, then?"

"Absolutely nothing until we have something concrete to support it. It could have been 'way,' 'may,' 'day,' 'say,' 'hey'—"

"It was pay!"

"—or nothing at all, just a distortion of sound crackled out of a mechanical box that you superimposed malicious intent behind, hoping for some good drama. I haven't gotten a look inside that box yet. It could be worthless, just a radio in fancy packaging that's picking up signals and broadcasting sounds through the speaker."

"I liked you better when you heard a ghost."

"Ha! No you didn't! That made you mad too. You took away my skeptic card."

"Well, you can have it back. The Audioxx—"

The lobby door opened, and Jillian walked into the auditorium. Head down, she rifled through her purse.

"Jillian! Hi!" Michael greeted her.

Jillian's head snapped up, her eyes wide. "Oh! Oh, you're here. I didn't realize."

"For footage review of course." Kimberly crossed her arms. "Michael said you had a meeting? Is it over? Because I'd love to visit with you about—"

"It's a phone meeting and I'm running late," Jillian said, pulling a set of keys from her purse. "I need to go to my office. Excuse me, please."

"I'll walk with you," Kimberly said and fell into step before Jillian could disagree.

Stan sidled into place behind them, camera up.

Jillian glanced over her shoulder. "I don't feel comfortable being on camera."

"An actor who doesn't like the camera?"

"Performing is different. This is real life. I suspect you know exactly what I mean."

She paused, slightly taken aback by the reminder. She did struggle to balance public and private life. Though determined to pry some information from Jillian and suspicious of the woman, she grudgingly acknowledged they shared this desire to keep personal information private. "I only want to ask you about your relationship with Donny."

Jillian tucked a sandy-blonde lock behind her ear. "What? Why? Just get him out of here. Isn't that what you do?"

"I attempt to resolve hauntings, yes. But resolution requires helping the spirit find peace, and to do that I need to understand their life and relationships. If I knew what sort of unfinished business he might have had—"

Jillian stopped abruptly. "Who opened my office?"

Kimberly looked around, reorienting herself. They stood in the dressing room, in front of the tiny office. "This is your office?"

"Yes. Who opened it?"

"I found it open last night."

"I know I locked it. I always lock it. How did you open it?"

"I pushed the door to open it a bit more, but I found it ajar. I heard a spirit—"

"You entered my office without permission. I have personal, private documents in here."

"The spirit—"

Jillian rushed into the room and sat at the desk, running her hands over everything, opening and closing drawers.

What in the world? Now Jillian was implying she might take

something? "No one mentioned this space was off limits, but I didn't touch anything."

"I don't want anyone in here. No one."

"But we—"

The phone rang. Jillian took a deep breath and slowly exhaled. "This is an extremely important call. Please show yourself out." She lifted the receiver. "This is Jillian."

Kimberly turned and walked in a daze back toward the stage. What could Jillian possibly be hiding?

CHAPTER ELEVEN

"I'M TELLING you it was weird and extremely suspicious," Kimberly said. She pulled her black peacoat tighter as a cool breeze lifted tendrils of hair and sent a shiver through her. They were walking from their hotel on the river through downtown Hannibal. The Hannibal History Museum, from where their ghost tour would depart, was only a few blocks away. Exercise sounded good and the weather, while not balmy, was clear and pleasant.

"We get it, girl," Rosie said. "You don't like Jillian."

"It's not that I don't like her, I just really think she's hiding something from us."

Michael lifted his eyebrows. "For the record, she never said anything to me about staying out of the office. But now I want to know what she's hiding in there."

"I wonder who opened the door," TJ said. "It was definitely open when we arrived."

"Can ghosts unlock doors?" Rosie asked. "Do you think Donny did it?"

Sterling shook his head. "Don't we think the likely explanation is that Jillian simply forgot? She seems extremely scattered to me."

Kimberly thought back to Jillian's reaction to finding the door open. "I don't know. You should have seen her. She's highly protective of something in there."

"We'll figure it out." Sterling draped an arm over her shoulders and squeezed. "For now, let's keep enjoying the evening."

"Okay." She took a deep breath and put it all aside, focusing on his warm brown eyes and the shiver of excitement they sent pulsing through her.

He'd treated her to dinner at a darling little bistro in town, about as opposite of pizza on the food spectrum as you could get. The owners had adapted an old house, adding another level of comfort. She could almost pretend she and the other diners had been invited to dinner at someone's house. In a town of fried foods and quick bites, the international flare had been a welcome relief. But the varied menu offered something for everyone, so while she enjoyed an appetizer of grape leaves and hummus followed by seared salmon and mixed vegetables, Sterling opted for chicken breast stuffed with mushrooms and cheese. The wide diversity did not impact the quality of the food one bit. She'd remarked on the skill of the chef. Even now she delighted at the content feeling radiating from her stomach, having eaten a healthy meal.

They arrived at the history museum and checked in, were given stickers to indicate they were part of the tour, then meandered around the room, perusing books and articles and pieces of the town's history. She liked that Sterling was excited to take advantage of their time here to soak up as much information about the town as they could. Seeing Mark Twain's home would be fun and when would she have the chance again? She also couldn't wait to see if she could detect anything supernatural at the purportedly haunted locations they would visit tonight.

Underlying the anticipation, however, she noted a sense of ease and felt more relaxed than she had in a long time. She took a deep breath and exhaled. Perhaps simply doing something fun, unrelated to the investigation, which would also result in a shorter work shift later tonight, was the reason. Maybe she should strongly consider a vacation. She'd spent so many years focused solely on the show, giving every second of her life and devoting every ounce of energy she possessed—and sometimes more—to ensure the show was a success. She'd heard and ignored advice about burnout. Initially, she couldn't imagine reaching that point. The show was new and exciting, and she thrilled at the opportunities it brought to her life.

The success of the show was not merely a benefit to her. The entire crew depended on her for their livelihood. If she didn't succeed, if the show failed, they all went down with her. That was a weight she carried every day and she had no intention of letting that happen. Not if she could help it. And she didn't care how much she had to sacrifice to ensure success.

But perhaps pushing herself so hard and functioning at one hundred percent all day, every day, was finally catching up to her. Could that be why she didn't realize the nun was a ghost when they crossed paths? Had she so completely worn herself out in her drive to succeed that she had burned out her psychic abilities? Was that a thing? She definitely charged up for investigations and felt drained following them. Was this the same thing but on a larger scale? And if so, could she permanently damage them?

If so, she could be negatively impacting the show without realizing it. In which case, she couldn't win. Hard to consider taking time off now with so many exciting things closing in fast —the potential of learning family history in New Orleans, investigating her childhood home back in Albuquerque. She couldn't quit now. Not when she was so close. Not when she might actually be about to learn the truth of her past. And not when her mother could be trying to communicate with her—or, God forbid, need her help. She was too close after all these years.

But what if she caused damage to her psychic abilities? Then what? The show couldn't continue. What would she do then? What would any of them do? And for that matter, how could she go through life no longer receiving little nudges and tugs from the spiritual plane? If she lost her connection to the Nightshade, she would have nothing. The majority of the population might get along just fine without a sixth sense, but such a loss would devastate her as surely as if she lost any other sense. She shuddered at the thought.

Sterling curled an arm around her. "Are you cold? What's wrong?"

She shook her head but nestled into his embrace. "Just thinking."

"Stop thinking." He squeezed her side. "Tonight, we have fun. I think our ride is here."

A red trolley rolled up to the curb outside the building. A man hopped off and joined them inside.

"Hello, everyone! My name is Darren and I will be your guide during your Haunted Hannibal ghost tour this evening. Whoever is joining us, please queue up here at the door to follow me. And also please make sure your sticker is easily visible so I can identify our party without too much trouble."

They followed him to the bus and clambered aboard. As she moved passed Darren, he looked for her sticker, then smiled and welcomed her—and did a double take after making eye contact.

Sterling kept a hand on her back as she climbed the stairs and chose a seat on one of the wooden benches. She scooted in next to Rosie, with Sterling on her other side. Seeing Rosie mostly back to her normal self added to her general sense of ease, better than she'd felt in some time. She leaned against Sterling's shoulder. "This was a wonderful idea. Thank you for doing this."

Beside her, Rosie heaved a sigh, pulling her back out of the euphoric mood a bit. Her empathic nature knew exactly why Rosie ached, and she felt the stab to her heart as sharply as if she herself suffered the loneliness. "You should invite Lorenzo to come join us, Rosie."

Rosie shrugged. "He wouldn't be able to leave now. October

and Halloween? The ghost tours at Crescent are always popular but they fill to capacity this time of year. He'll be working extra."

"He can't work twenty-four, seven, though. He has to get a couple days off. Let's make arrangements for him to come visit."

Rosie offered a smile that didn't quite reach her eyes. "It's a nice idea but I know he will say no."

"You should at least ask. If he can't, he can't. But then at least he knows you miss him and want him here."

Rosie shook her head. Kimberly opened her mouth to argue, but the tour guide hopped up the steps and welcomed them. She opted to let it go for now but not give up on the idea.

"Welcome, everyone," Darren said. He glanced at her repeatedly. "This is probably the most unusual tour group I've ever had. I'm a little nervous about leading a ghost hunting team on a ghost tour, but I'll do my best for you and hopefully not embarrass myself."

The trolley driver pulled away from the museum and navigated through the streets. They drove past old buildings, well preserved and quaint, though she felt sure renovated to include modern indoor plumbing. Still, the small-town atmosphere allowed her to transport herself to another time and imagine what life used to be like.

"We're going to focus on the old haunts here in the main downtown area, and I'll be sure to point out some of the historical sites as well, plus give you a brief history of our city. While we travel to our first stop, does anyone have any questions for me?"

She heard TJ yell from the back. "Have you ever seen Mark Twain's ghost?"

Darren smiled. "That's a great question. And one I hear quite a bit. I have not. And there is a good reason for that. Although Mark Twain grew up here in Hannibal, and in fact believed in ghosts and the supernatural, he did not die here. He moved his family to Connecticut. He had a rather tragic life and lost three of his four children at relatively young ages, which you can imagine struck a tremendous blow. But to encounter Twain's ghost, you'll need to try his home in Connecticut."

Michael posed the next question. "Have you ever seen any ghost?"

The tour guide laughed. "Another question I get quite a bit. I don't know that I've ever actually seen a ghost, but I have heard footsteps and I've noticed things moved around. I like to say I'm open to the idea, but unlike your fearless leader, I do not claim to hear from them or interact with them." He grinned at her. "Super excited to have you on my ghost tour. Love the show. I'm trying really hard right now not to geek out and make a total fool of myself. By the way, you are just as lovely in person as you are on the screen."

Heat crept up her neck and flooded her cheeks. "Oh. Thank you."

Sterling slung an arm around her shoulder and tugged her close.

Darren flushed a bit. "And of course, Sterling Wakefield. I didn't watch *SpookBusters*, but it's super cool to have you here."

Sterling offered a tight smile and rested his hand on top of hers.

Rosie leaned across her. "But apparently you're not as lovely in person as on television."

She elbowed Rosie. "Shh! Stop it. You two behave!"

The trolley pulled over by a dilapidated old brick building which Darren explained was the old firehouse, where many people reported seeing apparitions in the top window. They drove past the Old Catholic Church, which she already knew plenty about. Next they stopped while Darren pointed out the Stillwell Mansion.

"The Stillwell house is the site of Hannibal's oldest unsolved mystery," Darren said. "Amos Stillwell made a fortune in the pork packing industry. He lost his first wife in his forties. On a trip to visit family, Fannie, though only a teenager at the time, caught his eye. She was thirty years younger than Amos, and yet due to issues with her stepmother had been contemplating joining a convent."

Rosie dug an elbow into Kimberly's side. "There's one thing you have in common with Fannie. You used to threaten to join a convent yourself."

Sterling squeezed her hand. "Glad you didn't."

Kimberly shook her head and laughed. "I never meant it."

Darren went on. "Fannie must have decided being the wife of a wealthy widower would be better than being a nun because she accepted his proposal of marriage. Fast forward twenty years. The Stillwells appeared happy. On the night of December 29, 1889, Amos and Fannie had been to a party at a neighbor's house. Amos went to bed, according to Fannie, and she followed shortly thereafter. The couple slept in separate beds, Fannie sharing her bed with their children. Fannie maintained that at around two in the morning, she woke to hear Amos cry out, 'Fannie? Is that you?' She further claimed that she saw a dark figure in the room, standing over Amos' bed. She heard a noise and then the figure took off running. Fannie claimed to have discovered her husband with his neck severed, lying in a pool of blood. She said the children began screaming and she ran for help. A neighbor summoned the town physician. Fannie returned to her room and promptly fainted. The physician realized Amos was beyond help and worked to revive Fannie."

"But they didn't find the murderer?" TJ asked from the back of the trolley.

Darren smiled. "Now the story gets interesting. The police investigated, determined the intruder had fled through the back door, run across the yard and into an alley. They found a five-dollar bill in the yard which they assumed had been dropped. In the alley they found a bloody axe, determined to be the murder weapon, as well as more five-dollar bills and Amos' wallet. The police concluded theft had been the intention of the break-in, that Amos had awakened, causing the intruder to use the axe and flee, dropping evidence along the way."

"If the intruder was intent on burglary, why go in the bedroom at all?" Sterling asked. "Surely the safer course would have been to stay away from the mansion's occupants and take valuables from other rooms."

Darren smiled and pointed at Sterling. "Quite a few people in town didn't much care for the conclusion the police came to either. They raised a reward for the suspect, but no one was ever found. The Pinkerton Detective Agency was called in to investigate. The case had grown cold. But they did discover that Fannie had been seeing the town doctor quite regularly despite having no medical ailments. Tongues wagged and gossip brewed. Keep in mind this is the same doctor who attended to Fannie the night of the murder, claiming he did not treat Amos because he could tell it was hopeless. One year later, Fannie and the doctor married, which raised eyebrows and suspicion all over again. The case grew colder and colder but seven years later Fannie and the doctor were arrested, tried, and found not guilty. The two had divorced by that point. The case was never solved. Theories included that either Fannie or her doctor lover hired someone to murder Amos, that a true burglar murdered him, and that Fannie or the doctor committed the murder and then staged evidence to make it look like a crime. But nothing was every proved."

Kimberly shivered. "Wish we'd been asked to solve that one."

"You want to go toe to toe with an axe murderer?" Rosie asked. "No, thanks. Hard pass."

"Oh, hey," Sterling said, pulling up Twitter on his phone. "Speaking of the Stillwells, we tweeted about Trunk or Treat for this Saturday afternoon."

"If we must," she muttered.

"Hoffmeier insisted," he reminded her. "But, come on. Handing out candy to kids? That's not so bad, is it? I think it'll be fun and I'm the one who hates Halloween."

"Saturday afternoon?" Rosie said. "So I have three days to pull together costumes and makeup for you two? Great."

The trolley cruised down a small residential area, which

seemed quite familiar. She realized why when it pulled to a stop in front of LaBinnah Bistro. "This is one of the most haunted locations, with the owner and diners alike reporting more instances of paranormal activity here than anywhere else."

She looked at Sterling. "This is where we ate dinner."

"And you didn't get so much as a twinge? Must not be as haunted as they claim."

The tour guide kept talking, but she didn't hear anything else he said about the bistro.

How could that be? One of the most haunted locations in town and she'd felt nothing? She sat there for over an hour enjoying dinner and didn't feel a single tug at her psyche? Not one shiver down her spine or tingle over an arm? Something must be off. And how could she resolve a haunting if her abilities weren't functioning properly? If only she could go in for the psychic equivalent of an eye exam and have her sixth sense checked.

Rosie tipped her head and raised an eyebrow. "What is it, girl? You look lost in thought. Something wrong?"

She shook her head and forced a smile. "No, it's nothing." But it wasn't nothing. A cold knot of worry formed in her stomach. Something was wrong with her and she had no idea what.

"Our final stop today is the Old Baptist Cemetery. Dating back to eighteen forty-four, you'll find graves of Civil War soldiers, freed slaves, and average citizens. You can also see the tombstone of Agnes Flautleroy, inscribed with the notation, 'slave of Sophia Hawkins.' Sophia Hawkins was the mother of Laura Hawkins, who was the real-life inspiration for Mark Twain's character Becky Thatcher."

"Very cool," Sterling said.

"This site has long been a source of paranormal interactions. People have reported a young boy peering at them from behind that old tree over there. But when they go to look, no one is there. A Civil War soldier has been seen plodding across the graveyard. And some people have all described the exact same man in a long coat, watching them from the edge of the property. They all reported feeling unwelcome and that the man wanted them to leave but wouldn't come out and say so. In fact, one particularly annoyed gentleman stormed over and asked what his problem was but received no reply. He didn't realize he was interacting with an apparition."

"Sure," Sterling said. "And what proof do we have of this story?"

Darren glanced at Sterling but didn't reply. "We will stay here for about thirty minutes. Dusk is the perfect time to interact with restless spirits rising for the night to prowl the graveyard."

"False," Sterling replied. "Even Kimberly says ghosts are around us all the time, not just at night."

She elbowed him.

"What?"

Darren plowed on, ignoring the interruptions though appearing slightly unnerved. "I'll give each of you a pair of copper dowsing rods as you exit the vehicle. These have the ability to receive EMF signals in the environment around us, allowing us to converse with the dead who wish to speak. Let me demonstrate how to use them."

"Have you ever used dowsing rods?" Rosie asked.

She shook her head and whispered, "I have not, but I've heard of others using them."

Rosie rubbed her hands together. "Maybe we can all hear from spirits tonight."

Startled, she almost asked Rosie if she wanted her to try sharing her psychic energy, as she did with Sterling. Rosie had never said anything to indicate she wanted to connect with spirits. Did she want to address someone specific? Or was her best friend simply curious? Then again, if her energy was already low or her abilities weren't working properly, sharing was probably not the best idea right now.

Darren held up the metallic, L-shaped rods. "Hold each rod loosely in one hand by the shorter end, so that the longer ends rest on your fist. But don't grip it. They need to be free to move without your intervention, inadvertent though it may be."

"Sure," Sterling said. "Because no one would move them without realizing it. No, wait. Yes, they would."

"Sterling, please," Kimberly admonished.

"This is like using a Ouija board. People don't intentionally move it but subconsciously they do. It's called the ideomotor effect. Nothing moves by itself."

"Not by itself," Darren said, maintaining a smile that no longer seemed genuine. "The spirits move them. When you approach a grave, invite communication, then establish your rules. For example, closed rods means no and open rods means yes. Something like that. With as many tourists as come through, these spirits are accustomed to interacting, so they probably won't need much prompting."

"So it's basically a ghost petting zoo?" Sterling asked.

"One final thing," Darren said, this time looking directly at Sterling. "Please be mindful and respectful of the fact we're moving among final resting places."

"Hey, I'm not the one pestering them and harassing them to talk."

"Please remain on established walkways, in front of the gravestones, and avoid standing on the graves themselves."

"We will. Of course," Kimberly said.

Darren descended the steps ahead of them and handed sets of dowsing rods to each of them as they stepped off the trolley. When Kimberly reached for her pair, the tour guide held them out, then pulled them away again.

"You don't need these," he said, holding the rods over his shoulder, out of her reach.

She blinked. Of course she wanted a set. Why would he—

Darren laughed and extended the rods. "I'm just kidding. Here you go."

"You're hilarious," Sterling said, reaching for the final set of rods. "If anyone doesn't need them, it's me. But I paid for this tour, and by gosh I'm going to participate fully. Besides, I want to demonstrate these things don't work at all."

She raised an eyebrow. "And I can't wait to see the look on your face when they do. Let's see if any ghosts want to talk."

She rested a hand on his back, ready to send psychic energy flooding into his system, but thought better of it and patted him instead.

Please, let my sixth sense work.

CHAPTER TWELVE

KIMBERLY WATCHED her crew fan out, scattering across the graveyard. They were not alone. A few couples and families, presumably tourists, also explored the site. A trolley full of people, all carrying unfamiliar devices, was sure to garner attention. Sure enough, most of the other people nearby watched them. One man did a double take, nudged the woman beside him, and pointed. He said something, and the woman nodded furiously.

Great. She'd been spotted. She fought the urge to duck her head and hide behind something. Sterling, however, waved at them. The couple beamed and waved back.

"It's okay," he told her. "They're excited to see you, that's all. And surprised. They didn't expect to spot a celebrity ghost hunter in the graveyard."

She took a deep breath and nodded. "Yeah, you're right."

"How many years has your show been on? I can't believe you haven't adapted yet."

"I don't think I'll ever adjust to people being excited to see me. I don't get it. I'm just me. Nothing to be worked up about."

His face softened into a half-smile, half-frown. "I beg to differ. So do a lot of other people."

The usual butterflies jittered around in her stomach at his compliment and the intense look he pierced her with. If they were alone right now . . .

But they weren't. She shook her head and blew out a breath. *Focus.* "So. Where do you want to begin?"

"Show me how these things work?"

"I thought you were going to show me they don't work."

"I have to follow the prescribed rules to be able to trust the results. If I don't use them properly, I cannot claim to have disproven them."

"Seriously, though, you gave that tour guide kind of a hard time. I thought I'd convinced you paranormal activity is at least a real possibility. Thought you were open to it."

He scrubbed the back of his neck. "That was mostly for the show. Stan of course is recording. Hoffmeier isn't ready for two believers yet. He told Michael to maintain the current format for now. Though I don't need to continue with the side bar Confidential Corner bits if I don't want to, I do need to resist and offer scientific explanations as much as possible."

Real disappointment settled like a cloud over a sunny day. Her dreams of a supernatural investigating couple, working side by side, evaporated. Ironically, her producer Randall Hoffmeier had been the one to bring Sterling into her life to begin with. She'd balked and refused to no avail. Now that she'd adapted and even welcomed his presence, Hoffmeier once again interfered— this time forcing them to remain antagonistic in front of the cameras. Would she ever get to call the shots on her show again? She longed wistfully for the good old days when no one knew who she was and she and Michael spent their weekends resolving hauntings in people's homes, primarily in Albuquerque and nearby communities.

"Hey." Sterling bumped against her and smiled. "It's only for the show, right? We're okay, yes?"

She pushed aside her thoughts and focused on the case at hand. Wishing and daydreaming accomplished nothing. "Of course. Here, I'll show you. One rod in each hand. Good. Relax your grip. Let them spin freely."

"This might actually be worse than the Ouija board," he said. "I may be open to new ideas, but this is ridiculous."

"Well, it's less precise for sure. All we can ask is yes and no questions."

"I feel thoroughly foolish. Now what?"

"Wander around, wherever you feel drawn. Not every grave will have a spirit and not every spirit will want to speak with you. The dowsing rods might pull you toward a grave, if a spirit wants specifically to speak with you."

"Might pull me, huh?"

As if on cue, her rods both turned, pointing off to her right. "Like this. Let me know if you need me." She stepped carefully, guided by the rods, until they pointed at a small stone square. She squatted and read the inscription chiseled in the gray rock.

Anna, wife of James

"Hello, Anna. I'm Kimberly." The rods moved to a neutral position. "We can chat if you'd like. You can move my rods to answer questions. Open the rods for yes, and close them for no. Okay?"

Her rods shot apart in opposite directions, wide apart.

"That was an emphatic yes. Let's see if I can figure out what you want to tell me." She started with an easy one. "Were you married?"

The rods drifted apart, open for yes.

"Okay, but you know the answer to that," Sterling said.

She jumped. "You startled me! I didn't know you were there."

"I'm observing. Still unclear how these work. But you know she was married. You can see it. So you could have directed the rods to open."

"Okay, smart guy, no cameras around right now, so why the attitude?"

"I'm only trying to understand. And ideomotor effect is a

real, documented, proven thing. I know you're not intentionally moving them, but subconsciously you could be."

"Okay, let's try something else. Anna, were you happy?"

The rods crossed. *No.*

"Interesting. Did your husband hurt you?"

"Really?" Sterling asked. "You go right to domestic abuse?"

"It was quite common."

But the rods crossed a second time. *No.*

"Now that is interesting," Sterling said, "because you clearly expected an answer of yes."

"Did you have children?"

The rods drifted apart. *Yes.*

She blew out a breath. "And here lies the flaw with this system. We could ask questions all night and never figure out why she was unhappy."

He chuckled. "Yes, that's the flaw in this endeavor. So why not use your special talent to connect?"

She sucked in a breath. How could she explain her concerns that her psychic gift seemed to be functioning subpar? Should she even admit such a thing? Sterling was only beginning to accept that she might possess abilities he did not and could not understand. Had sharing her psychic energy with him somehow caused her own system to break down? Without understanding what was happening, she didn't want to discuss it.

He leaned back and cocked his head. "Don't want to waste your energy here? Saving yourself for tonight? I get that."

She jumped on his assumption, glad for the excuse. "Yes, exactly. I want to be at my best tonight." That was not a lie. She did want to be able to fully function at the actual investigation.

"I'll make a deal. I'll try my rods on a different grave. You can go work the crowd. Let people take selfies with you. Check on the others. Don't stress over this. Tonight is supposed to be our fun night, and this graveyard has nothing to do with the investigation. Okay?"

"If I agree, will you give the dowsing rods a real chance?"

"Absolutely. If I don't commit completely, I won't produce reliable data." He crossed his heart. "Scout's honor."

"Hope to die?"

"Nope. Not the slightest bit. Hope to live. And I refuse to hunt down a dead cat to swear on or cast a spell with or whatever the heck Tom and Huck used a dead cat for. You'll just have to trust me."

Sterling had a great point—she did not need to connect with any of these spirits. Who cared? Another example of how she took on stress she didn't need to shoulder. What difference did it make if Sterling didn't connect either? In the grand scheme of things, it made no difference at all.

She squeezed him tightly. "Thank you. Come rescue me if I get stuck in a crowd."

He held out a crooked pinky finger. "Pinky swear."

They hooked fingers, and she left him to cross the graveyard, stopping to greet and take photos with anyone who looked about to burst with excitement as she approached.

In between fans, she sought out her crew, all of whom appeared to be having success—even Rosie, she happily noted as she saw Rosie's rods move together and cross. But when Rosie leaned forward and yelled at the tombstone, Kimberly changed course and beat a hasty retreat. Leave it to Rosie to get into an argument with a ghost.

Looking around to see if she'd missed any other potential fans and photo opportunities, she caught sight of a man standing beside the gnarled old tree. Didn't Darren say a young boy played peek-a-boo from behind the tree? Or was it a girl? This was clearly neither. An old, grizzled man in overalls, he rested one hand on the tree trunk. In his other, he clutched a rusty pair of wooden-handled sheers, open to expose their sharp blade edges.

Her mouth dropped open. Was he a real, living person? Or a ghost, long dead and wandering aimlessly? She closed her eyes. *Please go away. Please go away.*

She opened her eyes. The figure remained. His thatch of gray hair stuck out at weird angles and appeared clotted with dirt, as if he'd just crawled out of a grave.

Stop it. She shook her head, aware she was letting her imagination run away with her. But she felt exposed and vulnerable, unsure of her psychic abilities. Was he a spirit? Perhaps a previous caretaker of the grounds, still roaming in death, trying to continue his earthly duties? She tried to reach out, to connect, to determine for sure what this figure represented. Nothing.

He lifted his sheers and leered at her.

Oh, God. He saw her. This was an intelligent manifestation, interacting with his current environment, not merely a playback recording looping over and over.

Her heartbeat raced, thudding in her ears. He meant her harm. She could tell, even without being able to feel with her sixth sense. His eyes glistened with malice.

Why couldn't she feel anything? Never in her life had she been without her gift, her peek into another realm which gave her a unique perspective on situations.

Stepping back, a voice in her mind screamed at her to get out, to go get help.

Someone yelled. She gasped and whirled.

Darren called to the group, tapping his wristwatch. "Time is up. Everyone back on the trolley."

Thirty minutes had lapsed already? Just as well. She wanted out of here and away from the man in the overalls. She glanced back over her shoulder.

He was gone.

She whipped her head back and forth and turned in a circle. No sign of the man in overalls. He'd disappeared.

Shivering, she returned to Sterling, noting with slight irritation he hadn't budged since she'd left him.

He graced her with a bright, I-told-you-so smile, which melted the moment he took in her countenance. "What's wrong?"

For someone who claimed not to have a sixth sense, he struck her as remarkably perceptive. But she wasn't ready to share. Still shaking, she tried to brush it off. "I'll tell you later. I thought you were going to try another grave."

"I did! Look."

She squinted at the grave marker he indicated.

Hannah, beloved daughter of Anna and James.

"I think this worn stone is probably marking James' grave, though I can't really read it. But it makes sense the family would be buried in the same area."

She crouched in front of the daughter's tombstone, running fingers over the chiseled letters, worn smooth with time. "Is there anything sadder than the grave of a child?"

"Watch," Sterling directed. He held his rods over the grave. "Would you like to talk with me?" The rods didn't budge. "No reaction whatsoever. The entire time I've been trying to interact. They don't even wiggle."

She stood and checked his grip on the rods. "If you clutch them tightly . . ." But the rods dangled loosely in his fists. That wasn't the explanation. "Or maybe the little girl doesn't want to talk to you."

"Or maybe this is silly and everyone else is answering their own questions, subtly guiding the rods in the direction of the answer they want."

She frowned. "I'm sure that isn't it. There's another reason."

The other members of her crew joined them.

"It's getting dark," Michael said. "And we do still have an investigation to conduct tonight. What's the holdup?"

"Sterling's rods don't move. At all."

"Big surprise." TJ stepped forward. "He's probably holding them so they can't."

"Okay, smart guy, you try it." Sterling stepped back and gestured to the grave.

Darren tried again to herd them to the trolley. "Time is up. We need to head back."

"Hold on," TJ said. "I need to prove Sterling wrong first."

"Good luck with that."

TJ stepped forward and held his rods over the grave. "Hi, there. Would you like to talk to us?" Nothing happened. He looked to her for guidance. "Maybe you should try, Ms. Wantland."

And what would it prove if she received no response? That the girl's spirit didn't want to communicate? The mother, Anna, had responded to her. But Sterling would surely use a lack of response as evidence that the rods were nothing but a silly parlor trick. None of them knew she was worried about her psychic abilities. How could she explain she didn't currently trust herself? She couldn't. Not without opening herself up to questions about why. She didn't have answers to that. And she was afraid to know, afraid to discover she'd somehow damaged her psyche permanently.

To make matters worse, several of the people she'd chatted with and snapped pictures with had wandered over to watch. They whispered to each other, things like, "I can't believe we get to see her connect with a ghost."

They might not get to, unfortunately.

She adjusted her dowsing rods, one in each hand and traded places with TJ so that she stood at the head of the grave. She took a deep breath and tried to relax, tried to still the doubts swirling through her, the nagging fear that something was seriously wrong with her and what she would do if indeed that turned out to be the case.

"Hello, Hannah," she began. "Would you talk with us today?"

The dowsing rods remained inert in her hands. Moreover, she felt no pull or tug at the psychic invitation she sent out into the spirit plane. Nothing at all.

"See?" Sterling bounced on his toes. "They don't work!"

She felt the pressure of at least a dozen eyes on her, waiting for something exciting to happen. "That's not true, though. The rods were quite active at Anna's grave."

"Mine worked for me," Rosie said. "The spirit was a guy, and he was incredibly rude. But the rods worked."

"I spoke with a Civil War soldier," Elise said. "So much history. Wonderful."

This was ridiculous. She connected with Anna earlier. She had no reason to believe she had lost her psychic abilities. She was being silly. Even her crew members established connections in this graveyard.

She passed her rods to Rosie and squatted down beside the little grave. She didn't need those copper sticks. Placing her hands over the earth, she closed her eyes and breathed deeply, refusing to allow doubts to overtake her. Reaching out, she probed for any bump or disturbance in the spiritual plane, any blip in the static that could indicate someone trying to communicate.

Nothing. Nothing whatsoever. What was happening?

"Kimmy?" Michael prompted her.

She glanced up. "I . . . I'm not sure. I'm not getting anything at all from this grave."

"What are you thinking?"

All the fans of the show that had gathered around looked gravely disappointed. The thought of disappointing them was too grim. Briefly, she entertained the notion she could invent a story or a conversation and no one could disprove her. Just as quickly, she dismissed it. Never had she faked an encounter with a spirit, and she wasn't about to start now. The idea of deceiving anyone ran so counter to everything she believed and stood for, she'd rather lose her ability entirely than misrepresent it.

She stood, brushing dirt from her hands. "Not every spirit stays behind after the body expires. This one must have successfully crossed over."

Sterling raised an eyebrow and gave her a look. "Really? That's awfully convenient."

"But it's true. You simply selected a quiet grave. That's all." She turned to the gathered fans. "I'd be happy to move to another grave for a presentation, but our tour is already running long."

Darren nodded. "Yes, we're behind schedule. If everyone will please reboard the trolley, we will head back to the museum."

The small crowd offered a smattering of applause. A few people snapped more photos. She waved and then strode to the trolley.

Her heart thumped. She didn't know for sure that what she told Sterling was true or wasn't. And that terrified her. She couldn't say anything with certainty as long as she suspected her sixth sense was not functioning properly.

And if she couldn't connect, if she couldn't communicate with spirits, how would she ever complete this investigation? Or any future investigation?

CHAPTER THIRTEEN

AFTER LEAVING THE MUSEUM, they walked back to the hotel and piled into cars to continue on to the Old Catholic Church. Technically they could have walked to the church. Most everything in the historic downtown area was within walking distance. But they needed their van of equipment. Besides, Kimberly knew once the investigation wrapped at two or three in the morning, she would want to fall into bed as quickly as possible. Walking back to the hotel in the middle of the night would not appeal. And probably wasn't safe, either.

She rode the short distance with Sterling in his i8, taking in sites like the Mark Twain Dinette and Becky Thatcher's Diner—and wondering how to determine if her sixth sense was working properly or not.

No one had ever offered guidance or training. She'd always explored her abilities on her own, primarily in secret since her parents either considered her mentally unstable or desperate for attention. Either way, they'd never approved and had forbidden her to so much as mention hearing voices.

Hearing voices. Why did everyone describe her gift in such a vulgar, insulting way? As if she belonged in an institution or on lithium at the very least. She couldn't explain it, but it was simply part of her. For as long as she could remember, she'd been aware of the "invisible people" as she'd dubbed them around four or five years of age. Sometimes the invisible people simply drifted past her, seemingly unaware. Sometimes they appeared shocked when she looked right at them and greeted them. Sometimes they sought her out, needing to connect, lonely ghosts who longed for someone to hear them and see them. As a child, unaware this phenomenon was unique rather than ubiquitous, she'd been happy to chat with any of them who desired conversation. When her parents assumed she'd invented imaginary friends, they'd been mildly amused, commenting on how precocious she was. As she grew older and insisted the invisible people were real, everything changed. Her parents no longer looked at her the same way. At school, she learned to keep her secret, but not before the other kids ostracized her, having labeled her weird.

Her contract with the show, in order to maintain an insurance policy on her to guard against financial ruin should anything happen to her, stipulated she must subject herself to a rigorous battery of physical and mental examinations annually. Not once had a professional mentioned so much as the slightest concern about her health or well-being.

But, whispered the voice of doubt, what if they're wrong? What if they're merely returning the results desired by the executives and producers to ensure their own future paychecks?

Neither the success of her show nor the validation of countless professionals could erase the memory of her parents' concern—rejection even—of her gift. Of her. The playground jeers and taunts, the refusal of her classmates year after year to commit social suicide by interacting with her, remained firmly lodged in her emotional state, displacing anything that might allow her to feel stable or likeable, much less vindicated.

Was she crazy?

Sterling swung into a parking space near their trailer and shifted into park. "You're very quiet. You okay?"

She nodded quickly but couldn't meet his eyes.

He caught her chin in his thumb and forefinger and turned her face toward him. "Hey. It's me you're talking to. I can't be deceived, remember?"

Right. Always intuitive, of course he saw straight through her. She turned away again, reaching for the door handle. "It's nothing."

He grabbed her hand and held her back. "You aren't taking the skeptic stuff seriously, are you? We promised not to let on-camera personas impact our real personal lives."

Her on-camera self was simply her own self. Anything she did or said in front of the camera or on her social media reflected only her true self, unlike his carefully constructed persona that shared and highlighted only what he wanted people to believe. Considering that was the furthest thing from her mind, she opted not to raise the issue. After all, their producer had insisted he continue with the skepticism, regardless of Sterling's slowly softening view. She couldn't criticize him for preserving the show.

"No, not at all. Really. It's for the show and I get that."

"What is it then?"

She shook her head. As much as she longed for someone to confide in, someone who might even be able to advise her or at least understand and support, Sterling couldn't be that person. Though she suspected him of some level of latent psychic ability, he remained unconvinced. His recent softening toward the idea of paranormal activity notwithstanding, his initial dogged refusal to consider, combined with his attention-seeking internet ploy, challenging her to face him in person, had touched a deep nerve. More so than he could know. The only thing that could make her feel any worse right now was to see a remnant of that skepticism, any delight whatsoever, dancing in his eyes at the thought she could be doubting herself.

Perhaps Sterling would see her as improved without her psychic abilities. But she would lose all sense of herself. She would no longer be the same woman. Her ability to connect with spirits in this world was too much of her identity. To lose it would render her a shadow of herself. It would be too huge a change.

And then she realized she'd been hoping for the same type of change in him. She'd always fantasized about a ripped, psychic partner to team with—someone who could understand her on every level. Someone who would feel her chakras resonate within her and pulse with desire. Someone who could match her emotional well and commune as no one else could.

Along came Sterling with his broad shoulders, cut abs, and bulging biceps, plus his playful attitude and clear interest in her. As a celebrity in his own right, he completely understood the demands of the show and had never begrudged her that. Now that he'd joined the show, he was always close, synching easily into her life, able to fill the tiny slots of free time. Was she trying to shoehorn him into her fantasy role? Certainly he'd seen a ghost and heard one speaking. But maybe she was leaping to the conclusion he possessed psychic powers he remained in denial about. And if he didn't harbor latent abilities, then she was trying to turn him into something he wasn't. And that wasn't fair.

She buried her face into her hands.

"Hey, hey, hey." He scooped her into a hug and rubbed her back. "I knew you were upset. What is it?"

"Do you think I'm crazy?"

"What? No. Why would you think that?"

"I'm starting to think I am."

"Ah. Well, allow me to allay those fears. The simple fact you're wondering if you're crazy negates the possibility."

"What do you mean?"

"Crazy people never think they're crazy."

She considered for a moment, fairly sure she'd heard this somewhere before. Still, hearing it from Sterling soothed her in a way reading it from a document online never could. "Are you sure?"

"It's a fact."

She lifted her head from his shoulder, taking in his sincere concern. "You and your facts."

He stroked her cheek. "I feel like there's a lot more here to discuss, but I also think we should probably join the others. Shall we table this for later?"

She nodded. "Yes, let's go inside."

"I'm not dismissing you." He cradled her face. "I want to hear about this. But I want to talk when we're not distracted and need to think about work. Okay?"

She rested a hand over his and reveled in his warmth. Even if he possessed no sixth sense, he possessed the ability to always make her feel better. And that in and of itself was a remarkable gift, something she'd never experienced before.

She couldn't bring herself to tell him her darkest fear though —that her psychic abilities weren't working properly, or worse yet that they were fading away. She had no idea why she had this sixth sense so few people seemed to be gifted with. Maybe she could lose it as inexplicably as she gained it. Saying the words out loud might make them true. Like a monster under the bed, so long as she ignored it, it couldn't hurt her.

They held hands as they crossed the deserted parking lot. The old building's windows flashed with a strobing black light. Disjointed figures blinked across the glass panes in the flickering light, appearing and disappearing as though bouncing from one spot to the next.

"Looks like some haunted house participants are still inside," she warned Sterling.

"Great."

They opened the spider-web-ringed door, ready to be welcomed by a costumed ticket-taker. Instead, a prolonged squeaking door and deliberate, echoing footsteps greeted them.

Not a soul to be seen. Or felt. A slamming door caused her to jump and whirl around. But it was only from the soundtrack.

"Jump scares," Sterling muttered through gritted teeth. "The cheapest, basest form of fright possible. And generic canned spooky sounds to add insult to injury."

The hallway went silent. An owl hooted.

Something felt off.

"Where is everyone?" she whispered.

In the dim light, Sterling shrugged. "Must be inside already. I saw the van in the parking lot."

"But no one is taking tickets. Someone should've been here to greet us." She shivered, grateful for Sterling's presence.

They crept forward as a quiet cackle filled the hallway.

"I don't remember hearing a soundtrack last night," Sterling said.

"Ian told me they change it up so people can come again and again and enjoy it. He says it's never exactly the same experience."

"Terrific. So something different will jump out at me and fall on my head this time."

She laced her fingers through his and squeezed. "Come on. We know the way. And we know this is all for show."

Though he agreed with her, she felt his primal fear manifest in his base chakra. He nearly glowed red, so entirely did fear rule his emotional state. Knowing something to be true in your mind did not force your emotions to follow suit. Mind over matter was great in theory but almost never plausibly applicable in the real world.

Her crew scattered and left her behind without even bothering to brainstorm and strategize? They always waited on her. Had they lost all faith in her? Could they tell she was losing her sense and thus her ability to lead and guide?

Crickets chirping accompanied them down the hallway—she couldn't be certain if it was the soundtrack or actual crickets.

Not a soul materialized as they made their way to the theatre—no witch, no Grim Reaper, no gauze-wrapped Ian mummy.

"Where is everyone?" she wondered again.

"If they all leap out at me at once, so help me . . ." Apparently Sterling couldn't think of a terrible enough form of retaliation.

Starting to feel a bit as though she'd landed in the midst of a Scooby-Doo cartoon, she stopped suddenly and retrieved her cell phone from her purse. "This is ridiculous. We have technology."

Michael picked up on the third ring. "Hey, sweetie, where are you?"

"Where am I? Where are you?"

"We're all in the theatre of course."

"You started without me?" She heard the betrayal in her voice, though she'd tried to keep it light and play it off as though teasing him.

"With a shortened timeframe tonight, we wanted to get all the equipment set up and be ready for you. About here?"

"Oh. You're setting up for me?" The relief underscored how incredibly tense and concerned she'd been. "We're almost there. About to come downstairs."

"Hang on a second." She heard him as if he spoke over his shoulder. "What is it? What's wrong?"

She heard ruckus in the background, an animated or possibly agitated voice, rising in pitch, along with additional voices joining the fray. "Michael? What is it? What's happening?"

"I can't—" His garbled voice broke into unrecognizable fragments.

The connection terminated. She called back but the call failed.

What had happened to Michael?

CHAPTER FOURTEEN

GRABBING STERLING'S HAND, she picked up the pace, dashing past bubbling cauldrons and leering skeletons. She didn't pause once, not even when a Jack-in-the-box burst from its lid, cackling and bouncing right in front of Sterling.

"Damn it! Not a clown! I hate freaking clowns!"

She pulled him on, regardless. Her crew had gone ahead to prepare and now something sounded like it went horribly wrong. They needed her. Nothing else mattered.

They passed a group of teenage girls, on guard for the next scare, who eyed them in anticipation. When they hurried on without interacting, Kimberly caught the looks of disappointment on the girls' faces but didn't have time to pause.

"I think that was Sterling Wakefield!" one of the girls said.

"Oh my God!" was followed by squeals of delight.

Sterling flew along behind her like a kite caught in a gust as he tried to turn and wave at the young fans.

She nearly tripped on the stairs, her feet a blur. No nun in the lobby this time.

Once again ignoring crime tape, she pushed open the door and hurried to find her group in the theatre.

The auditorium sat empty, but she heard voices. Hushed, subdued voices. But she still detected a note of excitement.

"Michael?" she called.

"We're all in the apartment, sweetie," his voice drifted from above.

"I came as fast as I could. What's wrong?"

"Wrong?"

"On the phone it sounded like something was wrong. And then the call dropped. I was afraid you were experiencing problems."

"The increased EMF may have interfered with the phone. Who knows. But get up here quick. We need you."

"I hope you're charged, girl," Rosie called, "because this place is hot tonight."

"Hot?" Sterling asked. "Lots of activity?"

"Right." And she felt completely unprepared for it. What if she couldn't connect? What if her sixth sense failed her when everyone needed her most?

They found the secret panel open, the passageway gaping, waiting to devour them. The steps creaked under their weight. As out of sorts and jumbled as her tangled emotions were, she worried she would be unable to reach out and connect at all. If she couldn't, if they couldn't discern what the spirit needed, then how would they ever piece together how to help?

They stepped into the little apartment, converted from the choir loft. Everyone hovered around Elise, circled around the Audioxx which she clutched in her outstretched hand.

Elise beamed at her. "It's been producing words since we arrived. The spirit seems eager to connect."

They all turned to her, probably for confirmation. "What has it been saying? Anything helpful?"

"I think it's saying, 'wave,'" TJ said. "Like maybe it's waving at us?"

"I disagree. Sounds like 'save' to me," Michael said.

"Not this again," Sterling muttered. "The exact same sound that no one can agree on?"

"I think it's saying 'behave,'" Rosie offered. "But that's just me."

"Nah. It's a one-syllable word," Stan said. "But no one can agree what word it is. That's why we need Kimberly."

She didn't need this stress. Relaxing and calming down were the only possible ways she might be able to connect. Additional demands on top of the percolating anxiety she already dealt with would only further detract from and muddle her abilities.

"This is just like in the cemetery," Sterling said.

Every head swung from her to him.

"What are you talking about?" TJ asked.

"Didn't anyone else notice how strongly influenced by your own personalities your individual ghost interactions were? Elise 'chatted' with an historical figure. Rosie got into a fight with a guy she says was inappropriate with her. Kimberly heard from an unhappy woman she imbued as needing help and resolution. All of these 'experiences' are filtered through your own personal prisms, creating the type of interaction you typically have with real people. Or the type of interaction you expect to have with a spirit."

"What about you?" TJ asked. "You claim to have heard a nun praying."

"I was probably influenced by our current surroundings as well as my upbringing."

"Wait," she said, startled by his change of heart. "Are you saying you think that was all in your head? That you didn't actually hear a spirit?"

"I think we need to be realistic about it and acknowledge we're all impeded by our own desires and experiences."

"But you said . . . you were so sure." In her heart, that had been their most intimate moment, when she shared her energy with him, allowing him to experience something he couldn't on his own, to feel for a few moments what she sensed routinely.

She had never experienced anything like it with anyone else before. And now he simply wrote it off? She may have hurt herself sharing energy with him, and he dismissed it like it was nothing?

"And a good scientist doesn't let emotion cloud his thoughts. We need to consider every possible explanation."

"But I thought we—"

"*Kimberly*." The Audioxx crackled, producing a robotic version of her name.

They all gasped.

"She wants to talk to you!" Elise said.

TJ jumped, hands covering his mouth. "Whoa! That was new! And clear. No question about that one."

Stan swooped in with his camera, ready to capture the next communication.

"Kimmy?" Michael said. "Sounds like you're up."

Sterling shook his head. "The obvious explanation here is that the machine produced an echo of someone else speaking her name."

"Except we've been talking quite a bit since anyone said her name, dude," TJ pointed out. "Didn't hear any other echoes."

Michael lifted the KII. "Nothing extraordinary. No temperature or EMF spikes. You getting anything?"

"No noticeable images on the FLIR," TJ reported. "What about you, Ms. Wantland?"

She grasped her quartz and breathed deeply. *Please*.

A gentle nudge offered relief so great, she nearly cried. "Yes. Someone is with us. She wants to tell us something." That much she could perceive, no deception required.

"What's she saying?"

"I'm not sure yet." The elusive moment evaded her, the connection evaporating. Like a fish bumping the lure but then swimming away, the intrigued spirit drifted off.

Come on, talk to me. She fought to reach out, struggled to scrape together more energy to offer to the spirit, enticing it with the opportunity to communicate. Sure she felt the manifestation circling, frustration consumed her. Why couldn't she connect? Was the spirit particularly shy or did something inhibit it? Or did the fault lie squarely with her? Did she imagine the weakened state she currently coped with? Was it all in her mind? A psychosomatic condition brought about by her own self-doubt?

The Audioxx crackled and hissed.

"*Anna*," the electronic voice said.

"Okay, that was clearly Anna," Michael said, "but so what? No one here named Anna. Kimmy, what does she want?"

A cold shiver ran down her spine. Had the spirit moved to the Audioxx in response to her inability to "hear" properly? She moved closer to the equipment. Elise handed it to her.

"Anna?" she asked. "Or Hannah?"

"*Hannah*," came the reply. Then, "*Anna*."

"It's clearly repeating sounds from the surrounding environment," Sterling said.

"*Hannah*."

"Wasn't that the grave that wouldn't respond to the dowsing rods?" TJ asked.

She nodded. "And Anna was the unhappy mother in the grave right beside her."

Sterling looked at her. "That can't possibly pertain to the investigation. It must be coincidence. Right?"

She'd agreed with him in the graveyard. Nothing could have prepared her for this. "In that I don't think this has anything to do with Donny, I agree with you. But for some reason this spirit wants to discuss the graves we just saw."

As much as she hated relying on the Audioxx, tonight she seemed to have little choice. "What about Hannah?"

A noise from below grabbed their attention.

"What was that?" Michael asked.

"Sounded like it came from the auditorium," Sterling said.

"Or the stage," Michael said.

"We have cameras elsewhere?" she asked.

"Sta-cams all over the stage and backstage areas," Stan confirmed.

"Maybe we should shift down there?" Michael asked. "Or do you want to finish here first?"

"I . . ." A tough question to answer when the Audioxx had fallen silent and the spirit either wouldn't or couldn't connect with her.

"Let's split up," Michael suggested. "The KII isn't detecting so much as a blip here. Let me see if it indicates activity around the stage."

"What about the Audioxx?" Elise asked.

Kimberly stared at it a moment and then passed it back. "You take it and go with Michael. It's not doing anything up here anymore."

Stan followed them while Sterling, Rosie, and TJ remained with her.

"Okay, girl, what's up?" Rosie asked. "You are off tonight. I can tell."

"I noticed in the car," Sterling said, "but she wouldn't tell me."

"I don't want to talk right now. Let me work."

Rosie clicked her tongue. "You just resorted to listening to an external device over your own psychic connection. So I ask again, what's up? I have my emergency bag if you're depleted."

"Maybe? I don't know." She sank to the floor, trying to relax and get a grip. The additional pressure was not helping her current flustered state, which made it even more difficult to focus.

Sterling squatted beside her. "Want me to try again? If it's the nun, maybe I'll have more luck, like the first night."

She shook her head, not sure where he even stood on the issue. Did he believe he connected the first night? He'd just denied anything had happened, claiming he was susceptible to his Catholic upbringing. Was he simply curious? Trying to repeat? He swung wider than a pendulum, and she couldn't keep up with his extreme shifts.

Holding up both hands to quiet them, she breathed deeply. This had to end. She took five deep breaths, holding for a count of five on each and instructing her erratic heartrate to calm down before exhaling with purpose. Once grounded and capable of clear thought, she sought the restless spirit who had seemed so eager to tell her something.

I'm here. I'm listening. What is it?

No connection clicked into place. No voice responded to her invitation to converse. But the image of a tiny gold cross emerged in her mind. What did it mean? As Sterling postulated, was she falling victim to suggestion from their surroundings? That hadn't happened to her before. Why would this investigation be any different? Then again, something was off and she had no idea what.

After five minutes of silence, she gave up. "Let's join the others. This room has gone cold." Why it had been hot before she arrived and grown cold after, she didn't know and didn't like.

Elise's excited voice from elsewhere in the building rose to meet them. "It said 'spotlight!' I'm sure of it!"

She glanced at Sterling and Rosie before hurrying down the secret passageway to join the action.

The haunted house must have ended for the night, she deduced as she saw Ian standing beside Michael. He was talking as she reached the group. "I mean, Donny said that quite a bit. The box doesn't sound at all like him. But he did say that."

"Of course the Audioxx doesn't sound like him. It's an electronically produced voice. It doesn't sound like any human." Michael glanced up as she approached. "Oh, good. Kimmy, what do you think? Is it Donny? Can you tell?"

Though she deemed it likely, she could not confirm the presence or hear what he wanted to tell them. "I'm . . . having trouble focusing tonight."

Michael raised an eyebrow. "Trouble? Are you—"

A thump in the wing drew her attention off stage.

"I'm fine. I'll go see what that noise was."

"What noise? You don't sound fine. Kimmy? Talk to me."

She left him behind and followed the thumping. Perhaps if she could get away from everyone, she would have better results from her sixth sense. In the wing, she listened, relieved to be away from everyone else's expectations. She relaxed and tried again to reach out.

A whisper slithered into her ear, garbled but insistent. She retraced her steps from the night before, farther into the theatre, led on by an emphatic voice beckoning her onward along with the gnawing feeling something eluded her, just outside her grasp.

What is it? What are you trying to tell me?

She found herself in front of Jillian's office. Why did the voice keep leading her here? The door clicked and swung open. Heart hammering, she stood in the doorway and peered into the room, hesitant to enter. Jillian's insistence they stay out still rang through her memory.

Papers on the desk fluttered, drawing her attention. Jillian had been so upset they'd been in here. What was she hiding?

She stepped closer. One glance at the papers on the desk couldn't hurt. And maybe they would offer some insight.

A hand rested on her shoulder. Blast it. Just as she was making progress, someone interrupted. "I really think I need to be alone tonight."

She turned, ready to ask Sterling to go back to the auditorium.

A rotund man stood before her, hand resting on her shoulder. A shock of gray hair crowned his head. Pale and clammy, his skin appeared to be actively decaying, sloughing off his frame.

She shuddered and leapt away from his grasp. Her mouth moved but produced no sound. She shook her head.

The man's mouth moved as though with great effort. "Jillian . . . must . . . pay."

CHAPTER FIFTEEN

IN THE DRESSING room the next morning, Kimberly watched Rosie root through rolling racks of costumes. Her dry eyes scratched like sandpaper every time she blinked. She lifted a cup of coffee to her lips and sipped. Her third cup and yet she felt no better, no more alert. She hadn't slept at all after her encounter with the gruesome spirit threatening Jillian. Certain it was Donny trying to communicate with her, she could not fathom what Jillian could have done to the man to cause such a visceral response after death. Ian said she'd allowed him to stay in the apartment, for crying out loud. That seemed like a gesture of goodwill. Thoughts of a possible affair sent a shiver down her spine. Just thinking about any woman with that hideous thing made her retch.

She set down the paper cup of coffee. Her hand shook and she wasn't sure if it was due to far too much caffeine or fear of encountering the spirit again in her weakened state. She should have felt him coming. Should have been able to connect with him and get some idea of what he wanted. As fully formed as the spirit had manifested, every hair on her arms should have stood on end. Every fiber of her being should have prickled with the ectoplasm formed in the air by the spirit burning energy. She should have felt her sixth sense connect.

Instead, nothing. She'd genuinely believed a member of the crew had come looking for her when the hand touched her shoulder. She shivered at the memory and glanced again at the open office door. They ought to shut it. If Jillian discovered it open again, the woman would surely pitch a fit. Perhaps even threaten to fire them and send them away. Kimberly wasn't sure that would be such a bad thing. For the first time since she was ten years old, she was scared of a ghost.

"Kimberly?" Sterling's gentle voice pulled her attention back to her current surroundings.

Rosie stood with a skirt and blouse, held out for her approval. "Hello? Where are you this morning?"

"Sorry. That ghost last night . . ." She shuddered. The spirit had so startled her, she had forgotten to look over the papers. She didn't find anything out from that.

"I don't understand why you wandered off on your own," Sterling said. "No cameras. No one to help if you needed it."

"I just needed to be alone."

"I know there's something you aren't telling us, girl," Rosie said. "And I don't like it. But right now, we need to make sure you're ready for Trunk or Treat. Jillian told Michael we can use any costumes we want. I think this will work for you. Then we need a prop axe."

"Are we certain the Stillwells are the way to go?" she asked. "Won't small children come to Trunk or Treat? Are a headless man and his axe-wielding wife really the best costumes for us?"

Rosie lowered the outfit and considered. "I should have thought of that."

"I'm not the only one distracted. You've been off since we got here this morning. What's going on?"

Rosie returned the clothing to the rack and sat, sighing heavily. "Lorenzo told me he loves me last night."

"But that's great. Isn't it?"

"I don't know! It's only been a month. We're still trying to figure out the long-distance thing . . ."

Sterling peered around the curtain of a changing stall. "You said it back to him, didn't you?"

Rosie buried her face in a costume blouse. "I . . . may not have been able to actually say those exact words."

"Rosie!" If she'd been drinking coffee, she would have spit it out. "You just left that hanging there?"

"Well, he surprised me! Have you told Sterling you love him?"

Her heart skipped a beat. She glanced at him but they both looked away the moment they made eye contact. "Well, I think we . . ."

Rosie turned to Sterling. "Have *you* said it?"

Sterling rubbed at the back of his neck. "I think . . . before you say those words to someone . . . you need to know for sure they're ready to hear them and ready to say them back. Otherwise, it could get awkward quick."

Rosie held out a hand. "Exactly. See?"

She picked up her coffee, suddenly not sure what to do with herself. "But if both people wait for the other one, no one will ever say it. Lorenzo took a chance. He must be feeling devastated."

Rosie grabbed both sides of her head. "I haven't heard from him yet today. I don't know what to do."

"You've reached out to him?" she asked.

"Yes. And nothing."

"What did you say?"

"I said good morning! What was I supposed to say?"

"Oh, geez." She turned to Sterling. "You're a guy. What should she do? How do we fix this?"

"I don't know Lorenzo. I have no idea what he's feeling or what he needs to hear. But if I told you"—his intense gaze pierced her—"and you didn't answer back, I'd be devastated and probably need some time alone."

She squirmed under the weight of his searching stare. He

seemed to be trying to gauge her response to the suggestion he could say such a thing to her. How would she feel? Her heart hammered.

"More importantly," Sterling continued, "does Rosie want to fix it?"

"Of course!" Rosie said. "I think so. I really like him and I'm not ready to call it off. He just surprised me, and I didn't react well."

"Okay, then, you need to call and tell him that," Sterling said. "Exactly that."

"I don't know if I can say that."

"You just did."

"But I mean to him."

"He's the one who needs to hear it."

Kimberly could understand where Rosie was coming from. She still marveled that she was in a relationship for the first time in years. And she wanted to continue and see where it went. Was she ready for Sterling to tell her he loved her? She hoped they didn't find out for a bit longer. Although, she thought she could say it back to him. He affected her in a way no man ever had.

"Sometimes, the things we need to say the most are the most difficult to say." She spoke to Rosie, but she looked directly at Sterling.

Sterling held her gaze. "And sometimes what we need most, can be the hardest thing to ask for."

Rosie wrung her hands. "I always blow it. Always. Usually I jump too quickly and scare them off. This time I tried to wait and ruined everything. Here I've found a nice guy, a guy who also works in the paranormal field and actually treats me well and totally gets me, and I've ruined it!"

"You don't know that," Kimberly said. "Maybe he's sleeping in. I'm sure he had ghost tours late into the night."

"But he always tells me goodnight before he goes to bed. He knows I'm up during an investigation. And he didn't last night.

Besides, *we* sleep in! He must be awake by now. He's just not answering me."

"Okay, let's put the costume search on hold for now and go join footage review. You can relax for now." She rubbed Rosie's back. "It will be okay. I promise."

In fact, she had an idea. But it would have to wait.

As they left the dressing room and headed for the stage, she pulled Jillian's office door closed and hoped it locked automatically. Jillian didn't believe a ghost opened it the first time and seemed less likely to believe it a second time.

Her crew was already hard at work reviewing everything they'd captured on audio and video the night before. No one lit up and commanded her to come listen or come watch, however, so they must not have found anything too exciting yet. Too bad. She wanted to wrap this up and go.

Elise, on the other hand, jumped from her seat. "Ms. Wantland! Guess what? Come see!"

She knew Elise well enough to know her enthusiastic researcher never really expected her to guess anything. It was merely her way of announcing she had something to share. She crossed to Elise's laptop and looked over her shoulder. Elise appeared to have accessed newspaper records, and from long ago. Kimberly had learned early on not to try to maintain everything in her head that Elise managed to mentally juggle. Kimberly had enough on her own plate. She'd brought in Elise to relieve some of the workload and it made no sense to micromanage.

"What are we looking at?" she asked. Had she discovered the connection between Jillian and Donny? But no, this looked extremely old. And seemed to be something about a lost little girl. Oh no.

"I wanted to find out about the graves from last night," Elise began. "So I started digging. That little girl, Hannah? The one who wasn't interacting? She went missing."

"Went missing?" Sterling asked. "You mean grave robbers or . . ."

"No, her body was never found. She was presumed dead and declared dead, but no one ever located her body."

Something clicked. "You mean, the grave is empty? There's no body in it?"

"Exactly," Elise said. "The family opted to hold a funeral and burial, probably to offer some closure. As you can imagine, the mother was distraught. I think her husband hoped it would help her move on."

"The mother. Anna. She told me she had an unhappy life." All the pieces came together. She turned to Sterling. "And that's why no one answered from the girl's grave. She isn't there. See? It makes sense. Anna was unhappy because she lost her daughter and never knew what happened to her. And we didn't get a response from the grave because she isn't actually buried there."

"You couldn't tell the grave was empty, Kimmy?" Michael asked.

"Yeah," Sterling said. "You told us the spirit didn't want to interact. Not that there was no spirit there."

Her previously infallible gift was failing her. No doubt about it. She hadn't lost it completely—Anna had interacted with her, a creepy dead guy had approached her last night, determined to make Jillian pay. But things were getting by her. She was losing control.

"I thought she was just shy," she offered. Even she heard how pathetic the excuse sounded. "Besides, we were just having fun last night. It doesn't have anything to do with the investigation. The tour was running over time, and we needed to get to work."

"Still, seems like you would have been able to tell." Michael lifted an eyebrow, clearly offering the opportunity for her to share.

"Here we go," TJ said. "This is more like it. Ms. Wantland, I have a figure upstairs in the apartment."

She turned from the uncomfortable conversation and went to his side, leaning over his shoulder. "Let me see. Do you think it's Donny?"

TJ shook his head. "I don't know. It looks like the hooded figure the girl described at our initial meeting with the troupe."

"Oh, right. The hooded figure she was convinced was an axe murderer. Though in all likelihood that axe murder was an angry wife. Why would she be hooded?"

Sterling, who had maneuvered himself between her and TJ to view the monitor, cocked his head. "Hooded? Or habited?"

"What does that mean?" she asked, squinting at the silhouette image TJ had isolated from their recordings.

"I mean, doesn't that look like a nun's habit? The covering a nun wears. Not some creeper in a hood or a cloak."

She looked again and suddenly she did see what he was talking about. "I do see that. You think that's the nun you heard praying? But why would the nun interfere with a teenage girl when she was . . . here with her boyfriend . . . all alone in the dark."

"Well," Rosie said, "I know what I would have been doing all alone in the dark with my boyfriend when I was her age. Or now for that matter."

Stan laughed. "Maybe you did hear her say 'behave' last night."

Rosie shrugged and batted her eyes, sparking more laughter from the group. Kimberly stared at the image while the others joked. Were they wrong about two spirits? That couldn't be. Why would a nun say anything about a spotlight? That sounded much more like an actor. But an actor who craved the spotlight and demanded attention should be more eager to connect with her. And so far, Donny had not been approachable. He seemed to be avoiding her to some extent. Why? Maybe her psychic energy wasn't strong enough and he couldn't detect her beacon, couldn't tell she wanted to help him. She always visualized herself as a lighthouse, sending out a welcoming light into the darkness of the Nightshade, inviting lost and battered spirits who were ready to rest. What happened if the light went out? What use was she if spirits could no longer find her in the dark?

Burying her fear as much as possible, she talked through the bits of evidence they'd collected so far. "Okay, so we already suspected the nun remained in the church, repeating daily activities as she did in life. Interrupting a teenage make-out session makes some sense in that context. But why would she reach out to us about the graves? What does that have to do with us? I would think nothing. Jillian believes Donny is the one harassing her and her troupe. But so far we haven't successfully connected with him to determine what he wants. All he says is Jillian must pay. And on top of that Jillian won't share anything specific that might help."

"I really wish you'd had a camera with you when he appeared to you last night," Michael chided her. "Don't do that again. We might have recorded something important."

"Or not," she answered. "The cameras don't always capture anything."

"Kind of seems like you're not getting anywhere with this investigation," Michael said.

"Hey! I'm trying like always. Some spirits are less cooperative." Anyone but Michael she could have dismissed a comment like that. From her partner and staunchest supporter, that stung.

"I'm just saying. What's the deal? You don't have any readings on this guy?"

She whirled around, hot words on her tongue. She didn't need his criticism on top of everything else. In fact, with her current fatigue and emotional state, it was the very last thing she needed. "'What's the deal?' Really? You're implying I'm . . . what? Not trying?"

Sterling rested a hand on her arm. "Okay, okay. No one thinks that. Deep breath."

Michael exaggerated a shrug. "Seems like you ought to be able to offer some insight."

"Insight? Why don't you take a turn? How would you like to deal with the half-decayed, decomposing, upset, lost, and confused dead things for a change? And have everyone always pulling and tugging and wanting something. I never get a break. Never. Someone is always there, needing something."

"Whoa. Whoa. Whoa." Sterling curled an arm around her and pulled her to his chest, stroking her back. "No one is criticizing you."

TJ spoke up. "Kinda sounded like Michael—"

"Nope." Sterling stroked her hair. "No criticism here. You're tired and overwhelmed and need a break. We can see that. It's okay."

He began to rock her, and tears flooded her eyes. It felt so good to be held and soothed. She wanted to crawl into his lap and listen to him tell her everything would be okay. Because right now, she couldn't believe it would be. Something was wrong. The others were starting to suspect but didn't yet understand the extent of the problem. If Michael was this unhappy with her thinking she was slacking off and not trying, how would he react to hearing her psychic abilities were deteriorating? She could not handle the look in his eyes. Everything they'd worked for together had been established on her gift. If she lost that, everything fell apart. Who was she without her sixth sense?

"Kimmy, I didn't mean it that way. You know I love you."

She stayed buried in Sterling's chest, unable to face them, much less tell them her dark suspicion.

"I think Kimberly and I are going to do some sightseeing today," Sterling suggested.

"What? Now?" Michael asked.

"I think now sounds perfect. You guys can finish here and let us know what you find."

"But we always sit through footage review together."

"But today she needs a break from it. If you want to come, or catch up later, everyone is welcome. Just no cameras and no discussion of the investigation." Sterling tipped her head back and wiped tears away with his thumbs, searching her eyes. "Okay?"

She sniffed and nodded. Getting away sounded perfect.

CHAPTER SIXTEEN

THE NATURE of the show meant she and her crew traveled together the majority of the year, spending nearly all their time together. She loved every one of them dearly. But the afternoon felt like a breath of fresh air, even as she felt a bit guilty that she'd ditched footage review. Sterling was right—what would she really contribute to it anyway? And if she went back refreshed and recharged for tonight, it would be better in the long run.

She watched Sterling watching her and marveled that he still sent butterflies through her stomach. How did he always know exactly what she needed? He'd whisked her away from the old building and into his i8 before anyone could strongly object. They'd seen Mark Twain's boyhood home, pretended to white-wash a fence, stood by the river and watched the steamboats chug past, their huge paddles churning the water.

Sterling clutched a bag with souvenirs he'd purchased for them, so they could remember their time here—T-shirts and mugs with famous Mark Twain quotes on them.

She needed to make sure Rosie fully charged her tonight. Surely after an afternoon relaxing, if she was fully charged up she could move beyond this ripple she'd experienced in her gift.

The wind whipped strands of hair into her face. Sterling pushed them aside and tucked the loose locks behind her ear. She cupped his cheek in her hand and tiptoed to meet his lips. A shiver ran through her, as if the two of them sparked electricity. Heat flushed her cheeks and rushed through her limbs. She pulled him closer, wondering if they could spend the rest of the afternoon in their hotel room. *Their* room. She knew she should be too old to feel giddy and silly about that but being close to Sterling filled her with golden light.

He pulled away, dark eyes shining. "Feeling better?"

"Much. Thank you." She leaned in for more.

"There you guys are!" Michael yelled from across the street. "I've been texting you both. Why didn't you answer me?"

She dropped her head back and sighed. She suspected she knew how parents of toddlers felt at that moment.

Rosie crossed the street, irritated drivers honking at her. "I told him you were probably at the hotel. Figured 'sightseeing' was code for getting it on. But, no, you actually appear to be sightseeing."

"Thanks, Rosie. Your timing is impeccable." She didn't admit she had been about to suggest that very thing to Sterling.

The rest of her crew followed once the traffic cleared.

"Well, how did it go?" she asked, ignoring Rosie's grin. "You guys find anything helpful?"

"A few odds and ends. No smoking gun," Michael said. "Elise wants to go tour Mark Twain's cave. Which seems appropriate while we're here. You two up for it?"

She looked to Sterling, wondering if he'd been thinking along the same lines she had before the others showed up.

"Actually, I was about to suggest we head that way. So your timing truly is impeccable." He rested a hand on her waist and squeezed. "We will meet you there."

He hadn't said a thing about touring a cave, but he merely shrugged in response to her lifted eyebrow. Oh well. They could make time alone later. Maybe skip dinner. Although Sterling needed his regular meals.

"What's that look for?" he asked as he held the i8's passenger door open for her.

"I was going to suggest we spend the rest of the afternoon in the hotel. Now I'm trying to decide when we can squeeze that in."

"Damn. If I'd known, I wouldn't have agreed to the cave tour. Although, how often do we get the chance to see that?" He climbed in and started the car. "I will definitely find alone time later, though."

They drove in silence for a few minutes. She breathed easily and noticed the serene calm settle over her again. Ridiculous she didn't recognize the feeling of happiness when she first noticed it recently. The little bud of contentment bloomed fully around Sterling.

"This is nice," she told him. "I love seeing other places, but I get out and do more now that you're here."

"Really?" He glanced at her and put on his turn signal to follow signs to the cave parking lot.

"I'm embarrassed to admit it, but yes. I mostly stayed around the hotel or investigation, hanging with the others. Don't get me wrong. I'm not throwing shade at them. But today was nice."

He parked the car and turned those vivid brown eyes on her. "I'm glad." He stroked her cheek and leaned across the emergency brake. "Now what should we do while we wait for the others to catch up?"

"Oh my gosh! It's Sterling and Kimberly from *The Wantland Files*!" someone nearby shouted. "I heard they're in town!"

She laughed because the only other option was to cry. "Looks like we take publicity photos."

He shook his head and smirked back. "Sorry. We are not meant to be alone right now."

"I blame your car for this one. If you didn't drive this flashy sports car, no one would notice us. A shabby, ten-year-old POS we could hide in."

"At least I'm moving up in the world. Did you hear that? I've graduated to 'Sterling from *The Wantland Files*.' I like the sound of that."

"Don't you forget it. You're all mine now. Let's get this over with."

They lifted the butterfly doors and waved to the small group crowding close, hoping for a glimpse and a photo. Where she had once loathed this sort of thing with every fiber of her being, she found herself joking and laughing along with Sterling, posing for photos and then returning to conversation—not as seamlessly as Sterling managed, but not as clunky and awkward as she used to be either.

When the van pulled in, his face now staring alongside hers from the side, they extricated themselves, having chatted with everyone at least once, and joined the crew.

"Look at you!" Rosie's lips twisted into a wry grin.

"What?"

"If I didn't know better, I'd say you were enjoying yourself around fans, Miss She Who Hates Publicity." Rosie elbowed Sterling. "It's your influence. I knew you'd be good for her."

"I hope so."

She could have lost herself in the depths of his dreamy eyes. But the cave waited.

Fortunately, the next tour had room for them. Their wait would be short. They wandered the parking area, taking in the wooded hillside they would soon plunge deep inside. She tried to imagine the area unpopulated, imagined happening onto an opening that expanded into a vast and unexplored series of caverns and tunnels.

They stopped to study a large map which indicated the current entrance as well as an original entrance no longer in use.

"Can you imagine Mark Twain and his friends wriggling

through tiny openings in the hillside and shimmying into the dark spaces inside?" Sterling asked her.

"I was just thinking about that myself. Nope. And with nothing but candles? They were lucky they always made it back out." She shuddered as she considered how those adventures could have ended.

Sterling seemed to intuit where her thoughts had gone and rubbed her back.

Shortly before their tour time, she and her crew amassed in front of the modern-day entrance, along with other tourists. A couple of them gaped and pointed, but everyone kept their distance.

Unfortunately, no one in her crew had listened to the advice to bring a jacket or sweater, and she shivered as she left the sun behind and delved into the chill of the cave.

Sterling took off his leather jacket and draped it over her shoulders. "Skinny thing," he murmured in her ear, brushing her cheek with his lips. He pulled her close and enveloped her in his arms. He sent a completely different type of shiver down her spine and a flush of heat that dispelled the chilliness.

The tour guide gathered them into the entrance and welcomed them. Electric lights lit their path, an easily navigated walkway that led them through some of the most famous rooms —The Parlor, with a rock formation that resembled a piano, Aladdin's palace, with its glorious outcroppings, Jesse James' hideout. They sidled past a formation that looked much like an alligator without too much imagination involved.

Along the way, the guide offered them historical information and interesting tidbits. Turned out Samuel Clemons' signature had recently been discovered in another cave, not on this tour. The walls of the caves were emblazoned with more scratched, burned, and chiseled names than she could count. Before the cave system had been designated a national landmark and control over such graffiti had been implemented, untold numbers of visitors to the caves had left their indelible mark on it.

The farther they moved into the interior of the hillside, the more Kimberly noticed a pulling sensation. It started in her stomach, a quivery feeling as though she was nervous. But she wasn't anxious about anything. It increased until overwhelming her with dread, sure something terrible waited around the next curve in the cavern.

Sterling gave her a look and tipped his head. "You okay?"

When she nodded, he looked like he didn't believe her and took her hand.

She heard Rosie squeal in delight. Her best friend needed to get over the initial glee of a new relationship. It wasn't even Rosie's relationship for crying out loud. That reminded her, as soon as the tour ended and they got back to the hotel for a brief respite, she needed to make a phone call. She had a surprise she hoped to spring on her best friend.

The tour guide continued with his presentation, but she had trouble focusing. Her pulse kicked up a notch. She pulled quick, short breaths and realized how narrow the passageway had grown. Minerals sparkled and glittered from the walls of the caves. She knew better than to believe any of it was worth anything but imagined herself chipping away and discovering gold, taking it home to her mother and father and saving the family from the financial problems that always plagued them. Her parents could barely feed their six children. She wished she could help.

Kimberly shook her head. What was happening? She didn't have money problems. Or parents waiting at home. Or five siblings. Her vision blurred and she threw a hand out to grab Sterling.

He curled an arm around her, supporting her as she stumbled.

Rosie pushed through the crowd. "What is it?"

She shook her head, nausea brewing in her stomach to the point she didn't trust herself to open her mouth.

Something tugged at her, insistently, as sure as if someone grabbed the front of her blouse and pulled. She fought the urge to leave everyone behind and turn down a tunnel. They weren't supposed to leave the group. She knew that. She refocused on the tour guide.

"And this is the part of the tour," the guide said, "where we let you see what Tom Sawyer, Huck Finn, and Becky Thatcher would have experienced when they got lost and the last nub of candle flickered out. I'm going to flip off our electric lights for a moment. Don't worry. I'll turn them back on."

The lightbulbs went out, plunging them into the most complete darkness she'd ever known. Her eyes strained even though her brain told her it would do no good.

I can't see. I can't see. Her breathing quickened. Sheer panic clouded her senses.

She pulled away from Sterling and groped for the cave walls, lost, terrified she would never see her family again. She needed out. She had to get out.

"Kimberly?" she heard Sterling's voice, muffled in the darkness. "What are you—"

She had to find her way back out. She didn't mean to go this far into the caves. She needed to get back home for dinner. She clawed at her throat, unable to breathe, sure the air around her had grown thick. Her oil lamp had burned out. She couldn't tell which way she was going. If she just turned around and retraced her steps . . .

Wait a minute. She ran fingers over her throat again. Her necklace. It was gone! Mama had given her the necklace. She couldn't lose it. *No, no, no.* Where did it fall off?

She stumbled and fell, dimly aware of voices around her but unable to discern what they said. *I'm here,* she tried to call out, but her dry mouth and lips couldn't form words.

The lights flipped back on.

"You can see how terrifying being lost and alone in the caves could be," the tour guide picked back up. "Is everyone okay?"

"Where's Kimberly?" Sterling asked.

Kimberly opened her eyes. In the darkness, she had veered off the main path and into a tiny side corridor.

"Kimmy!" she heard Michael call.

"Oh my God, where is she?" Rosie asked.

"Did we lose someone?" the guide asked. "We all really need to stay on the path, folks."

She shook uncontrollably. Her vision blurred. The sense of anxiety permeated every fiber of her being. Something drew her on, an inexplicable need to search the passageway. Her fingers scraped over the rough rock, sifting through dust that lodged under her fingernails as she clawed. *Where is it? Where did it go?*

Underneath it all, the pulling sensation continued to tug at her. Laughter filled her ears—the ugliest, most malicious sound she'd ever heard.

"Kimberly!" Sterling stood in the crack in the wall, reaching for her. "What are you doing in there? How did you even fit, you skinny thing?"

She opened her eyes and blinked. What was she searching for? What had happened to her? Who had she heard laughing? She shuddered at the memory of the sound. She looked to Sterling and reached for him, fighting the growing sense she was going crazy.

He grabbed her extended arm and pulled while she pushed against the rock wall.

The tour guide and the entire group watched as she emerged from the fissure. Rosie hurried to her side, looking her over for injury.

"Are you okay, girl?"

"Sorry. I . . . couldn't breathe and I—"

"Claustrophobia can hit you hard in the caves," the tour guide said. "Panic attacks sometimes follow. Take a deep breath and go slow."

Kimberly knew she wasn't claustrophobic but was so relieved to be over the episode that she didn't argue. Besides, easier to let him believe her bizarre behavior was the result of a panic attack brought on by claustrophobia than to try to explain she couldn't currently control her psychic abilities.

And someone had just hijacked them.

CHAPTER SEVENTEEN

KIMBERLY CLENCHED her fists in frustration. Not only was she unsure what exactly had happened to her in the caves, but also her team, her staunchest supporters, seemed reluctant to agree.

The certainty she'd lost something still clouded her memories, a sad fog weighing on her. She tried again to impress upon them the significance. "This means something. I know it does. I don't know how, but I know it's important. Someone dropped something in there."

Michael's face twisted into a convoluted mix of concern and doubt. "That could have been anything. Do you know how many people traipse through there every day?"

"And I'm supposed to be the skeptic. She veered way off the main path. How would a tourist drop anything there?"

She threw a grateful glance at Sterling. "Right? How can you explain that? Plus, I felt a presence. Something called to me. Or maybe a spirit wanted to lead me to something. I'm not sure."

Michael lifted an eyebrow. "And you think it's important to our investigation? Sorry, but I have a hard time seeing a connection. Or do you not suspect Donny anymore?"

"I do think Donny must be trying to contact Jillian about

something. But clearly we have another spirit, probably a nun who lived here while it was a church, communicating with us as well." How much should she admit to him? She already struggled with guilt using her fragile energy reserve on a side venture. She knew she really ought to focus everything she had on the main investigation and piece together what Donny needed to resolve to be able to rest in peace. She pulled in a breath. "I saw a gold cross the other night."

"Saw?" Sterling asked.

She sighed. "In the apartment. I wanted to connect with the nun. I hoped she would explain why she wanted our attention on Anna's and Hannah's graves. She didn't connect, but I saw a vision of a tiny gold cross. And then in the caves today I experienced stress about a missing necklace." Her hand drifted to her décolletage as if searching for it again. "It's hard to explain."

Elise grew animated, her hands working the air in front of her. "The Audioxx . . . we thought it was saying 'wave' or 'save' but maybe it was saying 'grave' so we would check the graves."

"Or 'cave' so we would go to the caves," TJ postulated.

Sterling shook his head. "Or maybe this is all a coincidence and we're applying evidence to support a baseless theory that we didn't believe five minutes ago."

The possibility he was correct crossed her mind. But she still believed it factored in somehow. "We have to adapt as we gather additional information, Sterling. That's how this works."

Michael crossed his arms and grabbed his chin as he contemplated. "Maybe. But in the cave, no spirit reached out to you? The owner of the necklace didn't connect and share some explanation?"

She shook her head. "I think maybe they tried to but . . ."

Michael mimicked her head shake. "But?"

"I experienced anxiety and stress. Fear. I felt lost and scared I'd never get home. But I couldn't actually connect."

"That sounds like claustrophobia, honestly," Sterling said.

"I'm not claustrophobic. This was . . . I think someone wanted to communicate but I'm . . ." She couldn't bring herself to say the words.

"You're what?" Michael asked.

"I'm feeling . . . depleted." *Damaged. Weak. Terrified I'm losing my gift.* "Rosie, can you please make sure I'm fully charged tonight?"

"You got it, girl. I'm here for you."

Michael eyed her. "Hold up. What do you mean, depleted?"

"It's hard to describe." She shrugged, not sure how much more to divulge until she better understood what was happening.

"She has to be exhausted," Sterling said. "I'll take her back for a quick nap. Then this evening Rosie can do her thing and by tonight she'll be refreshed and good to go." He looked to her and though he smiled, his eyes sought approval.

"Yes, that sounds great." She smiled back, glad for his intervention.

"I wouldn't mind a quick 'nap' myself," Rosie said. "See you two later."

"Have you heard from Lorenzo?" Kimberly asked.

Rosie waved away the question. "Nah. I blew it. It's fine. I'm over him."

"You've gotten over him since this morning?" Kimberly could feel the intense sadness rolling off her friend and knew Rosie wasn't remotely over anything. The relief her ability to read others' emotional states still worked, at least at some level, was overshadowed by Rosie's grief.

Rosie shrugged.

Kimberly pulled her into a hug. "It'll be okay. I promise."

Rosie forced a smile and a quick nod. "I'm sure you're right. See you two tonight."

She accompanied Sterling into the street, tingling from the high levels of energy he threw into the environment. His orange chakra pulsed so powerfully, she noticed other women they passed in the street gasp slightly. Sure, perhaps crossing paths unexpectedly with a celebrity caused the reactions, but she didn't think so. This was more akin to pheromones. His desire resonated so powerfully that he sent shock waves radiating around him. He was the equivalent to a cat in heat.

He tossed an arm around her shoulders and kissed her head. "Maybe we can finally carve out a little slice of alone time, huh?"

"That sounds good." Her orange chakra throbbed in response to his, but feebly. What was happening to her? Maybe he was right. Maybe some rest would rejuvenate her.

"You were nice to reassure Rosie back there. She looks devastated."

"I meant it. It will be okay."

He looked at her sideways. "Your psychic powers tell you that?"

"I wish," she mumbled. "No, I have a plan in place. And the psychic thing is really more of a gift or ability than a power."

"You're stronger than you realize. I see the good you do. Psychic or not, look how happy you made everyone at the caves."

"Maybe the fans. But that's not anything I did."

"Of course it is. Just you being you, touching hearts and caring about others. That's the beauty of it."

"Until I looked like a complete nutcase on the tour." What might happen next? Until she knew what was happening, she was at the whim of this capricious fluctuation. "If I had true power, I'd be able to sort this out and solve the mystery. I wouldn't be groping in the dark for tidbits and scraps of clues to piece together."

"Groping in the dark for tidbits. I like the sound of that."

"*And*, I wouldn't need someone else to recharge me all the time."

"What did you do before Rosie?"

"What?"

"How did you stay charged up without her? I mean, she was intended to be your stylist, right? Makeup and hair and clothes?"

"Well, yes. But she also knew some massage techniques and she learned Reiki for me."

"What did you do before she was hired?"

"She got hired on for the show. Before that, it was only Michael and me taking on investigations around town. Little things, mostly. I don't know. I never felt totally drained back then. Am I getting old? Am I losing my edge? What's wrong with me that I need help all the time?"

"Don't be silly. You're working much harder now, obviously, taking on a new investigation every other week. You run yourself ragged, I've seen it. And you don't get much downtime. No one can run full throttle all day, every day. You'd burn out. Stop beating yourself up."

"What if I already did?" She stopped and watched him carefully.

"What do you mean?"

"What if I have burned out? I don't know, something feels off. And Rosie is in no shape to help. She's falling apart over Lorenzo."

"You said everything will be okay with Lorenzo."

"It will. I think. I hope. But not by tonight." Her breathing picked up, her heartrate accelerated. She stopped walking and breathed deeply, trying to regain control. "I might be having a panic attack."

Sterling pulled her into a hug, cradling her head to his chest. "Shh. Okay. I don't know what 'feeling off' means to you exactly, but frankly you've seemed off to me. I'm glad you said something."

"You are?"

"I'm relieved. I thought you might be mad at me about something and didn't know how to tell me."

"No, it's not you. At all. I feel . . . weak or . . . I don't know."

"I'm here. We can figure it out together."

Her eyes watered. "Really? I thought you'd scoff at me. Say it was all in my head."

"Nope. I'll never scoff at my little psychic again. We're one now. A team. And if you feel off, I can't function properly either. So we need to get you operating at full throttle again."

They arrived at the hotel, crossed the lobby, and pressed the button for the elevator.

"I feel a little better already," Kimberly confided.

"Good. I want you to know you can always rely on me."

The elevator pinged and opened.

"It may take some time to adjust, but I will work on learning to lean on you," she told him.

"Good. First order of business is nap time."

They stepped inside, and he pushed the button for the top floor. "Good thing this hotel doesn't have a thirteenth floor."

"No hotel has a thirteenth floor. They always skip and go straight to fourteen."

"Which is silly, since in that case the fourteenth is really the thirteenth floor."

"Know what's even sillier? Thirteen isn't unlucky anyway. That's just an old superstition."

He grabbed her waist and pulled her close, sudden intensity burning in his eyes. "Say that again."

She giggled, confused, and stared into his eyes, trying to read him. His attitude clearly skewed playful, though he seemed completely serious. "What?"

"Superstition. Say it again." His orange chakra spun with desire so vividly, her own was helpless to resist and thrummed in response.

She leaned in, placing her hands on his chest and peered up at him. "That's only a *superstition*." She dragged the word out, her tone low and visceral.

He sucked in a breath. "I love it when you talk dirty to me."

"Is that a KII in your pocket or are you just happy to see me?"

"You know I don't carry a KII. I don't need any equipment other than my own."

She could not get him into the room and out of his clothes fast enough.

CHAPTER EIGHTEEN

THE BREAK HELPED IMMENSELY. Kimberly couldn't remember a time she'd felt so relaxed, so content. Sterling held her hand as they walked back to the site to prepare for the evening.

"Look at that blue sky," he said and breathed deeply. "What an absolutely glorious day."

She had to agree. When a woman hesitantly approached and asked for a photograph with them, Kimberly's smile stretched wide, a reflection of her genuinely improved mood. Nothing could bring her down now.

They discovered Michael and Elise in their trailer with Rosie. They sprang up out of their chairs like Jack-in-the-boxes.

"Well, well, well, here's our wayward couple," Michael said. "Did you two 'nap' through dinner?"

Sterling stretched into a huge and clearly exaggerated yawn. "We had an incredible nap. And we just grabbed a quick bite."

"Mmm-hmm. I'll bet you did," Rosie said, patting the massage table. "Come on. I'm here for your health. Not mine."

She glanced around the space, but no one made any movement toward the door. Odd. Normally, everyone understood to leave her alone when Rosie helped her prepare for investigations.

And yet here they all lingered. "Can everyone please leave so I can undress for my massage?"

"Girl, everyone here either knows what it looks like, has seen it, or doesn't care." Despite her chiding, Rosie held up a sheet to offer some privacy.

Sterling turned his back, followed by Michael and Elise. She wriggled out of her clothing, flushing at the memory of Sterling undressing her earlier.

Rosie helped her get situated, covered her with the sheet, then applied rejuvenating oils and began their ritual recharging massage and relaxation technique she had employed and honed over the past few years. Rosie had developed just the right touch, working out the kinks, loosening the knots, stimulating all the chakra centers while also replenishing Kimberly's waning energy stores with a boost of her own. "Wow. You are noticeably less tense. Well done, Sterling."

Without opening her eyes, Kimberly could picture his dimpled, boyish grin she knew he responded with.

"To pointedly change the subject," he said, "I'm going to make coffee for Kimberly and myself. Anyone else want a cup?"

"We had coffee after dinner," Michael said, "which you would know if you'd joined us. Elise also shared some interesting information at dinner, which you would also know, had you been there."

Kimberly raised up on her elbows. "What information?"

"Bup bup bup," Rosie fussed at her. "Lie down. You made clear how important it is we fully charge you for tonight. Sterling, can you start some water boiling for a tea infusion, please?"

"I can't relax knowing Elise made a breakthrough. What is it? Something about Donny?"

"No, it's—"

Rosie pressed harder than necessary. "I said lie down. Breathe, relax. Don't let anything impact your calm, centered state."

She lowered herself to the table. "I'm relaxed! Elise, what did you discover?"

"Hannah, from the empty grave?"

"Yes?"

"Her name was Hannah Atkinson. Ten years old. Her family attended the Catholic Church. She disappeared while her religious education class was preparing for First Communion."

"She was only ten?"

"After the parish celebrated the Rite of First Holy Communion, they all travelled to the graveyard to hold a ceremonial burial and perform Last Rites for the girl, who by then was presumed deceased."

"What do they think happened?" Sterling asked.

"The group of communicants all went on a picnic and campout together for prayer and reflection. She presumably went swimming alone and got carried away by a swift current and drowned. That's the official cause of death anyway."

"You don't think so?"

"Her mother never believed it. Said Hannah never learned to swim and was terrified of the water."

Sterling finished one cup of coffee and started another. "And not one of the other children saw what happened to her? Nobody noticed her wander off?"

"Apparently not," Elise said. "Or if they did, they were too scared to speak up."

A disturbing thought occurred to her. "Do we think the girl might have been abducted?"

"My research doesn't suggest that was considered, but anything is possible. Certainly wouldn't have been for financial gain. The family never heard from her or about her after her disappearance. They were never contacted for ransom. Besides, they were poor. Nothing to ransom anyway."

Sterling paused, his tone sober. "Little girls are rarely abducted for ransom. I don't even want to think about what might have become of her."

"Ick," Michael said. "And on that depressing note, I will take my leave and go make sure everything is ready inside."

"Definitely killed the buzz," Sterling agreed. "We'll be inside soon."

"I'll try to keep digging," Elise said, pushing her glasses up her nose, "but so far that's all the information I could find." She followed Michael out of the trailer.

Rosie finished the massage and switched to Reiki, holding her hands over Kimberly's chakras, checking for weak points. "How are you feeling?"

"I feel pretty good, honestly. Of course, I didn't feel bad before, just—" She remembered she hadn't shared her concerns with Rosie and stopped.

"Just what? What aren't you telling me?"

She wasn't sure she wanted to tell her yet. She'd only hinted at it to Sterling. If she kept confiding her concern, pretty soon the entire crew would know she was worried something was wrong. And then what would they think of her?

"Why?" she asked Rosie. "Did you find something of concern?"

"Your energy feels really low to me. Like it does at the end of a night's investigation, not headed into one. Considering everything I just did to energize you, this seems odd. Let me try again."

Her heart pounded. If Rosie could feel a difference, that meant it wasn't only in her mind. But what could have caused such a thing?

"How reliable is this Reiki thing?" Sterling asked.

"We've never had problems before," Rosie said.

"Maybe your own emotional state is impacting your ability to feel Kimberly's energy level."

Rosie paused briefly but then continued. "I might consider that except that you're forgetting one thing."

"What's that?"

"My emotional state varies between slight hot mess and total train wreck pretty much all the time."

Sterling laughed. "If you say so."

"I feel warmth along my spine," Kimberly said. "I can feel the influx of energy."

"Good," Rosie murmured. "Focus on the energy, the world around you, maintaining and strengthening that connection between you and the spirit world. You're the bridge. They need you."

"We all need you," Sterling said.

He rested a hand on her back. A jolt shocked her body so thoroughly, she jumped.

Rosie and Sterling both pulled their hands away.

"I'm so sorry," Sterling said. "I didn't mean to startle you."

"Girl, what just happened? That was not a startled reaction. You bucked like you'd been burned."

She pushed up on her elbows, heart hammering, and met their concerned gazes. "I don't know. I have never felt anything like that before."

What the heck was happening to her? And was it related to Sterling? He seemed to be the lynchpin—the new element she wasn't accustomed to coping with. All these years single, focusing all her time and energy on the show and the help she could offer other people. Partly this was out of necessity. Her limited time didn't allow for a relationship. She didn't know if this was something Sterling himself was causing or if it was related more to being intimately involved with someone.

Both of them appeared as confused as her. But neither of them knew the fear that gnawed at her. Something was wrong. She was sure. More than ever, she longed for someone who could offer advice. Someone who could truly understand.

"I'm scared," she whispered.

Rosie held out her hands, palms forward. "Well, you're fully charged again. To the brim. So take that, Sterling. Oh, ye of little faith."

He conceded, hands up in surrender. "Never should have

doubted you."

"You're fine now, girl. Go ahead and get dressed and I'll get Sterling's makeup and hair real quick."

"Yeah, all better," she said, trying to believe the problem had been solved that easily.

"Your coffee is next to the machine," Sterling said as he slid into his chair.

She drank deeply of the rich dark brew and then donned the ensemble Rosie had selected for her—a black blouse with bell sleeves and a white A-line skirt with black rose print. She spun in a circle and decided she liked it.

She joined Sterling for makeup. Rosie sized her up. "What do you think? I love it!"

"I do like the outfit, though it doesn't feel like my usual style."

"No, but this gives a hint of Halloween without resorting to dressing you in, say, a bright orange Jack-o'-lantern and black cat print vest."

"Which I would never wear," she reminded her stylist.

"Which I knew. This way you kind of exude an Elvira vibe." Rosie lifted a straightening iron and begin smoothing her wavy hair, rather than twirling her locks into long, loose curls on a barrel of a hot iron. "I won't tease the top of your hair into a beehive, but I can use a light foundation and dark red lipstick. It'll be close enough."

Sterling pinched his chin and considered, his gaze drifting to her chest. "I'm thinking more Morticia than Elvira."

"We're still in primetime, Sterling. I can only do so much, and we can't have her cleavage popping out of her blouse, Mistress of the Night homage or not."

"There's not that much to pop, anyway," Kimberly pointed out, squirming under the increased scrutiny.

"Actually, Morticia's hair would be more along the lines of what she'll look like when I'm done." Rosie stared off into space, then waved her hands and shook her head. "Never mind. People can assume she's whatever character they want. Speaking of characters, we still need to decide what you'll wear to Trunk or Treat."

"How about Michael Myers and Lori from the Halloween movies? That's iconic," Sterling said. "And how often do I get the chance to play a knife-wielding psychopath?"

"Again, small children and primetime slot, Sterling. Gotta stay family friendly."

"Okay, how about Jason, then?"

"Also a psychopath!"

Sterling smirked. "I meant her ex-fiancé, but I think that still applies."

"Hey! None of that," she insisted. "I could threaten to dress as Amber or any of the mindless models you used to date."

"Okay, okay. Truce."

"Don't dredge up the past, you two. Just be glad you have each other now," Rosie said, and Kimberly caught the wistful undertone. "We could dress Sterling as David S. Pumpkins and put Kimberly in a skeleton suit as your sidekick."

Sterling laughed. "She's tiny but not skeletal. She's got some curve to her."

She crossed her arms and scowled. "He would make a pretty good David S. Pumpkins, but I am not wearing a full body skeleton unitard and I am not a sidekick, so you can put that idea right out of your head."

"Well, you two have to coordinate with a couple's costume. If you won't be the skeleton to his David S. Pumpkins, I'll just have to keep brainstorming."

Rosie smoothed her hair once more, then applied powder, heavy blush, and far too much eyeliner and shadow.

She scrunched her nose. "Do I need to remind you I am not participating as a character in the haunted house?"

Sterling stood to leave. "It works with the ensemble. And I expect Michael any second, demanding to know what's taking so long. We should go."

"I'll be right there," she told him, glancing pointedly at Rosie.

Sterling got the message. He nodded his understanding and gave her a quick peck on the cheek. "See you inside."

Rosie continued fussing with her hair, lifting and inspecting the ends. "You could use a trim. Remind me next week while we're between investigations."

She knew Rosie and knew babbling about hair trims and other small talk was how she avoided discussing real issues. Was it better to let it go, allow her to avoid it? Or should she address it and offer sympathy?

"Did you hear from Lorenzo at all today?" she asked, deciding she could bring it up and then read Rosie's reaction.

Rosie's head dropped then shook. "What's wrong with me, girl? Why couldn't I just tell him how I feel?"

She rested a hand on Rosie's arm. "Nothing is wrong with you. Sharing can be difficult, especially when we're scared." She knew that. She felt a slight pang of guilt for not divulging the extent of her current concerns. This was Rosie. They'd always shared their darkest secrets. But this one was big. So big. And she didn't understand it yet herself. "It's still new and you're unsure where it's going. Add long distance and it's just more difficult. I get it."

"I'm embarrassed. And now I can't bring myself to text or call again. Not when he's basically ghosted me. I'll look like a crazy stalker."

I'm also scared to share, she thought. And yet neither had anything to truly feel ashamed of. "Listen. We will sort this out. Trust me. And if Lorenzo can't understand your mixed feelings and won't accept an offer of contrition, then he wasn't the one. You deserve someone who will cherish you, Rosie. Maybe more than anyone else I know."

Rosie pulled her into a hug. "This is the last thing you need to be worried about. Get inside and talk to some ghosts so we can solve this mystery. And then maybe we can solve my mess."

CHAPTER NINETEEN

Putting aside all concerns from other aspects of her life, Kimberly stood on the stage and envisioned holding her energy close, keeping a handle on it. She needed to devote every ounce of her attention and energy to Donny tonight. The third night of the investigation and she had learned almost nothing. She had to connect and bring something tangible to the table or let go of her theory and explore new ones.

Jillian had been less than forthcoming after initially proclaiming the target of their investigation. And Kimberly's current state helped nothing. Regardless, they simply could not afford another wasted night. No matter what, she needed a breakthrough.

Everyone waited for her to offer direction. She turned to Stan, desperate for a starting point. "Did you find anything else during footage review that I should know about?"

Stan's mouth twisted into a thoughtful frown. "We heard something that could have been attempts at communication, but no matter how many times we replayed and listened, we couldn't figure out what the voice was saying."

Interesting. That had also been her experience. Someone in this building definitely wanted to communicate and communicating with spirits was her specialty. She absolutely had to make progress tonight. She had to.

To help, she'd suggested they utilize the SEEPS, the Spectral-Enhancing Energy Power Source—basically a giant battery to energize spirits. She and her crew had developed it to offer a source of power to spirits without draining her, which would be particularly advantageous due to her tenuous energy level. She hadn't mentioned she thought they needed it because her own energy seemed to be misfiring and unreliable. No one else needed to know that. The black box rested on the stage, sizzling and crackling, spewing low-frequency energy into the environment. Her only concern was the possibility other spirits in the vicinity could be drawn to the power source and manifest as well. She couldn't control which spirits drank from the well. And what happened if she unleashed them and then couldn't control them at all?

She looked around the space. "The apartment and Jillian's office have been our two hotspots so far. We suspect the nun is the presence we're detecting in the apartment. But I was led to Jillian's office by a whispering spirit I couldn't understand. I think tonight we focus on the stage, the wings, and the dressing room. Jillian doesn't want us in the office, but we can get as close as possible and see if we can coax this ghost into speaking up a little more clearly."

And, hopefully, her sixth sense would cooperate a little better as well, now that Rosie had recharged her battery, so to speak.

They fanned out, spreading through the space, threading their way through the auditorium seats and aisles, checking for temperature fluctuations or anything to indicate a spirit hoped to communicate with them.

She climbed onto the stage and maneuvered around set pieces. Simply being on stage, surrounded by a set, kicked off a wave of profound nostalgia. Maybe someday when her schedule allowed, she would return to her roots and audition for plays again. She missed it so much.

Whispering.

She heard faint whispers and turned, ears straining as she moved in the direction the voice had previously led her. But in the wing, nothing awaited her but silence. She crept back out onstage. She heard it again. But what was it saying?

The others had joined her and watched expectantly for the break they so desperately needed.

"I hear you but can't understand you," she said. "Can you speak up? Or can you come closer to me?"

The murmurs continued, clear enough she didn't doubt herself, yet faint enough that it remained nothing but gibberish.

Taking a deep breath, grasping her quartz, and focusing on her indigo chakra, she gathered her energy and reached out. If the spirit couldn't come to her, she would have to reach him. Squandering her psychic energy could render her useless the remainder of the night. While blowing through her energy store so early in the investigation concerned her, she also knew that a timid approach wasn't getting them anywhere. And they simply could not continue treading in place.

She pushed. Hard.

A few words came through clearly. She struggled to catch and repeat them for her crew, hoping eventually to fill in the blanks. "Reports of . . . death . . . exaggerated."

"What?" Michael asked. She didn't need to open her eyes to picture his sassy little head toss that accompanied that tone.

"Shhh. I can hear him, but barely. Only a few words." She listened again, trying to shut out the rustles and shuffling in this world so she could catch the message. "Better . . . find out . . ."

"What do we need to find out?" Michael asked.

Frustrated, she pushed as hard as she could, fully aware she could be ruining herself for the rest of the night. "Do the right thing."

She heard someone gasp and spun around. Ian had joined them at some point. "What? What's wrong?"

Ian pressed his fingers to his mouth, eyes wide, and shook his head. "Donny worked as a Mark Twain impersonator."

Michael blew out impatiently. "Sweetie, I'm the only one allowed to drama. Get to the point."

"Those are lines from his act. He used those quotes. It's him. It's him for sure."

"You recognize what Kimberly is repeating?"

"Oh, yes. He opened with the famous quote about the reports of his death being greatly exaggerated. You know, suggesting he really was Mark Twain. For the duration of the show."

Michael looked at her. She couldn't help but smile. "Okay. Now we're getting somewhere."

Michael twirled his finger in a circle and directed the crew, "Keep going. All cameras on Kimmy. She's connected with our spirit."

"Connected" was a strong term to use in her tenuous state. But she pressed on, encouraged. She owed Rosie a drink later. Or an ice cream. "Donny? We hear you. What is it we can help you with?"

She felt herself fading and struggled to hold on. *Please, don't fail me now. Not when I finally made a breakthrough.*

More whispers. Behind her. Beside her, on both sides. Was this still only Donny? She couldn't tell. *Damn.*

Mark Twain impersonator. Even in death Donny continued to act, continued to present as a character he portrayed on stage. Why would he do that?

She'd never had anyone to discuss her psychic abilities with growing up. She'd learned early on to keep her mouth shut, to hide her secret. Her parents had insisted, but then ridicule at school had cemented the decision. No one understood. Until Michael, then Rosie, then the others, one by one. When she finally encountered people who accepted her, the relief had been indescribable. Her tribe. Friends. Community. A sense of belonging she'd never before experienced. Even if they didn't necessarily believe her, they welcomed and accepted her.

The theatre. That's where the huge shift happened for her. Many of her classmates had been ostracized, outcasts, the losers who ate lunch alone and navigated hallways alone, vulnerable to the primary predators at the top of the social food chain, constantly prowling for the next victim.

She no longer hid in the shadows on the fringe. Fate had smiled upon her and twisted her eccentricity into a conglomerate of like-minded souls, then a television show, then success. But she would never forget the isolation or the trauma the ridicule left in its wake.

What if Donny also found solace in the theatre? What if the stage had been the only place he could let down his guard? Hiding behind a character, ironically, had allowed her to share glimpses of herself—tiny facets of her own personality forged into the characters she shared on stage. Only someone with a deep emotional well, typically drilled by years of torment, could harness those emotions and channel them, finding the truth in the moments of the fictional story. Did Donny remain in the place he felt most comfortable? Still hiding behind a character to reveal his intent?

"Donny," she called, "I know you're hurting. Tell me what you need so we can help you."

The SEEPS crackled and buzzed, blue spark arcing from one coil to another.

"I know you want to talk to me, Donny. I'm trying hard to understand."

Whispering. Behind her. Beside her. All around her.

She turned in place, unable to pinpoint the exact location of the manifestation. *Damn.* She'd used up all her energy too quickly, as she feared she might. But why? Why did it drain away like water through a sieve?

A soft breeze, like a cold breath, brushed her cheek and neck. Tendrils of her hair lifted and danced of their own accord, as if toyed with by the wind. But she had no idea who encroached on her space and played with her.

"What do you want?"

Jillian.

Her skin prickled, and she swore a hand rested on her arm.

"KII spiking," Michael said. "EMF at one forty-five and climbing."

"I might be getting an image on the FLIR," TJ said.

"He's here," she told the others. "I'm sure of it. I just can't understand what he's saying other than 'Jillian.'"

"What about Jillian?" Elise asked.

"Pay." The Audioxx squawked.

"Why should Jillian pay?" she asked.

Silence. The hairs on her arms stood on end, and yet no matter how hard she worked to ignite the flame beacon in her spiritual lighthouse, it merely sputtered and extinguished. She could not light it.

"Jillian. Pay." The Audioxx mocked her, offering the type of intimate communication she alone previously provided but now, inexplicably, could not.

"Why should Jillian pay?" Elise echoed her.

"Jillian," the Audioxx crackled. "Jillian sorry."

"Jillian will be sorry?" Elise asked. "Why? What did Jillian do to you?"

The blue arcing lights of the SEEPS buzzed louder and louder, expanding in width, increasing in intensity until the entire crew crept backward.

"What's happening?" Michael asked, his voice echoing through the space. "The SEEPS has never done that before. EMF is over two hundred!"

She didn't know what was happening. Normally she could maintain a bead on the spirit they needed to talk with, and the SEEPS wouldn't get out of control.

"More orbs on the video than I can count," Stan said.

"Where are they all coming from?" TJ asked. "Cold spots all

over the stage. But also a massive heat source. I'm talking as red as possible."

Her sixth sense may be failing her, but she hadn't lost her common sense. "The SEEPS. We've energized every spirit in the vicinity. They're drawn to it."

Voices surrounded her, pulsing past as she spun in place, unable to identify, understand, or even separate one thread from the swirling cacophony.

The SEEPS hissed and popped, the most horrific sizzling sound she'd ever heard.

An axe appeared and swung at her head before disappearing into ethereal fog quicker than she could even duck.

A crying woman.

A yelling man.

A laughing child.

Figure after figure manifested before her, briefly animated before fading, disbanding into nothing but vapor, gray streaks trailing behind. The gray shade of the world around her took on a blue tint.

Briefly, she sensed a hostile presence. It pressed in on her, seemed to acknowledge her presence—and delight in it. But not in a happy way. She sensed a twisted and malicious pleasure before it disappeared.

Her crew. What happened to her crew?

But no, she could see them through the thick fog somehow permeating the building. Fog in the basement? She shook her head to clear it, but nothing changed. Shadow figures moved through the mysterious vapor. Were they spirits? People? Some of each? She reached out, both a hand and an attempt to connect.

The SEEPS squealed, long and loud, then went dark.

The fog lifted.

Her crew, every one of them looking as dazed as she felt, turned to her.

Except Sterling. Where was he? She didn't see him and in

that moment, she longed for his comforting reassurances, his level-headed calming influence. He alone could tell her it would be okay and she would believe it.

She sucked in a breath to call out for him.

But a new whisper tickled her ear. Soft. Gentle. Motherly. Repeating a string of words over and over. From somewhere above.

From the apartment.

"What happened down there?"

Sterling! His voice carried from above, presumably also from the apartment.

She raced for the secret passage and took the stairs two at a time, launching herself into his arms.

He stiffened as if startled, then pulled her close. "What's wrong? What happened?"

She shook, terrified of what had just happened, mostly because she couldn't understand what just happened. "The SEEPS overcharged spirits. I think. I could see them but . . . And Donny was there but I can't connect. I can't control anything. I saw fog and . . . I don't know what's happening to me."

"The SEEPS shorted," Michael called from below. "You okay up there, Kimmy?"

TJ caught up to her, his camera taking in the apartment.

Still shaking, she couldn't bring herself to answer Michael or face the probing lens constantly watching her every move.

"She's fine," Sterling called back. He cupped her face. "It will be okay."

She heard the soft, feminine whispering and turned her head, trying to hear. "I think maybe your nun friend is praying again." She would not admit on camera that she was at such a loss and couldn't control her sixth sense.

Sterling tipped his head. "I don't hear anything. Are you sure?"

Was she sure? The irony that her skeptic partner genuinely

questioned her ability to hear a long-dead praying nun, hoping she did, weighed against the additional irony that she wasn't, in point of fact, sure of anything. She almost laughed. Then she almost cried.

For the sake of the camera, she closed her eyes and took a deep breath, wrapping her hand around her quartz crystal. She breathed out slowly, anxious for a connection, the type of spiritual communion she'd taken for granted her entire life.

And she heard the woman. Heard her murmured words and even understood a few. "She says, 'eternal rest' and 'perpetual light' and I think I heard her say 'may she rest in peace' maybe."

Sterling looked thoughtful. "Eternal rest grant unto her, O Lord. And let perpetual light shine upon her. Could that have been it?"

"Yes! I think so. Did you hear her?"

"No, I didn't. But it's the Catholic prayer for the dead." He looked around the room. "Amen."

She thought she felt presences swirling about her but wasn't sure. She looked to Sterling and shook her head. The murmuring grew louder, a persistent buzzing in her ears. She sank into the floor, hands pressed over her ears. She couldn't comprehend, she couldn't connect. How did people live like this?

Louder and louder, voices hammered against her ears, and she couldn't block them out. Some of them seemed to mock her in her debilitated state.

She reached for Sterling, unable to process or cope. He grabbed her outstretched hand and pulled her into a hug. When he placed a hand on her back, a jolt flowed from him, flooding her with energy and lighting up her spine. She gasped.

The nun stood before her, hands clasped around a string of beads, lips moving in constant prayer. The ghostly image stared deeply into her soul and seemed to realize Kimberly could see and hear again.

The spirit nodded at Kimberly before a message hit her squarely, loud and clear. "Find her bones. May she rest in peace."

Michael, Ian, Elise, and Stan filed through the door. The nun dissipated, wicking into wispy swirls as the living entered her space.

Michael took one look at her and crouched at her side. "What just happened?"

"She . . . she asked me to find her bones."

"Whose?"

"The little girl's. Hannah's."

"Did she give you a tip where to look?"

Sterling helped her to her feet. She breathed deeply, one hand on her forehead. "No. Any ideas?"

Elise adjusted her glasses. "She was presumed drowned in the river."

Ian brightened. "So. River cruise?"

CHAPTER TWENTY

KIMBERLY WALKED WITH ROSIE, Michael, and Ian to the dock for a riverboat cruise. Michael and Ian had fallen behind, leaving her alone with Rosie.

"Where exactly is Sterling?" Rosie asked.

"He ran an errand for me."

"What errand?"

"Just an errand. He should be back any minute though." She glanced at her watch. Actually, he was late. Should've been back an hour ago.

"He better be, or he'll miss the paddleboat cruise."

"He'll be here."

"Frankly, I don't appreciate him bailing when I'm being forced to come. I don't do boats."

"You said that." She glanced at her cellphone again. Still no text. "He'll be here."

"If he doesn't show, I'm not going."

She stopped and clutched Rosie's wrist. "You have to. This is part of the investigation. I need you. Especially if Sterling doesn't make it back. What if . . . if I have trouble?"

Rosie raised a dubious eyebrow. "What trouble?"

"You know." She flapped her hands helplessly. "I don't know. You're always with me during an investigation."

Rosie sighed and glanced away. "Maybe you should text him."

"I did. He hasn't answered."

"Well, I don't—"

"—do boats. Got it. But today you do."

She knew the tight timeframe she'd mapped out would be risky. Any delay and her carefully constructed schedule would crumble. But she had to try. The potential payout was worth the gamble.

Rosie grumbled a bit, a low growl in the back of her throat. "Where'd he go anyway?"

"He just ran a—"

"—quick errand. Right. You know, I remember when I used to be your confidante. I think I like that better."

Michael and Ian caught up, both practically glowing.

"Soaking up the sun, ladies?" Michael bubbled over like a freshly poured soda. He moved on with Ian without waiting for an answer.

"Ick," she muttered.

"Now you know how I've been feeling," Rosie said.

"Well, it's just the two of us right now. Let's take advantage of it. We can talk about anything. Except guys."

They continued on in silence for another block.

Rosie heaved a sigh so heavy, it seemed to originate from the soles of her feet. "Yeah, but you still have Sterling tonight. And every night."

She gave up. Nothing she could say would cheer up Rosie.

Stan, TJ, and Elise climbed out of the equipment van, already attracting the attention of a small crowd, as they arrived at the dock.

Michael had pre-purchased tickets for the two o'clock cruise. He tapped his foot and glanced at her repeatedly. When he spoke, it was through gritted teeth. "You knew about this. Heck, it was your idea to go. But you sent Sterling on some mysterious errand? He needs to be here for the show. Where is he?"

She stared at her phone, willing it to throw her a lifeline. No text materialized on the screen. No communication at all. Nothing. She shrugged at Michael. Oh, well. If her plan had worked, it would've been great.

A revving motor at the intersection drew everyone's attention.

A steel gray BMW i8, blue accents curving over the wheel wells and bumper, sat waiting to turn into the parking lot. No way more than one of those existed. Sterling no doubt sat behind the wheel.

He slid the sleek sportscar into a parking space. The butterfly door rose into the air, and he stepped out, mirrored aviator glasses wrapped around his eyes. He scanned the crowd, grinned when he spotted her, and gave her a thumbs up.

Yes! Success!

Michael sighed. "Well, I don't know what errand was so important, but you got lucky, sweetie."

"Yes." She beamed as the passenger-side door of the i8 lifted into the air.

Lorenzo stepped out.

Rosie made a sound like a cross between a hiccup and a gasp and whirled to face her, mouth gaping. "What? He—"

"Yep."

Rosie threw her arms around her and crushed her in a fierce hug, then panicked. "Oh, my God! How do I look?"

"Sensational."

"No, I don't! I cried all night and barely put on any makeup! You should've warned me!" Rosie raked her fingers through her hair and smoothed her skirt and blouse. "Look what I'm wearing! I would have made an effort if I'd known! Why didn't you say something?"

Michael curled his lips and eyed the stiletto boots only Rosie would wear on a paddleboat. "I mean, I figured you were suffering enough and didn't need my wardrobe critique. But yeah."

Kimberly swatted him across the arm. "Michael!" She turned to her stricken best friend. "Rosie, he isn't here to see your makeup or your outfit. He wants to spend time with you."

"You . . . called him for me?"

"Called him, talked to him, and flew him here. For both of you. He missed you."

Sterling and Lorenzo joined them. Lorenzo looked every bit as awkward and nervous as Rosie did.

Sterling draped an arm around her shoulder. "Sorry. His plane was a little delayed. I made up as much time as I could on the drive."

She loved how easily he curled around her, loved the easy rapport they'd settled into. All these years she'd convinced herself a relationship would be difficult and messy and distract from the show, drain her of the energy she needed to give to her job. But with Sterling, that wasn't the case. "You made it. That's all that matters."

His heart chakra fluttered like a butterfly and filled her with happiness. She leaned her head against his chest.

Lorenzo and Rosie, however, looked like a couple of teens. Rosie twirled a piece of her hair and drew a circle on the ground with her toe. Lorenzo pulled at his collar and repeatedly cleared his throat. Kimberly had never seen Rosie like this around a man. Ever. Interesting.

"Hi," Lorenzo began.

"Hi." Rosie flushed.

"Listen, about the other night, I'm sorry I—"

"No! I'm sorry!" Rosie blurted. "I thought I made you mad."

"Mad? No! I thought I jumped the gun and scared you off."

"No. You surprised me is all."

The boat whistle blew, commanding everyone to board the ship.

Lorenzo nodded to Kimberly. "Thanks for this." He offered

his arm to Rosie. "I've never been on a riverboat before. I'm excited."

Rosie looked a bit queasy but hooked her arm through his. "I'm . . . excited you're here with me."

Sterling whispered in her ear. "I thought she doesn't do boats."

"She will for Lorenzo. I knew she would."

One issue resolved, she turned her attention to the probably pointless point of this excursion—attempting to detect and recover the century-and-a-half-year-old missing remains of Hannah Atkinson.

While Michael handed over tickets for the entire group, Kimberly took in the mostly white boat, three decks decreasing in size from lower to upper, ringed with a red stripe and festooned with flags draped from the side railings.

They wandered around the lowest deck, watching the Mississippi river running past them, lapping at the boat and inhibiting its race downriver. Small islands in the middle of the river, covered with trees, mimicked the edges of the river and narrowed the channel.

Rosie and Lorenzo said little, Kimberly noticed, while Michael and Ian chatted nonstop about anything and everything. She pulled Sterling away from the chatterboxes, bumping Rosie with an elbow.

"Ouch!" Rosie said, rubbing the offended limb. "What's the matter with you?"

Kimberly cut her eyes to Lorenzo, nodding her head. The guy couldn't stay forever, and Rosie wasn't usually one to waste time with a guy like this. Rosie bugged her eyes and scowled.

"So." Lorenzo cleared his throat. "We're on a triple date?"

Rosie cough-choked again. "Date?"

Michael and Ian actually stopped talking momentarily and stood blinking before speaking over one another as they scrambled to explain they were "just friends," "had a lot in common," "shared a love of theatre," and a "fixation with the New York City scene."

She squinted at them and held up a hand. "Mmm I don't know what this is, so I can't quantify it. But yes, Rosie, you and Lorenzo are on a date. And I'm pretty sure they are too."

Sterling shivered. "You said 'quantify.'" He hugged her from behind, burying his face in her hair.

Rosie rolled her eyes. "Okay, you two are in perpetual date mode, but we're here for the show. Right?"

"For the show but also a date. It can be two things."

The speakers squawked to life. "Good afternoon, ladies and gentlemen. This is your captain and over the next hour, I'll be guiding you down the great Mississippi River and sharing some of Hannibal's fascinating history with you."

He launched into the familiar story of the famous writer Mark Twain, born Samuel Langhorne Clemens, who based some of his most famous works on his life experiences growing up in Hannibal, Missouri. As a boy, like most boys at the time in the port city, he'd aspired to be a riverboat pilot, eventually adopting the pen-name "Mark Twain," the phrase used on boats to confirm the depth of two fathoms of water that allowed safe riverboat passage.

The captain next directed their attention to the island passing on their left in the middle of the river. "This is what's left of the island that was Mark Twain's inspiration for Jackson Island in his books set in St. Petersburg, the fictional town based on Hannibal where Tom Sawyer, Becky Thatcher, and Huck Finn lived. The island was larger back then but has been eroded by the river, breaking it into three smaller islands."

Elise, pen scrawling as she jotted down interesting facts, glanced up from her notepad. "You know, Mark Twain believed in ghosts and included spirits and supernatural lore in his writing."

Stan and TJ watched everything through lenses of cameras, recording their excursion and capturing the bits of history. The best footage would be included in the episode while the mundane bits would be edited out.

"Did Mark Twain really find a dead body out on the island?" TJ asked.

"I don't remember ever hearing that," Elise said, face contorted in thought. "That was Huck Finn and Jim in *The Adventures of Huckleberry Finn*."

"But based on true events, right?" TJ pressed.

"No, mostly fictionalized. The characters are based on people he knew, and the townspeople behave the way people behaved back then, but the story is invented."

"But—"

Sterling gripped TJ's shoulder. "Hate to be the one to break it to you, buddy, but 'based on a true story' is applied very liberally. He made up the story."

Kimberly watched the island glide by, disturbed by a sense of dread tugging at her psyche. She opened herself to the input, yet worried about attempting a connection. She allowed her senses to open wide, expanding into the realms where only her sixth sense offered feedback. The island teemed with life. She felt the hum and thrum of living, breathing activity—plants, insects, and animals all gave off an energy wavelength that broadcast their respirating, growing, reproducing selves in a vibrant green glow.

Below that, a lower frequency resonated, the bedrock of all else—darkness, decay, the loam of death, end point of the life cycle.

Between the two nestled another realm, the in-between, neither fully living nor fully dead plane of the Nightshade. Cast in hues of grays and blues, the Nightshade seethed with fear, confusion, and desolation—the gloomy dwelling of lost souls wandering alongside but separate from the living. Usually the soul simply crossed to the next plane of existence when the body reached the end. Kimberly had no idea what happened after crossing. She sometimes wished for a glimpse of the next life but had never seen beyond the portal.

But when something disrupted death, the process didn't always work. Unexpected violence that tore the soul from the body, absolute denial, or the need to right a wrong could all displace a soul and interrupt transversal from this plane to the next, resulting in a haunting. Those spirits who clung desperately to life remained in the Nightshade and sometimes managed to break through the flimsy barrier between our world and the netherworld—a place neither here nor there, but surrounding us, coexisting alongside us at all times.

The spirits who broke through and made their presence known typically sought help but primarily succeeded only in terrifying the people they reached out to. That's where Kimberly could step in. She possessed the ability to detect and communicate with those lost souls, to help resolve their unfinished business. Once satisfied, most spirits relinquished the death-grip on their previous life and crossed to the next.

Had little Hannah become lodged in the gnarled tree roots of the island? Had the innocuous-looking destination beckoned, the perfect playground getaway for adventure merely a short swim from her home shore? Had the water proved more than she could handle, sweeping her roughly to the island's edge where she grasped for something to hold on to, desperate to stop herself from being swept downstream? Once entangled, had the merciless current pummeled and smothered her?

Kimberly turned away from the rails, unsure if the vivid images playing out across her mind were the result of a connection with a young girl's spirit or merely her own imagination galloping away uncontrolled. Not knowing the source bothered her immensely. This lack of clarity was another symptom of her problem. Her sixth sense had never been so unreliable. Ever.

She turned away from the rails, unable to bear the frustration of not knowing. The captain pointed out a lighthouse on the shore. But as she turned to see it, a spirit nibbled at the lifeline she'd cast but hadn't reeled back in. The tug turned into a yank, pulling her, demanding attention. And she couldn't disconnect.

She couldn't breathe. A hundred souls, it seemed, clamored for her attention, their residual energy forces rising out of the watery depths to drag her down. Skeletal remains rattled far below, demanding she take notice, insisting she feel their final gasps.

She clutched her chest. Too many. Too many sought her out at once. As if she descended into the murky waters herself, the world around her blurred. Current carried silt, leaves, and detritus past her. Fish ogled her, gulping great gasps with their "o" mouths, as if confused by her sudden presence.

Shaking her head, she pushed the scene away. She could not be underwater. Could not. Though she didn't understand what was happening, she knew this wasn't real. At least not her reality. And yet she tasted dirt and choked on water filling her mouth and nose.

But the spirit who had connected and dragged her down had no intention of letting go.

Tell her I loved her.

The voice in her head rang as clearly as if one of her crew spoke to her. And an image surfaced—a woman in a flower-print dress covered by an apron, hair coiled on top of her head. Waiting. Waiting by candlelight. Waiting for this man who never made it back home.

I'll try, she assured him, knowing full well the woman had long since passed and no longer wondered what had become of her husband. The eased anxiety at her promise left her knowing she truly would try. She had to.

Her dollop of psychic energy, like chum in the water, attracted a feeding frenzy of other drowning victims, all desperate to send one final communique.

Tell Mom I'm sorry.

Tell Dad he was right.

Tell my kids I love them.

Bony fingers clawed her hands, stroked her arms, petted her head. No longer did she drown on water but on the incessant demands for attention that gulped down her energy in giant bites, leaving her drained and empty.

Her head lolled. This was the end.

"Kimberly!"

Her eyes snapped open. Bright sun burned her retinas and she squinted in the light after the darkness of the river.

Sterling shook her. Rosie patted her hand. Everyone else on the boat, including by the looks of it, every other passenger, clustered around her. Whispers wove through the crowd.

She sat on the deck. The boat had pulled back into the dock, the hour spent.

She'd been out of it for an hour? Where had the time gone? She took a deep breath but choked, her lungs congested. She coughed, each breath rattling through her chest. Rosie stuffed a tissue into her hand just in time. Her coughing fit produced a glob of thick mucus, tinged yellow-brown. *What in the world?*

Rosie wrinkled her nose. "What is that? Allergies?"

"I don't know. I feel like I swallowed water."

"Gross. Let's get you out of here." Sterling placed a hand on her back and scooped her into his arms. A crackle of energy sizzled along her spine at his touch. She could breathe again.

Michael held up his hands and addressed the crowd. "Just a little motion sickness. She's fine. And in good hands as you can see."

Though she abhorred feeling helpless, worst of all in public, she rested her head against Sterling's chest and allowed him to carry her.

The crowd clapped. She could imagine the Twitter posts that would result from this. But the truth was, she didn't trust herself to walk right now. And if she amended Michael's statement, telling the onlookers that spirits had dragged her into the river —well, she'd look crazy and she knew that. She'd been on deck in plain sight the entire time, whatever she experienced psychically.

Sterling threaded through the crowd, his chest rumbling

against her. "Excuse us. Please let us through. I need to get her to the hotel."

Nothing about his tone or his spectrum hinted at playing the hero or enjoying the attention. All she detected was genuine concern.

He settled her into the passenger seat of his car, leaning across to buckle her seatbelt for her. She started to tell him she could do it herself, but he smelled so good, she opted to enjoy the TLC and his musky, woodsy scent instead. He turned over his shoulder. "Rosie, you can walk Lorenzo back, yeah?"

"We can get back, of course," Rosie said.

Lorenzo nodded furiously. "Of course. I'm good with Google maps or Uber or whatever. I'll handle us. You take care of her."

"Welcome to my world," Rosie told him.

Kimberly hated that she'd had an episode like this during their triple date. She didn't want to run off Lorenzo before Rosie had a chance to spend time with him. And from Rosie's tone, she knew her best friend was worrying about the same thing.

Lorenzo took her hand. "It's an exciting world, and I knew that. Sterling, I meant what I told you. Meet you back at the hotel. Let us know if you need anything at all."

She watched them leave on foot then lifted an eyebrow at Sterling. "He meant what he told you? What did that mean?"

He tipped the chair back, letting her recline. "I had a little chat with him on the drive from the airport. Let him know Rosie hasn't had the best luck with guys in the past. Neither have you, for that matter. I asked him his intentions."

"His intentions?"

"Look, the last thing you two need is another loser trying to take advantage of you. If he was only interested in Rosie to get close to you or to get close to the show, if he doesn't have true feelings for her and intend to treat her right, I wanted to know. I would've dumped him back at the airport and not let him near either of you. But he convinced me."

She stared at his wrinkled brow as he pushed her hair away

from her face. When had any man ever stepped in to shield and protect her? Sure, she could get mad and point out she didn't detect any negative feelings from Lorenzo and wouldn't have invited him if she had. She was so accustomed to taking care of herself and handling everything. Someone else worrying about her was a new experience. And it appealed. "I . . . I don't know what to say."

"Nothing to say. I don't intend to let anyone hurt you." He felt her forehead and then rested a hand over her heart. Warmth radiated from him, flowing into her. "More importantly, how are you? What happened back there?"

"I'm not entirely sure. I don't seem to be able to control my psychic sense anymore. I still feel drained and worn out, like I can't completely charge. I keep fizzling out. Inviting connection is hit and miss. But then sometimes, like today, I feel like a spirit hijacks me and forces connection and there's nothing I can do about it. I've lost control." Her voice rose as she fought tears.

He lifted her hand and kissed the back of it. "Hey, hey. We will figure this out. For now, let's take you to rest. You need a break before we film tonight." He went around and climbed into the driver's seat.

"Thank you," she said.

"For what?"

"Not too long ago, you kept insisting I must have an under-lying medical issue causing problems. I appreciate you not repeating it, even if you are sitting there thinking it."

He smirked. "Well, you're not feverish and your pulse feels normal. And I've learned quite a bit about you in the time we've worked together."

"Can I tell you something?"

"Anything. Everything."

"I wish it was medical. I wish this was as easy to fix as going to the doctor for a prescription. Because I know something is wrong, but I have no idea what. And I don't know how to fix it."

CHAPTER TWENTY-ONE

THE PLAY WOULD RESUME TONIGHT. Kimberly didn't relish the idea of investigating a building brimming with people. On the other hand, if she struggled to connect with Donny, the interference would be an excellent explanation.

She tossed in the hotel bed, her lack of rest unrelated to the bed itself. What would she do if she couldn't resolve this haunting? Never once in the history of the show, or her personal history either, had she failed in an investigation. A time or two, she had found no paranormal activity during an investigation. But when a manifestation existed, not once had she failed the property owner. Or the spirit.

She needed to admit her current difficulties to her crew. They had always supported her and been there for her. They deserved the truth. She knew this in her mind and in her heart, and yet struggled with saying the words. Why? Why was this so difficult?

Perhaps her own lack of explanation played a part. She was the person they all turned to for answers, and this time she had none. They would want to know what was wrong, why it happened, how to fix it—and how they could help. And for the first time ever a massive shrug would be her only answer. In the aftermath, they would treat her differently. They would skirt around her, whispering behind her back, scrambling to appear occupied with some task or other whenever she entered a room. Their trust in her would be shattered.

How could the show survive that?

A quick knock on her hotel room door prompted her to sit up and check the clock. 6:15 p.m. The cast of *Blithe Spirit*, with a six o'clock call, would already be assembled. The *Wantland* crew needed to sneak in before curtain at seven.

She forced herself to her feet.

Sterling stood in the doorway. The look of concern on his face bordered dangerously close to pity. That was one thing she couldn't handle.

She waved him in. "I'll get my shoes."

He chewed his lip before speaking. "Are you better? Did you sleep?"

"I couldn't. Too restless. Out of sorts."

He blew out a breath. "Maybe you should sit out tonight and get some well-earned and much-needed—"

"Sit out? Not go to my own investigation? I have to at least—"

He grimaced. "Pretend?"

"Try! Never pretend. Never."

"Maybe if you rest—"

"No one will have a chance to connect. We're already deteriorating to the level of *Ghost Catchers* and *Paranormal, Inc.* All they do is yell, 'What was that?' and run around and look utterly preposterous. One of those fakes is who you should've issued your challenge to. Thad or Jeremiah would've crumpled under your scrutiny."

A half-smirk twitched his lips.

She held up a hand. "Yeah, yeah, I know. My show looks the same way to you."

"Not anymore. Really." He cupped her face. "Besides, I didn't want to go out with Thad or Jeremiah. Not my type."

She forgot about putting on her shoes as he bent and kissed her, slowly, gently. His soft lips eased her furrowed brow. Her breath caught. "That helped."

"Good. There's plenty more where that came from. Later. If we're going, we need to get you into Rosie's capable hands and inside the building before the play starts."

"I feel so drained. I hope she can reenergize me quickly."

"And cover the bags under your eyes."

"The what?"

"I know you'd be mad if I didn't tell you. You're looking almost sick."

She ran to the mirror. He wasn't wrong. In fact, he had down-played the purple half-moons under her eyes. "I'll need night vision goggles to cover this mess. Let's hurry."

THE HAUNTED HOUSE PARAPHERNALIA REMAINED, almost creepier dark and motionless than when active and lit. No people lurked in crevices waiting to jump out either. The cast worked on stage tonight.

Kimberly heard the shuffling and shifting of the audience punctuated by periodic ripples of laughter, along with the action and dialogue on stage. Apparently the auditorium was the only place that would see activity tonight, and not the paranormal sort.

Nothing happened in the building. Not a temperature fluctu-ation or a rustle or a whisper of anything. The second act was well underway, and they hadn't encountered a thing. Well, she had encountered Jillian, which she hadn't anticipated. But the woman had bid the cast, "Break a leg," and then declined to speak to her. "I'm sorry, but I need to get to the booth to help call the show."

"We all wear a lot of hats here," Ian had reminded her. "She directed and I'm stage manager, so . . ."

Jillian's continued refusal to engage really frustrated her. And now the ghosts refused to engage too. She would blame it on her out-of-sorts sixth sense except none of the equipment registered activity either. The old church was quiet as a tomb tonight. Why?

Ian burst into the room breathless, eyes wide. Between breaths, he managed to choke out, "Come. Quick. Bring every camera you have."

He grabbed her wrist and ran, pulling her along, down the hall, down the stairs. The noise from the audience grew louder as they drew near. The show was quite the hit, judging by the laughter and clapping. Ian opened the door into the booth where Jillian sat, headset over her ears, hands clamped over her mouth.

The play continued on stage and as her crew crammed into the space, Kimberly peered through the glass.

The audience members laughed and applauded. Cries of delight filled the air.

Confused, Kimberly looked to Ian. "What? What's the problem?"

Ian didn't answer. He pointed one shaking finger toward the stage.

"How are you doing that?" TJ whispered.

"We're not," Ian answered.

Kimberly followed Ian's arm, past his finger to the stage. Props rose into the air, drifting from table to table, from one surface to another.

"You're recording?" Michael asked.

"Zoomed in," TJ confirmed.

"I hope the motion-tripped cameras in the wings were triggered," Stan said. "This is some of the best activity we've ever witnessed."

Cast members maneuvered around the levitating items, avoiding collision while attempting to return the errant objects to their correct places—all while remaining in character and appearing to be working in a bit.

Kimberly had to pause long enough to appreciate the duress the cast currently worked through. She especially marveled at Marie, playing Elvira, the spirit of the upset first wife, who dashed about the stage pretending to move household items to antagonize the character Dan, played by Nate, who presumably didn't need to act to achieve the shock currently playing out on stage.

The audience burst into laughter as a pencil drifted toward Nate. Marie situated her hand under it, while Deborah, playing the second wife, went from looking shocked and scared to annoyed and plucked the pencil from the air.

Marie meanwhile noticed a coffee mug levitating above a table, looked startled, and pounced on it. The audience roared.

"Donny," Jillian whispered. "Donny, stop. You know we had to do this play. It's a Halloween staple. The show must go on. You know that."

Kimberly grabbed a headset and rested a hand on Jillian's shoulder. She heard only crackling and static. Was she tuned to the wrong frequency? Her sixth sense tingled but offered no actual input.

The stage lights began to flicker. Jillian fiddled with switches on the board until she gave up. Nothing she pressed stopped the craziness on stage. The woman formed fists. "Donny! Stop it!"

All the props fell to the floor. The lights returned to normal.

Kimberly's headset vibrated as a voice wove through the tiny speaker.

"Where's my spotlight?"

CHAPTER TWENTY-TWO

KIMBERLY FELT LIKE AN IDIOT. All the costume ideas they'd brainstormed and discussed and considered, and she was stuck in this. She wished she'd advocated harder for *The Matrix* idea Sterling had suggested. Although skin-tight leather head to toe probably would've been about as uncomfortable as a skeleton leotard. But instead of a hot, bad-ass Trinity costume, she stood in the Old Catholic Church parking lot clad in a gingham dress covered by a huge apron, hair in braids under a bonnet, with ridiculously exaggerated freckles dotting her nose and cheeks.

She'd already been mistaken for Raggedy Ann as well as Dorothy from the *Wizard of Oz*. Being forced to dress up and hand out candy to strangers' children wasn't enough—she also had to look like a fool doing it.

Rosie had been quite impressed with this self-proclaimed stroke of genius, which she claimed had been Lorenzo's idea. And then her best friend had bustled into the trailer with her arms full of this nonsense. Kimberly distracted herself from her current mortification by mentally planning all the ways to pay Rosie back for this humiliation.

Sterling had not fared any better—he stood beside her in pants with ripped and frayed cuffs, tied with a piece of twine, suspenders over a checkered shirt, straw hat perched on his head. He, however, appeared to be taking it much better that she. While she forced a smile and explained through clenched teeth for the umpteenth time that she was Becky Thatcher to his Tom Sawyer while thrusting handfuls of candy into outstretched treat bags, Sterling held a deck of cards and amazed an enraptured audience.

Local businesses that had opted to participate in *The Wantland Files* Boo-Ha-Ha Trunk or Treat lined the parking lot of the Old Catholic Church, trunks decorated, volunteer employees in costume handing out candy.

Her crew had decorated Sterling's BMW i8 with a flux capacitor and opened the butterfly doors so it more resembled the *Back to the Future* Delorian. TJ sported jeans and a puffy burnt-orange vest and gave his best Marty McFly impression. Elise, dressed in a 1950s poodle skirt and sweater, followed him around with puppy dog eyes, periodically repeating, "Isn't he a dream boat?" Stan had donned a wild white wig and a lab coat and told each trick-or-treating child, "Great Scott! We have to get you . . . Back to the future!" She couldn't tell if any of the giggling children understood the reference, but her crew were having a blast and she couldn't help but smile. Even if she resented her ridiculous costume when they all had such adorable outfits.

Rosie wore a sexy gypsy costume—of course she did—and sat behind a table near the rest of the crew, offering to read palms and Tarot cards.

Jillian had showed up and worked the crowd, smiling and visiting with attendees. A local news van interviewed her, and they stood near enough to the *Wantland Files* van that she could overhear the questions and answers. Jillian plugged the haunted house and encouraged everyone to come see the Halloween play.

Someone yelled, "Were the moving objects part of the show last night?"

Another person in the crowd shouted, "Is your building truly haunted? Why is *The Wantland Files* here investigating?"

Jillian laughed them off with her high-pitched, tinkling laugh. "We don't share our secrets. You'll simply have to come to the haunted house or the play or *both* and see for yourself."

Kimberly was unable to approach Jillian during Trunk or Treat. The continued avoidance and lack of communication irritated her, yet she couldn't manage to maneuver the woman into a quiet conversation.

Sterling's crowd of costumed short people gasped and clapped as he astounded them with another illusion.

"How'd he *do* that?" one little girl squealed.

"An illusionist never reveals his secrets," Sterling said, drawing his outstretched fingers across his face.

Someone tugged on her dress hem. "Miss?"

She looked down to discover a child in her space, peering at her expectantly.

"My mom says you can see ghosts, but my dad says that's stupid. So can you?"

Yikes. No way was she wading into that quagmire. She thrust a handful of candy at him. "Happy Halloween."

A man lurking behind the child, presumably the dad who thought her stupid, squinted at her. "So what are you supposed to be?"

She gritted her teeth. "Becky Thatcher."

"Huh." He raked his eyes over her. "That's not hot."

Sterling stepped closer and inserted himself into the conversation. "She's not here for your personal gratification. Can I help you with something?"

The man started, took the boy by the arm, and drifted on.

Her jaw fell open even as her mouth curled into a smile. "What about not offending the fans?"

Sterling squinted as the man retreated. "I can't stand bullies. And that man wasn't a fan. He called you stupid! If he comes back here—"

"You won't do anything that could cause negative publicity." She wrapped her arms around his waist and squeezed. "Thank you. Thank you for that."

He kissed her cheek and returned to performing. No wonder she was starting to feel better at public appearances. Sterling always kept watch and didn't let anyone sketchy get near her.

Michael showed up, sans costume. She squinted at him. "And why are you alone not in costume?"

He crossed his arms. "I am. I'm dressed as a television series director."

She rolled her eyes. "You're a riot. Since you're not participating in the Trunk or Treat you orchestrated and insisted I take part in—"

"Take part in? You're the star of this show!"

"—you can be in charge of corralling Jillian so I can speak with her. If you can ever get her out from in front of the camera."

Michael scrunched his features into his "ew" face and lifted one hand to his chest, pointing behind her.

"I'm out from in front of the camera," Jillian said.

She blanched, forced her features into a smile, and turned around. "Jillian. Finally we have the chance to chat."

"Why do we need to chat? Have you figured out how to make Donny go away?"

"See, that's exactly why I need your cooperation. Your reaction last night leads me to believe you know more than you're telling me, which I already suspected. I think you knew Donny better than you're admitting to. And I can't do my job if I don't have every possible bit of information."

Jillian kept her face placid, but her eyes couldn't hide the truth—the woman was concealing something and seemed to struggle with her next move. She opened her mouth as if to speak.

"Hey, Aunt Jillian!"

And snapped it closed again. "Cory! Hello, there!"

Cory joined them, a bashful-looking Kayla beside him staring at Sterling, and nodded to Kimberly. "How's it going?"

"We're making some progress," she hedged. She grinned at Kayla. "No axe murders so far."

Kayla remained entranced by Sterling's magic—and she suspected not only the illusions he performed. "How does he do that?"

"How's your dad, Cory?" Jillian asked. "You guys okay?"

"Yeah, we're cool."

"If you want to work at the theatre again next summer, just let me know."

"Can you even afford that?" Cory looked confused.

Jillian's high-pitched trill of a laugh pierced the air. "Now, you let me worry about the money. That's not your concern."

Cory frowned. "Okay, it's just I know you—"

"Cory!" Jillian scowled and shook her head.

"Cool. Okay, sure. What about Kayla? She loves theatre." He bumped the girl with his elbow.

Kayla jumped and turned to him, jolted from her Sterling-inspired reverie. "What the heck?"

"I told Aunt Jillian you love theatre."

"Oh! Yes! I do!"

Jillian cocked her head. "Are you two back together?"

"Just friends," Kayla insisted, glancing at Sterling and then anywhere but.

"Well," Cory said. "More than friends but taking it slow."

Kayla flushed.

Jillian nodded. "Do you prefer acting or backstage work?"

Kayla drew a circle on the ground with her toe. "Oh, I'd always rather be on the stage than in the wings, but I'll help any way!"

"Good attitude." Jillian smiled at the girl. "You can audition for *A Christmas Carol* this year if you'd like. We have parts for young women in that and always need community actors to fill the cast."

Kayla lit up like she'd just won the lottery. "Okay! Thank you!"

Cory jerked a thumb at Kimberly. "Well, let's see if she can get rid of your ghost problem. I don't want Kayla's life at risk."

Kimberly shook her head, startled by the extreme exaggeration. "No one's life is at risk. I can assure you—"

Jillian laughed her ear-splitting giggle again. "Oh, Cory, let's not—"

Cory crossed his arms. "I heard you tell my dad the ghost threatened you. And that a lamp fell from the catwalk and barely missed you. You said you're almost afraid to go inside the building."

Kimberly turned and lifted an eyebrow at Jillian. "Was this before or after your nephew's incident?"

Jillian looked around, noting the other people still present. "Fine. I'll tell you everything I know. But not out here in public. Come to my office when this thing ends. I'll wait there."

Kimberly wasn't sure she trusted the woman but agreed. What choice did she have? She watched Jillian retreat into the building, more convinced than ever that the two had shared an intimate relationship. And sure Donny felt Jillian wronged him and wanted to make her pay.

CHAPTER TWENTY-THREE

WHEN THE FOUR-HOUR Trunk or Treat drew to a close, only a few stragglers remained, making rounds for candy. Eager to move inside and learn something from Jillian, Kimberly tapped her foot. She'd watched Cory and Kayla accompany Jillian to the door of the building and then part ways—Cory and Kayla leaving after Jillian went inside.

Sterling pulled her close and held up his phone, Twitter open. "Look at this. *Wantland Files* Trunk or Treat is trending."

"Good. That's good." She glanced at the door again and passed candy to another trick-or-treater.

Sterling lowered his phone. "Less enthusiasm than anticipated. Why so anxious?"

"I want out of this costume. And I need to get inside and speak with Jillian before she changes her mind about sitting down with me. I've been watching the door, afraid she'll sneak off. I knew she was withholding important information."

"Your intuition still works then," Sterling said. "Boy, that kid really let the cat out, didn't he?"

"Yes, and I'm glad. My intuition may work but my psychic senses aren't. He proved me right, though. Big time. Jillian didn't think to mention she thinks she's been physically threatened and attacked? Really? Didn't consider that important enough to run by me? 'Oh, yeah, and by the way the ghost tried to kill me, and I'm scared to be inside my own building. Just in case that's, you know, important or something.'" She rolled her eyes.

"Whoa. That's some serious sarcasm. Someone is getting salty."

"I'm sorry. I just . . . I'm getting nowhere with this investigation and I need to solve it."

"Well, smile through the frustration because we're not quite finished here."

Two more children approached tentatively, encouraged by a mom. "Go on. Go ahead."

"That's a stage mom for sure," she muttered to Sterling. Then a sharp pang hit her, the early loss of her own mother yawning wide, the grief a fresh wave. How would it feel to have a mom to encourage through uncertainty, to buoy on down days, to murmur encouragement every day as needed? She swallowed her grief and smiled widely at the boy and girl. "I have good candy. No cheap stuff here."

The boy approached first, dressed as a superhero, she thought, though she didn't know it by name. She couldn't tell what costume the little girl wore until Sterling pointed out the necklace with a grin. "That looks familiar."

The girl wore earth tones, a loose blouse and flowing skirt, a retro seventies feel to it. And around her neck she wore a chakra necklace, links holding stones that worked to strengthen each chakra. A little quartz star merkaba pendant inside two gold rings hung from the necklace, with a quartz crystal point hanging below that.

Kimberly's mouth fell open. "Are you . . . are you me?"

The girl nodded and ootched forward a few more steps.

"Say hello to Ms. Wantland, Alyssa," the woman said. But Alyssa stood mutely, clutching her mother's hand. "She adores you. We watch every episode, even re-runs. And some of the old footage on YouTube from before the show when you investigated on your own. I made her costume to mimic an outfit you wore in one of those videos."

"Back before she had me to dress her," Rosie said. "One of her better combinations though."

"You made that?" Kimberly asked, ignoring her snarky best friend.

The woman nodded, chuckling nervously. "I hope that's okay. Hope I haven't infringed on a trademark or anything."

"Of course not," Sterling said. "Even trademarks aren't enforceable if copied only for personal use."

"I'm not selling any," the woman assured them. "Just the one for her. She wanted one so badly after you gave one to Kimberly. She tried to convince her brother to dress as Sterling today, but he refused since Sterling is your boyfriend."

"Your brother can't be your boyfriend. That's gross," the boy insisted.

"Good instincts," Sterling told him.

"I didn't even know any of the recordings of my old investigations were online." She looked at Sterling. "How can that be?"

"I'll talk to Michael. Maybe he knows. The two of you could make a channel, put all the old stuff on it."

The woman clasped her hands. "Oh, please do. Alyssa cannot get enough of you."

"I don't know how to—"

"You have me now," Sterling said. "You don't have to know how. I can make it happen."

She crouched down, and the extremely bashful girl, eyes wide, edged closer. Why was this girl fixated on her show? "Hello, Alyssa. I'm Kimberly."

The girl stared and nodded, then held out a hand.

The woman wrung her hands. "I don't want you to think we're crazy, but . . . she says she sees them too."

Kimberly took the little girl's hand in her own. A ripple of electricity buzzed across her skin. Was the girl . . .

Alyssa whispered, "You're sick."

She blinked in shock. "What?"

"You don't feel good. You're sick."

She sucked in a breath.

Sterling squatted beside her. "What did she say?" He fished his notebook from a pocket.

"I'm so sorry!" the girl's mother said. "Sometimes she says really odd things. She doesn't mean—"

"No, don't apologize. She's right. I haven't been feeling well lately." She smiled at the little girl, whose brown eyes softened.

Sterling scribbled. What was he writing?

The girl's mom looked startled by this response. "Well, she's always been a little . . ."

"Different? I was too. Still am." She shook her head. "I'm sorry. She startled me. I so rarely encounter someone else with abilities."

"You think she's . . . like you?"

Kimberly squeezed the girl's hand, prompting a shy smile. "Definitely. I can sense her energy. And she can tell mine is . . . a little off right now."

"I thought she was simply mimicking you. Which in and of itself seemed a little strange. Don't get me wrong, I've worried about her quite a bit. The other kids at her school watch cartoons. She's engrossed by your show. And threw a hellacious fit for a *Wantland Files* lunchbox and backpack when we went back-to-school shopping. Which by the way, doesn't exist."

"Ha!" Sterling scribbled furiously. "There's a marketing niche we haven't yet explored."

Kimberly raised an eyebrow. "Seems like an extremely narrow niche."

"Don't sell yourself short. If one child is pitching a fit, I'm sure there are lots more."

Dubious, she shook her head, adding a chocolate bar to each child's bag. Then she fished a business card from her purse and, without hesitation, wrote her personal email on the back before passing it to the children's mother. "Stay in touch.

Please. I know what it's like to be in Alyssa's shoes. But I'm so glad you seem open and accepting of her abilities. I wish my parents had offered me that support. What about her father? Is he . . ."

The woman shook her head. "Not in the picture. And that's for the best."

"I could suggest a couple of books to read. But seriously, if you need some experienced advice in the future, I'm happy to help. Please don't hesitate."

Alyssa's mom looked ready to cry. "Thank you. Thank you so much. I get so overwhelmed, trying to handle everything as a single, working mom. And then she . . . well, I didn't know what to think. Or what to do."

"She's an Indigo Child for sure. Some of us have supersensory perception, extrasensory perception, extreme empathy to the point of experiencing actual pain ourselves."

"Yes! A few times I've found her crying, and when I asked what was wrong, she said, 'Everyone is just so sad.' I had no idea what she was talking about."

"She feels pretty strong, like I was. And if she reports seeing spirits, that could increase with maturity. It did for me."

The woman clamped her hands over her nose and mouth. "Oh, my gosh. What do I do? How do I help her?"

Alyssa placed a hand on her mother in a gesture Kimberly recognized. "It's okay, Mommy."

Her mother appeared to calm slightly. Kimberly knew Alyssa had passed soothing energy to her mother. This girl was the real deal. "Alyssa, I'm so glad you came to meet me today. You keep looking after your mom, but remember, sometimes we need someone to look after us."

"Like Rosie!" the little girl cried.

"Like me," Rosie agreed.

"And me," Sterling said, curling an arm around her.

"But mostly me," Rosie insisted. The two stared each other down.

"But most important of all, when you and your mom need me, tell her to let me know, okay?"

Alyssa nodded.

She watched them move to the next trunk for more treats, fervently hoping she would hear from them again. If she could save the girl the trouble and heartache she'd experienced growing up, she would.

"Well, that was rather beautiful," Rosie said. "I just remembered why you're my best friend."

She rolled her eyes. "Oh good."

"It really was though," Michael said. "Hopefully we captured that heart-warming exchange for the show." He turned, looking for Stan and TJ who each gave him a thumbs-up.

"Okay, now I don't know if you're being sincere or sarcastic."

"Sincere, sweetie. But good footage never hurts."

Sterling's pencil scratched across his notepad. Elise had moved behind him, adjusting her glasses and bobbing her head, clearly attempting to read whatever he wrote.

Sterling slowly turned and looked over his shoulder at her. "Can I help you, ma'am?"

"It's just . . ."

"Yes?"

"Well, you've been taking a lot of notes this week."

So she wasn't the only who thought this new behavior curious.

"And?" he asked.

"It's just . . . usually I take the notes."

Kimberly pursed her lips, fighting the laughter that shook her body and struggled to escape. Rosie had confessed to feeling jealous of sharing her with Sterling. Now Elise appeared to be jealous of his notetaking.

Sterling shrugged. "More than one person can take notes."

Everyone looked at Kimberly. For what? Did they expect her to tell him to stop taking notes?

"I admit I'm also intrigued and would like to see what Sterling is writing. But I doubt you need to be worried, Elise. I'm sure it won't conflict with your notes."

"We don't really know that."

TJ stepped closer. "Yeah, she's right. Why the big secret?"

"It isn't secret. I'm just not ready to share yet."

"Oh yeah? Why not?" TJ leaned close and tried to see the pages. "You spying on us? Taking notes to start your own show? Or feed to a rival?"

Kimberly laughed and opened her mouth to dismiss such nonsense. Then again, why wouldn't he share with them if the notes were harmless?

Sterling stuffed the notebook into his pocket. "Back off, kid. It's notes for me and nothing more. If I have something important to share with the group, I will."

Michael crossed one arm over his torso and struck his thoughtful pose, one hand in the air. "Umm, okay, now I want to know what you're writing. And as director of the show—"

"You will be first to know if I have anything of importance to share." Sterling stared him down until Michael looked away. "Kimberly, didn't you want to speak with Jillian?"

"Oh, gosh! Yes! TJ, Stan, let's go!"

"But—"

"Not now! Jillian could leave any second." She turned to the building, ready to race inside.

She stopped in her tracks.

The man in overalls, the one she'd seen at the cemetery, stood at the edge of the parking lot. He raised his rusted, dirt-caked pruning sheers, leering smile across his face.

She spun around, collided with Sterling, and buried her face in his chest.

"What the—" Sterling's hard body jerked to a halt as she slammed into him. "What's wrong?"

Her voice wouldn't work. She shook and gasped but could not form words.

"Hey." He lifted her face to his. "You're terrified. What is wrong?"

She pointed behind her.

His eyes moved back and forth and back again, scanning the area. He met her eyes, searching for something, and shook his head.

"The . . . man. The man in the overalls."

His eyebrows scrunched, but he looked a second time.

Michael leaned close. "There's no one there, sweetie."

Sterling turned her slowly. "Do you still see him?"

No man, overall-clad or otherwise. No one at all. She shook her head.

She saw concern in Sterling's eyes as he took her hand. "Come on. Let's go talk to Jillian."

CHAPTER TWENTY-FOUR

THE AIR in the room crackled with anxiety, the level high enough Kimberly's less-than-fully functional sixth sense could detect it. As a result, her own anxiety skyrocketed as she watched Jillian pace the tiny office, cramped and claustrophobic already with camera crew and Michael wedged in like Tetris pieces. They lacked only Rosie, who presumably had opted to spend time with Lorenzo.

Kimberly glanced at her watch and decided the woman needed a nudge. "Cory said you think the ghost tried to harm you?"

The woman nodded but continued pacing.

"A lamp fell near you?"

The woman nodded again, gesticulating as she finally spoke. "Yes, but I probably overreacted, right?" Jillian glanced at Sterling, presumably for validation. "I mean, it could have been a coincidence, right?" Another glance at Sterling.

Sterling cleared his throat. "It could have, of course. But I can't help but wonder why you called a paranormal investigation team if you really believe that. Why don't you tell us what happened?" He gestured to a seat.

Jillian didn't sit but took a deep breath. "Okay. Here goes. I was onstage during *Noises Off* rehearsals, blocking. Early stage, right? Still blocking, no lights or anything."

"Right, right," Kimberly said, "Not until tech week—"

"Exactly. But Ian had started moving some of the instruments. We had a basic lighting plot. No spotlights or anything specific. But a general idea. That night, a unit fell exactly where I'd been standing seconds earlier. And I only moved because Marie couldn't remember which door I told her to go through the previous beat. I honestly was quite annoyed with her. We're all professionals. How did she miss that? But her negligence probably saved my life."

Negligence? Kimberly leaned forward. "Was she negligent in asking for clarification? I played Brooke in a college production. It was pretty complicated to pull off."

"This isn't college. This is a repertory theatre and I expect professionalism."

Elise scribbled furiously, her pencil scratching across the paper in the silence that once again settled over the space.

Sterling sat on the edge of the desk, one leg bent over the other. "You mentioned Ian moving some of the lights. Do you think he—"

"Ian has never made a mistake in the entire time he's been with us. But I'm ashamed to say I administered a pretty terrible tongue lashing in the heat of the moment. Turns out, that instrument hadn't been moved from the previous show. A spotlight. And the clamp was completely unscrewed. Not loose. Unscrewed. As if it somehow worked its way out. Plus, the safety cable failed."

"Failed?" Sterling asked.

"I don't understand it. The carbiner had detached somehow."

Stan lowered his camera, his brow furrowed. "Somehow the clamp unscrewed and somehow the safety line detached? That seems highly unlikely."

"And yet the entire troupe was present. No one had wandered off."

Sterling frowned. "Did you consider calling the police? Someone could have been inside the building and you didn't know it."

Jillian laughed, a dark, mirthless rumble. "So they could ask me if I have any enemies? Anyone who might want to see me dead?"

Kimberly wrinkled her nose. Not exactly a plea of innocence. "Do you?"

Jillian gave her a withering glance. "Don't we all?"

Michael's head whipped in her direction, his eyebrows high, corners of his mouth pulled down. Jillian had piqued his interest for sure. But Kimberly needed to stay focused, not veer down that rabbit hole.

"Ummm, no."

Jillian shrugged. "But to answer your question, no, we didn't call the police. We chalked it up to a scarily close near miss, but an accident. Nerves frayed, we resumed blocking."

"And yet you summoned a paranormal investigation. Something must've prompted that."

Jillian stared into the distance, arms crossed, as if struggling with this. "Everyone in the troupe kept telling me Donny's presence, his spirit, whatever you want to call it, is still here. I tried to discount all of that. I mean, come on. The entire town supposedly brims with ghosts, but I've never encountered a thing. Then one night I heard it too. Everyone else had gone home. I was looking over some paperwork, getting ready to lock up, and I heard my name. I heard someone calling out to me. I went to see who had come back inside, when I recognized his voice. I couldn't move. Couldn't believe it. And then I heard him ask, 'Where's my spotlight?'"

"That's when you called us? I thought—"

"No, I still didn't act on it. Tried to convince myself I'd imagined it. Until Kayla heard him too. That girl heard the same thing. She has no basis to even imagine that happening. None. Kayla never met Donny. She didn't know he had a habit of saying that, of insisting the spotlight operator was off, because he couldn't possibly be in the wrong place. Oh, no. Donny could never admit to being wrong, that attention- and adulation-seeking egomaniac."

Sterling had his notebook in hand and scribbled notes. Elise, watching him closely, bent over her spiral and redoubled her note-taking efforts. Sterling seemed oblivious. "Would you say this is fairly strong proof of paranormal activity? You became convinced once you were faced with this evidence?"

Jillian fiddled with her necklace. "That's when I reached out to you. To the show. I'm not sure I want to admit to believing it even now. I don't want to believe it. Don't want it to be true. Any of it. If he's here, why? Why can't he just leave me alone?"

Kimberly saw the woman's resolve beginning to crack. Finally, an opening. "That's why I've been trying to talk with you. So we can figure that out. I can help, but I need your input to get there."

Jillian's face twisted into a wry grin. "Help you help me? Is that what you're saying?"

"We do need your cooperation, yes."

"I thought you'd just get rid of him. You know"—Jillian waved her hands around—"like in *Ghostbusters* basically."

"Sorry," Kimberly said. She shook her head at Michael, who pressed his lips together to suppress a grin. Why did that comparison keep coming up? "I don't have any means of trapping ghosts and forcing them to do what we want. I need to understand why Donny is upset and then convince him he will be happier if he moves on."

Jillian puffed out a breath and shook her head. "This is so like him. I can't believe he's managing to pull this garbage even after he died."

She glanced at Sterling who lifted an eyebrow. "You knew Donny, then?"

"*Knew* him?" The woman scoffed again, looking at Kimberly like she was nuts.

Getting information out of this woman was like pulling teeth. "Ian mentioned to us that you let him stay here in the apartment when he moved to Hannibal."

"I did. And feel like an utter fool. No good deed goes unpunished. Especially not with Donny."

Sterling flipped pages of his notebook. "Are you having financial problems with the theatre?"

Jillian glanced at some papers on her desk, then scowled at the collective group gathered in her personal space. "I specifically stated I didn't want anyone in here—"

"You nephew Cory made some comments indicating the theatre is having problems. That you're worried about losing it."

"Oh. I see. Well, he probably picked up on that while he was working here."

"It's true?"

Jillian held her arms out. "Look at the place. It's pretty obvious, isn't it? Why do you think I'm working day and night, schlepping myself all over town pushing people to come see our shows, to come to a haunted house? This was supposed to be fun. My own theatre to run. I moved here to be close to Cory and his father, the only family I have left."

"You had some success in New York, didn't you?" Michael asked. "I'm sure I've seen your face."

"Some, yes. Decent roles off Broadway. Some commercial work. Even some minor bit roles in film. Never crossed over into television or broke out hugely in any area. Supported myself well enough. When my sister was diagnosed with cancer, I came down here to help out as much as possible."

A gray cloud of sadness passed over Kimberly. She knew how the battle with cancer had ended before Jillian told them. She could feel it. "I'm so sorry. That must have been devastating."

"Thank you. I stayed to try to help her husband with their son. Like I know anything about kids. But I needed to feel like I was doing something."

Something she and Jillian had in common. "I understand."

Jillian glanced at her and offered a wry smile. "Work for actors is pretty limited around here as you might have guessed."

"Ian said something similar," she said. "Earning a living as an artist is extremely challenging almost anywhere really."

"Don't I know that. I wasn't ready to go back to waiting tables, but I didn't exactly have a huge slush fund of savings. I learned this old church was for sale, cheap, about to be demolished. I invested in it with the idea I'd establish a repertory theatre. You wouldn't believe how cheaply I picked it up. But it was just this side of condemned and required a lot of renovation before we could even use it. I mistakenly believed I'd find other backers, people eager to save historic buildings from demolition. Especially in this old town."

"Not so much, huh?" Sterling asked.

Jillian sighed deeply. "People who will spend five dollars on a cup of coffee don't like paying so much as a dollar for a ticket to see a show. Or contributing that dollar to a 'Save the Old Catholic Church' fundraiser. No, we're not doing well and I'm almost at the end of my rope. I even reached out to my agent and asked her to let me know if she hears about any roles I'd be ideal for. Cory and his father seem to be back on solid footing now. I need to make some real money again."

"But they're your family," Kimberly said. "Don't you want to stay close?"

"Family can be a mixed blessing," Jillian said. "And if I can't turn things around and earn a living here, I won't have any choice."

"What about this place?" Sterling asked.

Jillian glanced at paperwork on her desk again. "I haven't had the heart to tell the troupe, but this is probably our last season. I'll put the building back on the market and hope to God I make my money back out of it. If it even sells."

She looked to Sterling for guidance. This was not at all what she'd expected. Nor was this helping their investigation. Now she felt bad for Jillian, who she'd assumed was hiding something nefarious. Once again, her sixth sense failed her. Sterling shrugged, looking equally baffled by this turn of events. He flipped through the pages of his notebook again, eyes skimming the notes.

She decided to press on. "During our investigation, the ghost we suspect to be Donny can be repeatedly heard to say, 'Jillian pay.' Why do you think—"

Jillian's head whipped to face her. "'Jillian pay'? He thinks *I* should pay? Seriously? That man's nerve simply has no end! I should pay? That's all I've ever done is pay!"

She leaned back. Whoa. She'd expected a reaction but nothing quite so intense. "You knew Donny well, then?"

Jillian looked at her like she was crazy. "Of course. I assumed you'd already figured that out."

"No. And I think some details could be helpful."

"I don't like talking about it. Frankly it's quite embarrassing."

She glanced at Michael, whose face had brightened. He had eyes on Stan and was twirling one finger, directing him to keep rolling. Michael never could resist a good scandal.

"You must have known there was bad blood between you if you believed he attempted to drop a lighting instrument on you."

"Bad blood? That's an understatement. With Donny, that's the only type of blood. I can't believe I—" The woman's phone rang. She glanced at the incoming call and stiffened. "It's the bank. Sorry, I really must take this call."

"But you can't believe you what? What were you—"

Jillian shuffled through papers as she answered the phone. "Hello?" She scowled at the group in her office and shooed them away.

She and her crew reluctantly vacated the space as instructed. Jillian closed the door behind them.

She looked to Michael. "Now what?"

"Now we have dinner."

CHAPTER TWENTY-FIVE

THE CLATTER of cheap plates and silverware reminded Kimberly of another reason why she steered clear of diners as much as possible. The bright lights, busy black-and-white checkered floor, loud chatter, and general frenetic pace set her nerves jangling. This was the complete opposite of the dim, soothing, quiet surroundings that allowed her to center and focus prior to investigations.

She'd tried to beg off and retreat to her trailer, but Michael had declared it a "working dinner" and demanded her presence since they'd be discussing the case. Knowing her input would be minimal to none, she knew this to be a waste of time. But since she couldn't bring herself to confide her concerns yet, she couldn't explain why her attendance would enhance nothing.

Stan wanted meatloaf and everyone else wanted to do something touristy. So the Tom Sawyer Diner it was. Meatloaf, burgers, fried chicken, biscuits and gravy—none of the options on the menu appealed to her no matter how many "Best of" lists the food topped.

She pressed her fingers against her temples as she waited for her salad—the only thing on the menu that didn't churn her stomach—to appear. Even pizza would've been preferable to this—and she was sick of pizza.

Sterling put an arm around her waist and whispered in her ear. "You sure you don't want the grilled cheese?"

She shook her head. "They only have American cheese here which is a processed cheese product, high in salt and additives. I'll pass."

"You can't just eat salad. I'll take you someplace else after this. We'll have time before the investigation starts."

Her stomach gurgled and she wasn't sure if it was hunger or nausea. "It's really not necessary. I'll be fine. But thank you."

"You've barely eaten today," he reminded her. "You need something."

"Kimmy?" Michael called from the other end of the table, and she realized everyone stared at her. "You okay? Something you want to share with the rest of us?"

What was this, middle school? He sounded like he'd caught her passing notes or something. "No, nothing to share."

His left eyebrow went up, and he gave her the look.

"What? What is that for?" Had he figured out her secret? Did they all suspect she was losing her abilities?

"She's just not feeling well," Sterling said.

"We can all see that," Michael said in his saltiest tone. "But what's the cause?"

He knew. He had to know. This was what he did. He never just flat-out stated suspicions. He hinted and goaded and pestered until you couldn't stand it and blurted it out. She forced her features into the most innocent expression she could manage. "I'm fine."

She glanced at Rosie. Had her assistant passed along intel? Did Rosie share with Michael that her energy levels were low and easily depleted? But Rosie was whispering to Lorenzo.

"We all have your back, sweetie," Michael coaxed. "Whatever's going on, you can share."

"Nothing to share. But thank you."

Michael stared her down but then cleared his throat. "Moving on. Stan, TJ, anything additional to add after reviewing the recordings again?"

Stan shook his head. "Nothing helpful. Whispers. Muttering. Same things repeated over and over."

TJ spoke up. "I've identified some images that appear to match the descriptions Kayla gave us from the night she thinks she saw manifestations. My theory is that we're hearing the whispered prayers and confessions from when the space was a church combined with actors practicing lines in the wings. But I can't be sure. We need Ms. Wantland to connect and figure this out for us. You know?"

"Kimmy? What else have you gleaned?"

"Everyone agrees Jillian must have dated Donny, right? That's what she was going to say, don't you think? She can't believe she dated him?"

"We didn't need a psychic for that, sweetie. What can you add to the investigation?"

She squirmed in her seat. "We already feel strongly it's Donny."

"But why?" Michael pressed.

"You know we intend to find out tonight." *I hope*. She twisted her fingers together.

Michael scrunched his nose. "I thought you were just building up suspense for the show. Giving us an excuse to bring Jillian in. You really don't know?"

"Oh. I mean, yes, of course I'm building suspense. But . . ." Okay, so apparently Rosie hadn't shared anything. If he didn't suspect her of having sixth sense issues, what was all that nonsense about? Her cell phone rang. *Thank goodness*. "This is Angela. I need to take it." She turned slightly and held a hand over her open ear to muffle the diner cacophony swirling around her. "Hi, Angela. Are you okay?"

The voice on the other end quivered. "I'm so sorry to bother you. I know you're busy. But I just saw a . . . a shadow or a figure or something. I'm not even sure."

Angela had never before expressed fear of the supernatural. "Tell me what happened."

"I was in the kitchen fixing my lunch . . ."

The kitchen. The location where her mother had inexplicably died. The kitchen of that house seemed to be a hot spot. Or perhaps the shadow belonged to her mother's spirit. After all, she'd seen her mother just after she passed. Perhaps she never left. This was part of the reason why she longed to conduct an actual investigation in the old house. Partly she wanted closure on the death. Why had her completely healthy mother died suddenly? Even doctors had no real answer. And partly she worried her mother's spirit could be trapped in the house. What if her mother needed help and no one else could hear her? She needed to know for sure. And now with her sixth sense possibly eroding away, what if she was running out of time to help?

She realized Angela had stopped recounting her story. "Go ahead."

"I'm afraid it will sound ridiculous to you. And I'm embarrassed how scared I was."

"You won't sound ridiculous, I promise you that. Any unexpected encounters are startling. I understand."

"Well, a shadow fell over the counter. I swear it was a person's shadow, as if someone had walked up behind me. It was definitely distinct from my own shadow. Obviously, no one but me lives in the house, so it really startled me. I whirled around, glad I had a knife in my hand, even if it was only a butter knife. I truly expected to discover an intruder behind me."

"But there was no one there?"

"No one! I let it go, assumed I had imagined it or somehow mistaken my own shadow, even though I really don't think I did. But just now I came down the hall and turned into the kitchen and I swear I saw someone! Only for a moment. I blinked and they were gone. I feel like a crazy person seeing things that aren't there."

"Did you have the feeling the presence was male or female?" She couldn't imagine her mother as a menacing presence. Remembering her mother's gentle nature, her quiet smiles, the way she read stories to her and comforted her, she teared up. No, her mother would never intentionally scare someone. But any sudden manifestation could be perceived as a threat.

"Male," Angela said without hesitation. "Though I couldn't explain why. I don't remember any specific details that should lead me to that conclusion."

"That's okay. Gut feeling means a lot in these situations. Are you still hearing footsteps from the attic?"

"Oh, yes. Every night when I go to bed. I've grown accustomed to it and forgot to mention that."

"Not a problem. Why don't you start logging every instance of activity you notice. I get the impression we're seeing an uptick in activity levels, but I'd like to have something in writing to back that up."

"Definitely increasing. I can attest to that. But I'm glad to keep track for you."

"Listen, Angela. I mean this. If you ever feel threatened in any way, leave the house. Okay?"

"Up until today, I would have laughed at that suggestion. But now I'm glad to hear it."

"Your safety is more important than anything. Remember that. And call me with updates. Anytime."

She hung up and shared the information from Angela with the others at the table. "I almost wish we could ditch the rest of our planned investigations and go back to Albuquerque now. I want to know what's happening in that house."

"But you know we can't bail," Michael said.

But what if her mother was there and needed her? She blew out a breath. The people on her schedule she'd promised to help needed her for sure. Her own house had waited this long. It would have to wait a bit more. "I know. But I want to."

Michael glanced at the time and then leaned forward. "Back to Donny. Are you serious that you're not getting anything when you connect with him? Why is he so reticent?"

This was the perfect opening to tell them. All she had to do was admit she wasn't connecting normally, that her psychic energy felt low, her abilities off. She had no idea what caused the issues, but didn't they all just promise they had her back?

"Once again, feel like you're not sharing something," Michael said.

Rosie slurped her soda through her straw, the noise as she sucked at the ice cubes remaining from the drained drink obnoxious enough to pull attention.

Michael squeezed his eyes shut, his face contorting as though being tortured. "That sound is the aural equivalent of driving a stake into my temple. Do you mind?"

Rosie knew he hated that. One look at her friend confirmed the distraction had been intentional.

Michael saw the glance Rosie shared with Kimberly, whose face must have reflected the gratitude she felt. "Enough is enough. What are you keeping from me?"

Before she could answer, the waitress arrived at the table, balancing a huge tray loaded with plates. Saved by the food. The waitress distributed one greasy, gravy-laden plate after another. TJ reacted with pure ecstasy to his breakfast-for-dinner biscuits and gravy. Stan had apparently ordered extra gravy on the side, which he poured over his slab of meatloaf. Chicken fried steak with gravy. Fried chicken with mashed potatoes and gravy. She started to worry her salad would come drowning in gravy instead of with dressing on the side. She gritted her teeth and willed herself not to get sick.

Sterling had ordered a burger—thankfully sans gravy—with steamed vegetables in addition to fries. "Here, I got a side of veggies for you. Help yourself."

The waitress finally plunked down a white plastic bowl of wilted iceberg with one sad cherry tomato and three croutons on top. The woman eyed Kimberly as if she might be hiding a bomb. "And just a salad, no dressing."

"Hold up," Sterling said, signaling for the waitress' attention.

Much to the waitress' apparent delight. She rolled her lips together and rested her fingers over his arm. "What else can I do for you, sugar?"

"She ordered dressing on the side, not no dressing."

Gravely disappointed, the woman retracted her hand and curled a lip at Kimberly. "I'll bring that right out."

"It's fine. Really. I can eat it without . . ." Too late. The woman and her swaying hips already made their way back to the kitchen.

Kimberly watched her coworkers descend on a virtual flood of gravy, picked up her fork, and pushed around the sad-looking lettuce shreds. Nauseated, she put her fork back down and pushed the salad away.

The pinch-faced waitress returned, two fingers and a thumb gripping the plastic cup of dressing like it was a urine sample. "Here's this. If you're even gonna eat."

Michael lowered his fork and knife and paused in the inhalation of his chicken fried steak drowning in gravy and scowled at her. "Okay, what is this?"

"She's just not feeling well," Sterling said.

"I can see that. Why not?"

Lorenzo whispered in Rosie's ear.

Rosie's face lit up, her hands rising to cover her mouth, which fell open. She waved her hands at her face and appeared to be tearing up. "Are your low energy levels due to . . ."

Kimberly watched her best friend gesture at her as if she should know how to finish that sentence. "Due to . . ."

Rosie stared at her intently. "You know. It would totally explain things."

Michael looked back and forth between them. "She clearly

doesn't know, Rosie, and I am so done with being left in the dark. What is happening?"

Lorenzo tried giving her a nudge. "You'd be protected under the PDA. They can't threaten your job."

She shook her head in utter bafflement. Of course her job would be in jeopardy if she lost her psychic abilities. Her entire job hinged on her unique gift.

Sterling suddenly gripped her hand and stared at her with an odd expression.

Elise flipped pages in her notebook. "I hope I didn't overstep my bounds, but I also looked into the possible effects on psychic abilities, just in case our suspicions turned out to be correct."

Rosie leaped up and rounded the table, crushing her in a hug. "I'll be Aunt Rosie! I am crazy excited for you two." She threw one arm around Sterling and pulled him into the hug.

Michael jolted as if startled by a glass of water to the face. "Oh my God, you're pregnant!"

She sucked in a breath. "What?"

Sterling looked like he might be sick. "You didn't tell me. You didn't tell me?"

She shook her head. "No, I—"

Michael sat up straight, his forearms resting on either side of his forgotten dinner. "Oh my God. A Kimberling baby will send ratings through the roof. Wait until Hoffmeier hears!"

Beside her, Sterling trembled. "Are you . . . are we having a baby?"

She shook her head again, trying to get a word in among the storm of noise breaking out over their table.

Michael fumbled with his phone. Elise began rattling off rare but documented instances of pregnancy inhibiting psychic abilities. Rosie promised to learn massage techniques specific to pregnancy. TJ, a forkful of biscuit smothered in gravy halfway to his mouth, looked shellshocked. Stan smiled at her and nodded knowingly—he and his wife were expecting their first.

"I'm not pregnant!" she insisted.

But the horse had left the stable and galloped gleefully through the open meadow of imagined delight.

"It all makes sense." Rosie smiled down at her, and where her best friend had just crushed her in a hug, now she rested a hand tentatively on her shoulder, as though afraid she'd shatter.

She didn't shatter. But she blew up. She slammed one palm on the table. "I am not pregnant!"

The diner went deathly silent the moment she raised her voice to be heard over the noise level which had only risen like an incoming tide from the moment they'd sat down. Of course it did. Perfect timing. Now everyone in the place drew a collective breath and almost as one withdrew cellphones and began snapping photos, perhaps texting the juicy gossip or maybe even posting it on all their socials, eager to be the first to break the news and gain all the attention such a bombshell piece would reward them with online.

Michael frowned. "Are you sure? I was trying to reach Hoffmeier. This could be huge."

"You're absolutely certain?" Rosie echoed. "Because think about it. This would explain why you've been so exhausted and why your energy has been drained. You have a little parasite inside you sucking your life force away."

"Rosie! Eww! What a terrible way to describe pregnancy." She clutched her stomach.

Sterling draped an arm around her. "You make our baby sound like a Xenomorph from the *Alien* movies!"

"Wait a minute," Michael said. "What do you mean your energy has been low? Why am I just now hearing about this?"

"I'm sorry. I didn't want anyone to know. I was hoping it would go away with some rest."

"Did it?"

"It doesn't seem to be. And it seems to be affecting my connections. They haven't been as strong."

"But you have no idea what's causing it?"

She glanced at Rosie and then at Sterling. "No."

Michael pointed at her. "So you could be pregnant?"

Elise flipped pages and reasserted her findings. "You know psychics are rare. Pregnant psychics even more so. But I did find some obscure references to women who believed their abilities were dampened during pregnancy."

"I'm not—"

"You are one hundred percent certain?" Michael asked.

"Yes, I . . . Well, okay so I'm not this second able to say definitively that I'm not. But I'm in between cycles right now. It's not like I'm late."

"You do seem to be coping with morning sickness," Lorenzo offered.

"I'm never hungry in the morning. I'm tired and need coffee first."

"You're more exhausted than normal," Rosie said. "Experiencing low levels of psychic energy."

She turned to Sterling and met his gaze, trying to gauge his reaction. "I don't think I'm pregnant."

He stood. "Kimberly and I need to talk. We'll walk back."

All eyes remained on her as she accompanied him out the door, past a dozen or more phones raised and taking photos or videos as they retreated.

The fresh outside air helped clear the funk of the diner. She breathed deeply, enjoying the quiet of the evening, the water lapping in the river, the quiet puffing of the steamboats chugging upriver.

"Let's get some ice cream," Sterling suggested and veered across the street to Becky Thatcher's Ice Cream Parlor.

"Ice cream on empty stomachs?"

"Just this once."

His mood was difficult to read. She couldn't get a good sense of his chakras or discern which resonated most vividly. Was he scared? Angry? His red chakra didn't seem to dominate. His phone began to ping rapidly, again and again. He tore his gaze from her and looked at the screen. "Oh no."

"What?"

"No one in that diner heard the 'not.' All they heard was 'I'm pregnant.' Hashtag Wantland baby is trending."

"But if I'm not pregnant—"

"*If* you're not? You seemed fairly sure back at the diner."

"There's always a chance until my time of the month. Nothing is one hundred percent effective."

He cupped her cheek, brow furrowed but eyes gentle. His phone rang. "Shit. It's Hoffmeier."

She laughed. "Take the call. This is your life now. You said you could handle it."

"I did say that." He shook his head and accepted the call. "Hello, Mr.— Well, it wasn't really a— No, we don't know— Of course. Of course, sir. Thank you." He hung up and raised his eyebrows. "Needless to say, he's delighted. Says next time to run it past him first. But he thinks it's genius. Especially if you're not."

"But how would we explain that? People will want a due date, baby pictures."

He blew out a breath. "Obviously we won't even acknowledge the rumor on the show. In fact, our best move right now is to remain silent on the issue and let speculation run rampant. When we know for sure one way or the other, then we'll deal with it."

She leaned back, not sure how to take that last comment. "Deal with it? What does that mean?"

"If you're not, one of two things. We either call it out as the unfounded rumor it is or go the sympathy route and announce you lost it."

"I don't love that. I'd rather come clean about the misunderstanding than manipulate emotions."

"They invite it. No one made them post false info for attention."

"I still don't feel good about exploiting it. But what if I am? How would you deal with that?"

He cupped her face again, his eyes misting. "I'd take you shopping for maternity clothes."

Practical, but also sweet. His heart chakra thrummed, buzzing sincerity in a way no one else could detect. She didn't expect this reaction. At all. He seemed almost . . . happy. "But what about the show?"

"What about it? You could easily finish this season. We might even get you through next season's investigations before you need a break, even if you waddle through a few episodes."

She punched his arm. "Waddle!" But the thought brought the possibility firmly home.

"Seriously, though, if you are pregnant, you're only just barely. We haven't been—"

The server called their number and Sterling went to the counter to retrieve their ice cream cones.

Noting all eyes on them and how preternaturally quiet the fellow customers and shop employees had gone, he jerked his head toward the door. "Let's walk. We can eat these as we stroll to the trailer."

The sun hung low on the horizon, glistening off the river while setting the sky a brilliant shade of orange, like a vibrant sacral chakra thrumming with pleasure and desire. Awareness of how familiar she'd become with Sterling's orange chakra resonating for her sparked a hum of interest in her own.

He held out his salted caramel cone. "Want a taste?"

"Sure!" She exchanged cones with him, allowing him to sample her brownie batter flavor. "I really appreciate how chill you're being about this."

He shrugged. "You seem pretty sure you're not. I'll confess I haven't given much thought to having a child. Wasn't sure that card was in my future. If it turns out we've been dealt that hand though, there are worse things in the world than having a baby with a woman I admire and respect and have come to—"

She stopped and waited, ice cream pooling at the edge of the cone, threatening to drip. What had he been about to say? The

"L" word? Had they reached a point they could love each other? Considering they were discussing a possible, no matter how unlikely, pregnancy, she must love him on some level. Right? She wasn't sure she was ready to hear or say it though. How well did he really know her? And she him?

He watched her intently, as if gauging her reaction to the near slip. A drop of cold splattered her hand, demanding her attention. She laughed and lapped it with her tongue. "Salted caramel was an excellent choice," she said between twirls of her tongue around the cone's edge. "It's a nice dark caramel, not too sweet."

He cocked his head, brow furrowing slightly before nodding and trying hers. "Brownie batter is also delicious. A little more direct, not so subtle. But I like it."

They traded back. She wasn't pregnant. She couldn't be. They'd been careful. The real concern was why her abilities seemed to be fading. Concentration and focus would be almost impossible tonight. Exactly why she'd refused to allow a relationship to complicate things. Sterling shoved his cone in front of her, offering another lick. She giggled and took him up on it, noting as she often did how his eyes sparkled when she smiled. She bumped him with an elbow. "I'm glad you're here."

CHAPTER TWENTY-SIX

KIMBERLY WAITED in the lobby of the auditorium. An exhausted and nervous-looking Jillian exited the booth after the show ended, but she worked the crowd, thanking people for coming and hovering as the cast mingled with attendees.

The audience members who milled in the lobby, however, seemed more interested in snapping photos of the paranormal investigation team and asking for selfies with her and Sterling. But many of them also grumbled about coming to see the incredible on-stage effects they'd heard about—and being disgusted by the lack thereof.

"We should have snuck in the back and waited for Jillian out of sight," she told Sterling.

He shrugged. "This is great publicity. And free." He accepted pen and paper and signed his autograph with a huge smile. "Who should I make this to?"

One man stopped to confront Jillian. "Listen, I won't ask for a refund, but I'd be justified in demanding one. I came tonight after reading and hearing how hilarious this fresh version of the show was and how impressive your special effects were. Everyone said you have to see it to believe it. I don't know how you pulled off this publicity stunt, but you better be able to make good on your promises."

Jillian hung her head. "I'm sorry you were disappointed. We had some technical difficulties tonight."

The puffed-up man deflated in the face of an apology. He twiddled his thumbs and looked away, apparently unsure what to do with himself since the expected rebuttal didn't materialize.

"Yes, well . . ." He turned and strutted away.

"Hey!" TJ yelled after him. "She didn't promise you anything! That was only online conjecture—"

"Don't antagonize him," Jillian pleaded. "Please. I appreciate it but just let him go."

"That's the spirit," Sterling said. "One disappointed person won't sink the show."

"Except he wasn't just anyone," Jillian said. "He's the reviewer for the local paper. Been trying to get him to come see a show for over a year. If he'd been impressed and reviewed us well, we would've sold out shows the rest of the month. So naturally he came tonight and is unhappy. This place is doomed to sink like the Titanic. Come on. Let's go inside the auditorium."

As they moved inside for the investigation, Kimberly couldn't help but draw a parallel between her "pregnancy" online conjecture and the firestorm it could create. What if people responded in the same angry manner when their bubble of excitement was burst as this man had to the lack of expected "special effects?" Jillian couldn't exactly tell him the truth—that a real ghost had ambushed the show the previous night. As much as she preferred the truth, always and in all things, she was starting to see why Sterling sometimes skewed it to prevent diffi-cult situations. And perhaps he had the right idea, eventually claiming she'd lost the rumored pregnancy rather than coming clean and explaining it had all been a big misunderstanding. Maybe she'd get lucky and the whole thing would fizzle, dissi-pating into nothingness like the phantom story it was.

"I'm so sorry," she said to Jillian. "I wonder why Donny was so quiet tonight after last night's big show."

"Honestly, he probably realized his little temper tantrum could benefit me and laid low out of spite."

"What in the world caused such a rift between you two?"

Michael cleared his throat and drew one hand across his neck in a classic "cut" motion. "Kimmy, save it for the show, sweetie."

She shrugged at him, an overly exaggerated gesture accompanied by a hard stare.

He pursed his mouth and glowered right back at her.

Sterling scribbled away in his notebook. Everyone stared at him, but he wrote on, either completely or willfully oblivious.

Michael tossed his head. "Okay, Sterling, seriously. What's the deal with the notebook?"

Sterling glanced up and nodded. "I told you I'd share when I was ready—"

Michael held up a forefinger. "That's not—"

Sterling mimicked the gesture. "Didn't let me finish. Now I'm ready."

Michael pinched the bridge of his nose and waved at Sterling to continue.

"If we ever want to be taken seriously outside of the paranormal community, by which I mean the scientific community, we need evidence."

Every mouth in the room opened, the accompanying frowns and furrows made clear hot words were about to follow.

"Let me finish. Actual, quantifiable evidence. Elise handles the research, I get that. I'm taking notes during the investigation and then extrapolating correlations and anything I can run data on. I know what skeptics will say, how they'd try to attribute everything to trickery and graphics manipulation. But I know what we saw last night, and I immediately documented the stage the moment the play ended. Ian accompanied me, so I know he wasn't able to change or hide anything. No wires were attached to any of the props we'd just witnessed levitating across the stage. Furthermore, no fly rigging is currently in place for stage work like that."

"And no one in the wings to operate it," Ian reminded him.

"Exactly. But the lack of hardware is irrefutable."

"We know the way you guys think too," TJ said. "We've listened to it for years. You guys never admit you could be wrong. Never even consider maybe—"

"Hey," Sterling said. "I'm on your team now, and I'm trying to be open to new ideas."

TJ rolled his eyes. "They'll still argue it's fake."

"They will. I know. But we will put the raw footage out there and dare anyone to find evidence proving it's faked."

"You and your dares," TJ muttered.

"The last one worked out pretty well." He glanced at Kimberly. "But the data and the dare and challenging the beliefs will come later. The reason I'm sharing now is because I've noticed a correlation I think we need to act on immediately."

Sterling allowed his dramatic pause to stretch on too long. Kimberly saw Michael's antsy shuffling develop into impatient gestures.

"Well, what is it?" he demanded.

"You all know from the discussion at dinner that Kimberly has been coping with extreme fatigue and lack of energy this past week. She refers to this as her psychic energy—"

"It *is* her psychic energy," TJ snapped. "Once a skeptic, always a skeptic."

"I can feel her energy levels," Rosie pointed out. "No offense, Sterling, but I've been taking care of her for years. We all have. You can't just breeze in and decide you know better. I get that this is all new for you, but we know what we're doing."

"Besides," TJ grumbled, "her condition may well be your fault. Why weren't you more careful?"

Sterling raised an eyebrow and every head in the room swiveled toward her. To referee this match. How could she make a call when she loved them all, agreed with them all, and needed them all?

Only a few months ago, she would have sided with her crew and delighted in watching them turn on Sterling. But things had changed. She'd grown accustomed to his presence in every possible way. Her crew would assume she sided with him due to the romantic relationship that had blossomed between them. And sure, that absolutely factored into the equation. But from a practical standpoint, they should see how much value he added to the show. For that matter, last month they'd all been reminding her of his fresh new energy, their improved social media presence, and the significant uptick in ratings. Sterling infused new life into the show.

And he infused new life into her. She blushed as she recognized the literal interpretation of that. But figuratively, she'd pushed her personal life to the back burner, cold and stagnant, for years for this show. None of the others felt bound to the same rigorous devotion. Rosie went through men as fast as she could pick them up. Michael was more discreet, but she knew he dated, particularly during summer hiatuses when he vacationed in New York. Stan was married with a baby on the way. Everyone but her was free to do as they pleased.

They were all jealous. That was the problem.

She finally had someone in her life who welcomed the demands of the show—because he was already accustomed to living under the barrage of constant public attention and scrutiny. He could let it all roll off. She hadn't yet developed that ability, but he often stepped in between her and overwhelming crowds and was there to help and support.

He deserved the same.

She breathed out. "How great would it be though to have Sterling fight those battles for us for a change? Come on, every one of you until very recently lectured me on giving Sterling a chance, how great he'd be for the show and for me. Don't turn on him now."

Their faces all contorted, and she didn't waste her precious, finite energy trying to read the emotional state of the room. She knew jealousy spiked all their emotions. They needed to recognize it and let it go.

Only Jillian spoke. "Well. If I'd realized you're not the prim and proper goody two-shoes I assumed you were, I would've suggested we go get a drink and commiserate over our personal dramas."

She started to explain that she never drank while working, which meant she never drank, when the gravity of the statement hit her hard, knocking the air out of her lungs. Goody two-shoes? Prim and proper? That was the vibe she gave off? To such an extent Jillian considered her unapproachable and didn't think she could confide in her? She squared her shoulders. "That sounds great. Let's do it."

Michael pinched every muscle in his face. "Umm, do we think drinking is a good idea in our present condition?"

"Oh, one drink never hurt anyone." Jillian waved away the concern.

Before her crew could lob a barrage of counterarguments, Sterling intervened. "I still haven't arrived at the point I'm trying to make, and we have an investigation we need to get moving on. You're all so busy declaring how well you know Kimberly, how in tune you are with her needs and what's best for her. But has anyone else noticed Kimberly's energy appears to wane fastest when I'm not with her? And picks back up when I'm near her?"

Silence.

She remembered the little shivers of energy through her spine the past few days whenever Sterling rested a hand on her back. Especially when her energy had been drained. If that was true, if he was correct, what could possibly be causing that?

"Wait, what?" Rosie frowned. "What would that have to do with anything? I'm the one who hones and recharges her energy. How would you be impacting it?"

"I'm not saying I can explain it. And correlation does not

always equal causation. But I do see a statistically significant correlation. I suggest I remain beside her tonight rather than do my own thing, in case I am seeing a pattern."

"I'll be there too," Rosie insisted. "Ready to recharge as needed."

"Good." Sterling smiled. "She needs all the support she can get."

"I'm right here," Kimberly reminded them.

"Right where you're needed," Sterling said. "And we're all here for you."

Though she sometimes fondly remembered and longed for the quieter days, before her little side project the Albuquerque Paranormal Society got picked up and turned into *The Wantland Files*, she couldn't pretend this group of people surrounding her was anything but incredible. More people meant more opportunity for differing opinions and strife and drama and complications. But it also meant more connection and ideas and support.

She climbed onto the stage, all cameras pointed at her, and watched Michael count her in. This would be roughly the halfway point in the episode, coming back from commercial break. Time to recap what they knew so far.

"The Old Catholic Church is proving to be a difficult puzzle to piece together. Numerous ghostly residents have reached out to us, but the owner of the building remains certain that a previous member of the troupe, who passed away on this very stage, is responsible for the recent phenomena in the theatre."

She didn't like going into the evening investigation without all the cards in her hand. Jillian had been on the verge of divulging something critical. After their earlier conversation was interrupted, Michael deemed it the perfect opportunity to catch drama unfolding on camera. And she reluctantly agreed his point was valid. How often were they gifted with the chance to witness something like this unfolding organically while the cameras rolled?

She didn't like to gamble though. She preferred to know

exactly what she was dealing with and what to expect. Which was why she didn't like to include anyone outside her crew in an investigation. And here they were, bringing in Jillian to face off with her former . . . friend? Lover? She didn't know. And that didn't sit well.

But she didn't make decisions about the show in a vacuum and Michael had pressed for Jillian's inclusion. So here went nothing. "Jillian? Are you ready?" She gestured for the woman to join her.

Jillian looked like she was being summoned for a root canal. "This is ridiculous."

Kimberly noticed Michael brightened and squeezed his lips together to keep from smiling. Drama made good TV. Hopefully the truth would come spilling out tonight. This level of resentment indicated something big. Jillian had admitted only to being embarrassed and not wanting to discuss it. Embarrassed because in retrospect he was so much older than her and gross? Had he played her for a fool? How was Jillian going to feel if part of this intimate information about her life wound up used in the show and aired nationally? No one liked having their dirty laundry aired in public. Actually that wasn't true. Some people would share anything. But she understood Jillian's viewpoint and the desire to keep her personal life private. She hoped the gamble of bringing Jillian in tonight paid off. Fortunately, they could always edit out any material that didn't help the show.

"Jillian is joining us tonight to confront the spirit she believes remained behind to torment her. Let's find out why."

"And cut," Michael said.

"Remember I'm staying with Kimberly, so I won't branch out on my own," Sterling said.

"You don't ever help anyway," TJ replied. "What should I do Michael?"

"Can I hang around again?" Ian asked. Kimberly hadn't even seen him join them in the auditorium.

"I brought my entire travel support kit," Rosie said, holding up her psychic support person version of a doctor's little black bag. "Also, Lorenzo asked if he could watch but he promised not to get in the way. I said yes. Hope that's okay."

"I'm going to check the motion-activated cameras," Stan said.

Michael shook his head. "I feel like the master of ceremonies of a three-ring circus. You all know what to do, and what you should be doing, so let's do this." He clapped his hands.

All the lights in the theatre went out.

CHAPTER TWENTY-SEVEN

"I'M ASSUMING this old building isn't equipped with a clapper?" Michael asked.

"No," Jillian's voice replied from the darkness.

Everyone pulled cell phones and activated flashlight mode.

"I'll go look for a breaker box," Stan said. "See if a circuit got tripped."

Jillian gave him directions where to find it. He wasn't gone two minutes when he stuck his head back in the auditorium door. "Only the lights down here are out. The upper floors still have power. I'm betting it's a tripped breaker."

"We don't need lights to work," Kimberly pointed out. "Do we wait for Stan or go ahead and continue?"

"I think we should—" Michael began.

But Jillian forced their hand. "It's not a tripped breaker. Unless Donny tripped it. Right, Donny? You're still looking for ways to get my attention, aren't you? Well, you have it!"

The strings of black and orange Halloween lights flickered. Everyone with a hand-held camera hustled to focus and record the activity. They killed their cellphone flashlights, plunging the room back into darkness, their shrouded lanterns and covered flashlights offering just enough light to maneuver safely. The flickering lights cast eerie shadows that seemed to chase them through the space.

Kimberly heard the Audioxx hiss and knew Elise had powered it on. She wasn't sure she wanted that equipment competing with her. Actually, she was sure she didn't. Donny needed to come through her.

"Donny," she began. "Can you talk to us? We're here to help you. You can—"

"You want to have this out, Donny?" Jillian goaded. "Come on! Let's settle it once and for all!"

She moved closer to Jillian. From past experiences, she knew antagonizing spirits didn't tend to end well. "I typically let them come to me. Let's not provoke him unless—"

"Jillian."

She spun toward the voice but knew the electronic sound indicated the Audioxx performed her usual function of communicating with the dead. Grasping her quartz pendant, she tapped her indigo chakra and attempted to intervene. "Donny? Can you come to me?"

"I'm right here!" Jillian cried. "What do you want now?"

"Jillian, please. If you'd let me try to—"

"Pay."

Again, the Audioxx won out.

"Elise, can we turn that off, please?"

"But it's working!"

She was losing control of her own investigation. How could she compete with the cool new gizmo when it was clearly working and she was not? "Elise, please."

"You think I should pay?" Jillian shouted. "You think I owe you after everything you did? Everything you took?"

"Jillian . . . sorry . . . pay."

"Oh, I'm sorry, all right! Sorry I ever let you move in here. Sorry I let you—"

"Pay!"

His tone grew more intense, more insistent.

Jillian matched his intensity, ratcheting up several notches. "Even after you've died you can't leave me alone! Just go away!"

Kimberly gripped Jillian's arm. The woman's red chakra spun wildly, vivid proof Donny had tapped into fear, flipping the woman into survival mode. "Jillian, you have to stop. Your emotions are out of control. You'll only further energize and strengthen him."

As if to prove her point, the Audioxx roared. *"Jillian! Pay!"*

Allowing Jillian to join them had been a terrible idea. She should have voiced her concerns and prevented this from happening. Until she could connect and interpret the intent behind the words, perhaps tap into memories tying Donny to this world, they were like two people screaming at each other in different languages. And getting louder did not help with comprehension. In fact, it hindered, adding frustration and apprehension to the mix, triggering more shouting and anger, spiraling in a perpetual cycle that would lead nowhere.

"What the hell could I possibly owe you?" Jillian yelled. "What did I ever do but pay? You took and took and took and it was never enough. I'm sorry you died disappointed and bitter. I know you wanted more out of life. But you created your own problems, and I did everything I could to save you."

Whoa. Michael was getting his drama, but this shouting match was not resolving the haunting.

"Elise, please turn that—"

The lights flipped back on, searing all of their retinas and blinding them.

"Damn!" TJ yelled.

"Guess Stan found the breaker box," Michael said. "Poor timing. Someone turn those off—"

Light bulbs shattered, showering broken glass all over the stage and auditorium.

Plunged in darkness again, Kimberly gasped, little shards peppering her skin, the fallout settling onto her scalp.

Sterling's hand flew out to clutch her. "You okay?"

"Oh, my gawd," Michael said. "No one move. We do not need injury liability."

"Well, we can't just stand here forever," Sterling said. "Jillian, where would I find a broom?"

"There's a custodial closet out in the lobby."

The auditorium door opened, and Stan returned, flashlight beam cutting a swath in the gloom. "Sorry, guys. Wasn't a breaker after all. I checked and triple checked—"

"Stay there!" Michael yelled. "The lights came back on and then, I don't know, exploded or something. There's glass everywhere."

"We're wearing shoes," Sterling pointed out. "Stan and I can go grab brooms and clear the stage at least."

She sucked in a breath as Sterling left her side. Dependency on anyone went against her every core belief. And yet she couldn't deny the moment of panic that burst through her.

"I'll be right back," he promised.

Alone in the darkness, something brushed against her. Whispering voices enveloped her, but she could not make out individual words. It grew louder, more intense, grating against her ears, frustration building as she strained to understand.

She wrapped her hand around her quartz, closed her eyes, and breathed in deeply, pushing all other concerns to the backseat as she exhaled. Nothing else mattered right now. Focusing on her crown chakra, she tapped her psychic energy and opened herself to connection. "What is it, Donny? How can we help you?"

A fresh burst of whispers encouraged her to continue. No matter how hard she tried, she could not pick out a single voice from the swirling threads weaving in and out of the space around her. Something bumped her again, leaching away warmth with each insistent nudge. Her breath fogged in the cold vacuum the spirits left in their wake.

Her vision began to blur. No, that wasn't quite right. The gray darkness of the room around her and the little pockets of light from flashlights and lanterns fuzzed, breaking apart into shaky little bits, a blue haze bleeding through the fractured pieces.

She shook her head and blinked several times, trying to clear her vision. She didn't feel dizzy or lightheaded, and yet the bizarre phenomenon continued. Like the picture on a television screen if the signal is too weak, the room around her could not quite resolve into clear images. The murky haze tingled against her skin, whispering an invitation of its own in response to hers.

And yet none of the voices seemed to belong to Donny. He was clearly here. He had just made his presence known. Why wouldn't he connect with her? Or was the correct question why *couldn't* he connect with her?

A shrouded figure approached. She had no problem understanding why Kayla had been terrified of the figure she described as wearing a hood. But the form morphed into the nun she'd seen in the lobby. And where the other ephemeral beings drifted past her as if unaware or disinterested, the nun approached with apparent intent.

Hannah.

The word burst into her mind. The nun clutched a necklace or something in her hands, her mouth moving in silent prayer as her fingers crept along the string of beads. Kimberly didn't feel threatened by this manifestation but couldn't gain any information from her either. The missing little girl remained a strong enough concern that the nun couldn't cross over and leave this world behind.

"How? How do I help Hannah? I know you want me to help, but I don't know what I can do."

"*Hannah.*"

This time the supplication crackled from the Audioxx. That

stupid box. She told Elise to turn it off. She'd lost Donny somehow and now the nun pulled at her. Distractions and split focus were the last thing she needed.

And where was Sterling? Staying close by her side had been his idea to begin with. She could feel her energy draining away. The spirits around her siphoned it away like little vultures, no longer drifting past as if unaware of her. Her presence had caught their attention. Or perhaps more accurately, her energy.

Hannah.

"I hear you! I don't know what to do. I need more information."

Ugh. Like Jillian, she was allowing frustration to take over. Uncontrolled emotions did not help. She knew staying calm and focused was imperative. She wasn't accustomed to not understanding though.

More spirits pressed in on her, the weight of their consciences smothering her.

I never told her . . .

Please let him know . . .

I know now I was wrong . . .

Too many all at once. Bleeding her dry like leeches, they gorged on her energy, bloating their final thoughts and regrets, while rendering her a husk.

Not one of them felt or sounded like Donny or the nun. This was not helping. She tried to pull away, to extricate herself from the demanding spirits clawing at her mercilessly, desperate for release.

The light surrounding her glowed a gentle, pulsing blue, and yet she saw no stage, no seats—only the cerulean blue which thrummed to her heartbeat. The sound of her pulse quickened in her ears.

Where was Sterling? For that matter, where was Jillian, who only moments ago had been near enough to touch. None of her crew was in her field of vision.

Where was *she?*

No voices but those of the dead. No Audioxx crackled in competition, a sound she would have welcomed at this moment.

A laugh, deep and harsh, rang in her ears. The horrible sound tickled a memory, triggering the sense she knew the sound, had encountered it before. Yet the memory eluded her, like a dream not quite remembered after waking. Despite her inability to pinpoint the origin of that familiar and hideous laugh, she knew the owner of the voice took glee in her growing terror.

Her fight-or-flight response triggered, she was compelled to run. This was not something she could fight, especially not now. She should get off the stage, out of the auditorium completely if possible. As if nailed or superglued, her feet wouldn't budge. With all her energy focused on her right foot, she pulled with everything she had remaining in reserve.

The floor pulled back. She swore the boards warped, stuck to her foot. A viscous and vicious supernatural quicksand, it stretched as far as she pulled. And tugged back when she'd spent her last ounce of strength.

Evil laughter, the kind that delighted in misery and sorrow, filled her ears as the entity pressed closer. It wanted her. She didn't know why but didn't need to. She had to get away.

She pulled again, willing her feet to move. She swore she could feel hot breath as the monstrous thing bore down on her, yet she couldn't see it.

Fingers entwined in hers. *Sterling.* She knew intuitively and squeezed tightly.

The blue haze leeched away, yanking her back to reality and leaving her blinking in confusion.

Everyone gathered around her, watching intently.

Sterling's brow furrowed. "You know I don't like when you do that."

Her temples throbbed. She squeezed her head. "What did I do?"

"You looked gone. Nonresponsive."

"I . . . I saw something. Heard something."

Jillian squatted in front of her. "Was it Donny? That bastard—"

"No." She shook her head almost violently. "This was something . . . different than anything I've ever felt. Cold. Evil."

Rosie clutched her little black bag, digging through it for just the right tonic and oils. "Everyone, step back. Give her room to breathe."

"No, it's okay," she said, drinking in the familiar sight of her friends. Remembering the lost desolation of the wandering spirits, she shuddered. So often she longed for solitude. This moment, she'd never been so grateful for camaraderie.

She shivered. Something had been coming for her. What was it?

Rosie pressed a travel mug of tea into her hands. "Here. Drink. I suspected we might need this."

While she sipped the soothing, rejuvenating decoction, Rosie held both hands over her, reading her spectrum, recharging her depleted energy store.

Sterling ran a hand over her back, comforting with slow circles, sending little jolts of energy sparking through her, more invigorating than Rosie's tea. Nothing could rid her of the chill that horrible laugh had filled her with, however.

Her crew had swept the floor and brushed and vacuumed as much lightbulb debris as possible from the surfaces. Stan switched off the little hand-held dust vac.

The Audioxx hissed and popped. *Cave. Key. Cave. Key. Hannah.*

Jillian stood from the chair she had sunk into, watching Kimberly like she might disappear. "What does that mean?"

Kimberly leaned forward, her energy partially restored from Rosie's reiki and Sterling's touch. "I saw the nun while I was . . . connected. I think she wants me to find Hannah's remains. I'm not sure what cave and key mean." And she didn't trust herself to reach out and seek the answer. Not with that shadowy specter nearby, potentially waiting to pounce. She shivered.

Movement above them drew her gaze up. "Is someone in the apartment?" A quick glance answered her question. Everyone in her crew was all here. Her heartbeat kicked up a notch at the thought the dark thing may have found her. More movement and sound convinced her someone was up there. Maybe not anyone living, but someone.

"*Jillian.*" The Audioxx's harsh, electronic voice demanded attention.

"Oh, not again. What do you want Donny?" Jillian spoke through gritted teeth.

Kimberly tried to stand up but remained woozy. Sterling rested a hand on her back, offering support. Another little burst of energy sizzled along her spine. An image of the apartment flashed in her mind, along with an urgent desire to go upstairs.

"I think Donny wants us to go upstairs to the apartment," she said.

"*Yes.*" A short burst of sound confirmed her suspicion.

"Well done, Kimmy," Michael said. "Can you tell why?"

Before she could answer, the Audioxx crackled again. "*Key.*"

"Key?" Michael asked. "Is the apartment the key to the mystery?"

"*Key.*"

The image of a small key appeared in her mind. "I think it's a literal key."

"To what?" Michael asked.

"*Cave.*"

"The key to a cave? That makes no sense," Michael said.

"Well, you are interpolating staticky noise produced by a box spewing out random sounds and trying to distinguish words in it," Sterling reminded them. "Are you really surprised it makes no sense?"

Michael didn't respond to him. "Kimmy? Can you interpret?"

She closed her eyes and hesitantly reached out but was met

only with silence. "I'm not getting anything else." Was Donny refusing to connect? Or unable to connect?

"He's fixated on Jillian," Michael said. "One might say obsessed. Jillian, you dated the guy. Did he ever mention—"

"Whoa! I'm sorry. What? Dated him? Eww no. He was my brother."

Brother? Well, there was something else she got wrong this week.

CHAPTER TWENTY-EIGHT

IN THEIR DEFENSE, Jillian never mentioned Donny was her brother. This only proved Kimberly's fervent belief that withholding critical information hindered the investigation. Still, she did think her crew rather overreacted.

"Your brother?" TJ practically yelled.

"All this time and you never thought that might be an important thing for us to know?" Michael asked.

Jillian shivered and made a *blech* noise, followed by gagging. "How could you possibly think I dated him? Even if he wasn't my brother, he's much older and he's . . . just no. Gross. Gross, gross, gross."

"How were we supposed to know? You didn't tell us. And you don't even have the same last name."

"I retained my ex-husband's last name. All my stage and television appearances were associated with it. But regardless, Donny used a stage name. He used it nearly his entire life."

"A stage name? I've never heard of Donny Bannister. I do know *your* work," Michael said.

Kimberly detected a frosty nip in the air. The ends of her hair lifted as a current swirled around her. "Careful, Michael. I think you're offending him."

"What? I haven't heard of him. Is he having trouble accepting the truth?"

Jillian scoffed. "Donny always had trouble accepting the truth. And was consumed with jealousy. Always."

The swirling current intensified. Kimberly's breath formed a little cloud as she spoke. "Seriously, Michael. He's upset."

"Oh, we wouldn't want to upset Donny," Jillian said. "It's not their fault you never hit it big, Donny. They haven't heard of you because you called yourself an actor but never put the work in. You didn't get parts because you never studied the craft. But instead of working harder, you preferred to jealously cut down and ridicule anyone who did."

Kimberly's ears detected a pounding heartbeat which grew louder as Jillian continued.

"I know. You were furious I succeeded where you failed. But it wasn't my fault. How dare you think I owe you anything!"

The Halloween lights blinked orange and black, pulsating along with the heartbeat.

"Jillian, maybe this isn't the best—"

"He left home for New York when I was still in middle school. I didn't even know him that well but remember adoring him. He was my big brother. I thought he was the coolest. And he was heading off to a big city to be a famous actor."

The chilly air continued to cloud her breath, but the intensity of the swirling settled. The heartbeat no longer battered her ears but pounded in a softer *lub-dub*.

"My parents worried, of course. The life of an artist is never easy. But they wanted Donny to achieve his dream. We all did."

The string of lights dulled to a low glow.

"By the time I was in high school, he had developed a terrible drug habit. Our parents tried to keep it from my younger sister and me, but we overheard them. Any time we heard from Donny, he was in trouble. Mom and Dad always bailed him out, so he never suffered any real consequences. Dad would fly off to New York and nurse him back to health, then drag him to a facility for help. My college fund went to his stints in rehab, over and over, one place after another. And yet he always fell back into his bad habits. They threw good money after bad, nearly bankrupted themselves. They'd planned to travel during retirement but of course, Donny's issues overshadowed everything. Decades of squandering money. None of this helped his career hopes—he couldn't hold an entry-level desk job, much less land a coveted part in a play. Much less a film."

"This would have been really useful to know from the moment we arrived," Michael said.

Kimberly agreed but remained quiet, hoping to maintain the tenuous connection she had established with Donny. She felt his demeanor calming, felt the icy anger transitioning to embarrassment, a dismal darkness overshadowing the righteous indignity that had dominated only moments ago.

"Would you want people to know he was your brother? He made the news sometimes, but only for drunk driving or crazed rants in the throes of manic episodes when he was high. Well, Dad had a stroke, died suddenly. Mom held on a couple more years but followed not long after. Any inheritance we might have seen he'd blown through long ago. I have always been left to take care of myself and handle everything on my own because Donny needed everyone's attention. And who did he come crawling to once Mom and Dad were gone? Me, of course. He said he had to get out of New York. He had gotten into trouble with the mob or a gang or something. Or so he said. I was here in Hannibal, tending to our sister who had cancer. I wasn't leaving her, but I told him if he could get himself down here, he could stay in the apartment upstairs. Then of course, he was thrilled with my little theatre project and thought he should star in every show. The troupe called him a jerk. Said he wanted attention. Always demanding the spotlight. They don't know the half of it."

Well. That certainly changed things.

"And your nephew? Does he . . ."

"No. Isn't that horrible? My sister was even younger than I

was when Donny left. She barely knew him at all. And when he moved here, she was sick. Donny was never one to care for or nurture. He didn't even go see her. We decided it was best if Cory not know him."

The atmosphere of the room had turned brittle and sour. The pungent odor of grief and remorse stung Kimberly's nose. Though everyone shifted uncomfortably, the strained relationship and the sad waste of potential affecting them all, she knew the majority of the discomfort bled from Donny's spirit, winding through the room like a caustic vapor.

"And somehow he still thinks I owe him? After everything he put us through, he wants me to pay? Wants me to be sorry?"

Kimberly struggled to maintain the tenuous connection with Donny. Rosie continued to push energy to her chakras. Sterling ran a hand up and down her back, firing up her spine and electrifying her senses. She closed her eyes and reached out, encouraging Donny to stay with them. Resolution was close, she could feel it.

The Audioxx rustled, then whispered, *"Jillian."* The desolate sound pulled at her heart, Donny's residual emotions as vivid as her own.

"He's sorry, Jillian. I can feel it." Confidence in her ability to confirm motivation felt so good.

"You can feel it? I can't. If he's sorry, why doesn't he say that instead of telling me to pay?"

Good question. "Donny, can you tell Jillian you're sorry?" That sounded like she spoke to a toddler. Ugh. She'd tell them to edit that line out. At least she was connected and moving the investigation along. Finally.

Ebullience at the successful spiritual connection lasted only fleetingly. Donny drifted away. She closed her eyes and focused, redoubling her effort to hang onto him.

When she opened her eyes, blue haze clouded her vision again. Staticky images of set pieces and auditorium seats blurred and faded, coming in and out of focus.

Spirits hovered around her, faceless entities with no destination. Except one slouched figure that she spotted drifting away from her. Donny. She knew it was him.

She fought the urge to shove aside the idle spirits. The wasted efforts would only expend precious energy and risk setting off a feeding frenzy with her presence. Since they'd returned to a static state, she didn't want to upset it in her impatience to catch Donny. She also feared drawing the attention of that horrific spirit again.

The blue tint and sudden reappearance of so many spirits confused her, but this wasn't the time to sift through possibilities. Right now, she needed to catch Donny and figure out what he'd been trying to tell them. The Audioxx might have allowed him to vocalize, but it didn't help communicate what was wrong. That was up to her. And while her psychic abilities were working, she needed to take advantage.

She turned to follow Donny, but her feet wouldn't move. Again? Reaching for Sterling, she couldn't find his hand. One glance confirmed he was no longer by her side. Again. Neither was Rosie. In fact, no one else shared the auditorium with her but the spirits.

Gulping down panic, she attempted to reassure herself she wasn't as alone as she seemed. How could she be? She'd only closed her eyes for a moment. Her crew couldn't have walked away two steps, much less left the room entirely. Her perception had changed, however. They were close, but she couldn't see them.

She opened and closed her eyes several times, hoping to switch back to the reality where her friends remained. Nothing changed. She couldn't blink her crew back into existence or blink herself back to where she belonged.

The auditorium warped around her, the floor pitching sideways to a nausea-inducing slant as if she'd stumbled into a funhouse. The walls skewed at odd angles and seemed to breathe, bowing and retracting as she struggled to stay on her feet.

Where was she?

She opened her mouth and called, "Hello?" Though she produced only a feeble whisper on a gasp of air, her booming voice bounced around the room, echoing off the still-seething walls.

Had she tumbled into an alternate reality?

And then she felt that dark, menacing presence. And it felt her. Malicious glee filled the presence, whatever it was, and somehow she knew it delighted in finding her again. And moved closer. She didn't want to connect with this. Shouldn't connect with this. She knew it inherently.

He was back. He found her again. Her stomach lurched and her blood turned to ice in her veins. She couldn't see anyone other than the zombie-like spirits beginning to notice her.

With another lurch of her stomach, she realized this place, this experience, reminded her of something. But how could that be? She couldn't—

A nudge against her back sent her sprawling onto the stage floor. An actual wood floor that did not twist or buckle or pull at her to inhibit movement. Her crew gathered around as she coughed and struggled to get her bearings. She could see them again though.

Sterling pulled her to a sitting position. "What happened? You looked like you fell asleep on your feet."

"I was . . . I couldn't see any of you. The room turned blue and . . . weird." She held her head in her hands. She felt sick and woozy.

Rosie grabbed a bottle of lemon essential oil, took one hand, and began gently massaging her skin with the invigorating oil. "I'm worried about you, girl."

"Me too," she admitted.

"Think maybe you fell asleep?" Michael asked. "And then fell over?"

She shook her head. "Someone pushed me."

"We were looking right at you when you fell," Sterling said.

"No one was near you, sweetie." Michael sounded more concerned than he had in a long time.

"I felt it. My back. Someone pushed my back."

Rosie paused rubbing her hands. "I'm sure you felt something, but nobody was there."

She breathed deeply and kept her eyes focused on the wooden stage to avoid the concerned looks shared among her crew. First she couldn't connect with spirits like normal, now she zoned out on them while lost in a spirit realm. What must they be thinking about her?

Why was she getting pulled into the spirit realm? Crossing over like that normally required extensive preparation and concentration. When she'd rescued Faith from the Nightshade during the last investigation, she made sure her crew was alert and ready to support her and would anchor her to the living world. She should not be able to slide back and forth across the barrier like this, with no effort and no control. As she thought about it, she couldn't think of any other explanation for what had been happening to her this week.

Worst of all, every sojourn into the Nightshade opened the possibility she would become lost there forever, unable to return. Without an anchor in place, the risk was real. And terrifying.

Movement above them distracted her from the thoughts flying threw her mind.

"TJ, can you focus the FLIR on the apartment? I think Donny has gone up there. Do you see anything?"

"Actually, yes. I'm seeing a shadow!"

"He seems to be beckoning us to follow. Let's see if we can figure out what the key is." She got to her feet and headed for the secret passageway. The unsettling concerns about the spirit realm would have to wait.

"Hold up." Sterling grabbed her arm and gently held her back. "I think maybe you need to stop for the night. We don't know what just happened, and I don't like it. I'm worried about your health."

She nodded and offered as much smile as she could manage. "I know. You're always worried about my health." He tried to interrupt but she continued. "I'm not saying it's unwarranted. Something does seem to be off this time. But we have a ghost trying to tell me something, so can you please help me to the apartment?"

"I don't like it," Sterling repeated. "I don't like seeing you like this, but I've come to realize you are the best judge of your current state. If you're sure it isn't medical, I'll believe you."

"It isn't medical. This is all related to my psychic energy." That was as much as she knew for sure. Once this investigation ended, she could focus on herself for a bit and hopefully pinpoint the elusive issue. How he would react to her claims she was crossing uncontrollably into the spirit realm was another issue.

He held out a hand. "Up we go then. I'll be right behind you."

"We're all here, Kimmy," Michael assured her.

They crept up the creaking staircase, TJ in front with the FLIR and Stan bringing up the rear, recording everything as it unfolded. Sterling remained directly behind her, step by step, so close she felt the heat from his body.

The apartment sat still and empty when they emerged into the space, dust motes gliding through the lights from the cameras the only thing that moved.

"Where did he go?" TJ asked. "Nothing on the FLIR now."

Michael spanned the room in a few steps. "KII stable. No spikes. Anyone feel any cold spots I'm missing?"

Kimberly could no longer detect a presence either. *Come on. Why bring us up here? What did you want to tell us?* They were close, she could feel it. "I don't know. But I'm sure he was directing us to follow him—"

Something scraped in the room, a strange, grinding noise. She spun around.

Everyone in the cramped space turned toward the sound, which seemed to originate in the corner where a small desk sat.

Kimberly moved closer, listening intently, open to any communication from the spirit realm.

One of the desk drawers was open.

She squatted for a closer look. "Was this always open like this?"

Michael knelt beside her for a closer look. "I don't know. I didn't ever look specifically at the desk when we were in here."

"Jillian, when was the last time someone was up here?"

"Not since Donny got his own place and moved out. At least to my knowledge. I suppose someone could've come up here without me knowing."

Sterling hunkered down next. "How many people know about the secret passageway, though? Not just anyone could slide up here without being noticed, could they?"

Elise brought a flashlight to assist with inspecting the tiny drawer. Kimberly pushed against the rough wood with one finger, nudging it closed, then slid it open an inch.

"That's it!" TJ said. "That's the noise we heard!"

"It snags," she said. "The track isn't smooth. Here, Sterling, you try it."

Sterling actually had to jiggle the drawer a bit to convince it to close and open again. "I will agree that this does not seem like something that simply slid open of its own accord or due to gravity or any other natural force acting upon it. Elise, could I see the flashlight?"

He shone the beam all around the desk and the drawer, then ran a hand over all the edges of the desktop.

"Anything?" Kimberly asked.

"No wires or fishing line or similar apparatus."

Once he'd completed his inspection, she opened the drawer again and peered inside. "It's empty. Another false lead."

"Seriously?" Stan asked. "I thought we'd found something for sure."

"Now what?" Jillian asked.

She shook her head, not sure if she wanted to laugh or cry. "I honestly don't know."

Sterling knelt in front of the drawer. He pulled the drawer as far as it would go then juggled and manipulated it until it disengaged from the track. He removed it completely and turned it over.

Something struck the floor with a metallic ping. He lifted the item in his fingers. "I believe you said we are looking for a key?"

CHAPTER TWENTY-NINE

KIMBERLY ACCEPTED the key from Sterling and inspected it carefully. She'd never seen anything quite like it—small, gold, but discolored from age. She held it out for Jillian to see.

"No idea. I've never seen it before."

"Could Donny have left it here?"

"He didn't say anything to me if he did."

"Is it a safe deposit box key?" Sterling said.

Jillian scoffed. "If it's a safe deposit box key, then there's no way it belonged to Donny. That would imply he had something of value he needed to protect. He didn't."

"That you know of," Michael said. "Maybe he—"

"Maybe he returned with a small fortune he needed to hide from the mob and lived like he was penniless to his dying day so they couldn't track him down? Maybe he opted to live in this building the city keeps threatening to tear down and bumming free meals whenever he could and subsisting on a couple hundred dollars' worth of food stamps every month because he was rolling in cash? I guess we'll never know." Jillian took a deep breath as if the diatribe drained her. The woman buried her face in her hands and broke into tears.

"Yikes," Elise muttered.

"Big yikes," TJ amended.

Jillian composed herself. "I know I sound like a bitter old woman to you guys, but . . ."

"But he hurt you badly." Kimberly, no stranger to unresolved family issues that would probably remain that way, patted Jillian's back and attempted to soothe her emotions. She couldn't detect any energy activation or transfer and Jillian appeared equally distraught—which only seemed to confirm her fear that her abilities were slowly fading. "I understand. I'll do everything I possibly can to help you through this."

Jillian took her hand and squeezed. "Thank you."

"Where's the nearest bank with safe deposit boxes?" Michael asked.

"How would I know?" Jillian asked. "I told you I'm broke as a joke. I have nothing valuable and will be lucky to even get my money back out of this place."

"I'll look it up!" Elise said. "First thing tomorrow I'll—"

"Here, I've got it," Sterling said, the glow of his cell phone illuminating his face. "Not far. Here in town. They open at ten tomorrow."

Elise clicked her tongue, clearly annoyed. "I do the research."

"This was a Google search, not research," Sterling said. "It's beneath you."

"Google search falls under research. It's in the word research!"

"Who cares where it is?" Jillian asked. "Haven't you been listening? Donny was even worse off than I am. I mean, I could theoretically lock up some old jewelry of mine for safekeeping. Sentimental value, not monetary, but I'd be devastated if I lost it. He literally had nothing."

"TJ," Sterling said, "note the correct usage of the word 'literally' and file away for—"

"Oh, come on, dude! We finally made a breakthrough."

"Not according to Jillian."

"You have to go see what the key opens," Michael said.

"Why would I waste my time?"

Michael shook his head, mouth hanging open slightly. "Aren't you the *least* bit curious what's in the box?" His tone conveyed he was dying to know.

"Nope. That could be someone's lost key he picked up off the ground, hoping he might pilfer the contents. Why else would he leave it when he moved out?"

"She has a point," Sterling said. "That makes sense."

"Well, I want to know," Michael said, his voice rising.

Uh-oh. She recognized that tone. The key had piqued his curiosity and he was worse than a dog worrying a bone once he detected intrigue.

"Michael, let's—"

"You *have* to figure out what that key leads to. At least for the show."

"I'm telling you it's a waste of time. And I don't want to let him have the last laugh. He probably hung around to make me look like an idiot one last time. I won't give him the satisfaction."

"But . . . We . . ." Michael floundered, looking for someone to take his side.

"You know what?" Jillian said. "You guys tried. I get it. This isn't your typical case. We can call it good."

Call it good? Was she being dismissed?

"Jillian, every case presents unique challenges. Don't give up. Let me help you. And help Donny. Please. I've caught glimpses of spirits who never let go and moved on. It's devastating to see."

Jillian heaved a sigh. "I just want to put this behind me."

Michael saw an opening and went for it. "And now we have this clue. At least see if it means something."

They stood in silence for a moment waiting for Jillian to respond.

When she didn't, Michael tried another approach. "Kimmy, see if you get something from the key! Then we'll know if it's important or junk."

Oh no. She might not get anything from the key even if it was important. But she couldn't admit that on the show. They could edit things however they wanted to, but she could not bring herself to say the words in front of a camera.

She pressed the key between her palms and closed her eyes, hoping against hope that something would come to her, some little twinge or jolt or whisper.

Nothing.

I've never pretended. Her words came back to haunt her, taunting her with her former arrogance, content in her abilities, never guessing she might struggle with maintaining them.

"Kimmy?"

She took a deep breath and grasped her crystal, squeezing the little key in one fist. *Come on. Is the key important? Talk to me.*

More nothing.

Should she pretend? Was she actually considering faking psychic visions? Faking a connection? No one would know but her. She could claim the key was important at least to placate Michael. She had to do this. For the good of the show. And if it came down to it, she might need to pretend to help Donny move on as well. She ignored her stomach squirming with repugnance that she was doing this and took a deep breath. "I—"

"Fine," Jillian relented. "I dragged you down here. We'll do it your way. But remember, I warned you."

"Yes!" Michael said, jumping up and down and clapping.

Yes. Thank goodness. Kimberly sighed in relief, saved from pretending on her own show. A slight gust lifted the ends of her hair as something whispered past her.

"*Where's my spotlight?*" The voice seemed to come from the secret passageway.

She looked around, analyzing each face for signs of a joke. No one was absent from the group and everyone stared at her like, *What?*

"Kimmy, you have that look on your face," Michael said. "You either just farted and hope nobody notices or you're sensing something."

"Michael! Don't be gross!" She noticed that Ian laughed, however, and realized why her best friend was showing off.

"Well, I don't smell anything, so I assume—"

"*Where's my spotlight?*" The voice was fainter this time as though moving away from her.

She jumped to her feet and ran downstairs into the auditorium.

And came face to face with the nun, full apparition in her habit.

"*Hannah.*"

"I know! I know!" she told the nun. "One thing at a time."

"*Where's my spotlight?*"

"Donny! Is it the key? What are you trying to tell us?"

"*Where's my spotlight?*" The question repeated again and again, ricocheting off the walls and battering against her, mocking her inability to deduce the solution.

She sensed the spirit gliding around the room as the intensity of his insistent voice increased. Then silence.

He was gone.

***

STERLING OPENED the door to their hotel room. Kimberly followed him, tingling at the thought of curling up beside him and falling asleep nestled in his arms. How about that—she shared a room with a man and the world had kept turning and the internet didn't break. Exhausted didn't begin to describe what she felt. Broken was more like it.

And yet, one glance from him started her heart pounding.

"You want in the bathroom first?"

He always offered. Always. Why had she thought sharing a space would impinge on her time in any way? He was too thoughtful. He could anticipate what she needed and make sure it happened. The relationship, the togetherness, was still too new for her to be in the bathroom with him at the same time. She'd been on her own too long. And that didn't seem to bother him. She appreciated that he allowed them to move at the pace she was comfortable with.

He sat at the little desk and took out his notebook. "I need to look over some notes anyway, so take your time."

She stared at him, this surprising man who had fallen into her life and made himself at home—and whom she now didn't want to leave. Ever. Just a couple of days ago she'd been contemplating how perfect everything was, how good she'd felt. Now nothing was going well with the investigation. She had no idea why her psychic senses were muddled and was terrified they might never return to normal. Everything had seemed perfect. Too perfect, apparently.

But Sterling, with his dark eyes and mischievous grin, remained steady. He was here for her no matter what.

Instead of taking him up on dibs on the bathroom, she moved beside him, compelled to be near, and brushed aside the lock of hair that always managed to flop over his forehead.

He turned his gaze up to her, his eyebrows scrunched. "What? No shower?"

"I should. I need to wash my makeup off. My face will break out if I don't." She glanced at the clock and cringed. Three in the morning. She really should hop to it. The sooner she rinsed off and got into pajamas, the sooner she could climb into bed—and snuggle into Sterling's warmth.

He nodded, having learned her habits. "Right."

She should go wash up. She really should. His unruly hair kept flopping back over his forehead no matter how many times she pushed it back. Giving up on the stubborn lock, she ran her fingers through his hair.

He lifted an eyebrow, somehow frowning in confusion but smiling in delight at the same time. "What about your shower? Don't you want to get cleaned up?"

She answered by dropping low for a kiss, the need for his soft lips on hers outweighing the concern for her complexion.

He grabbed her hips and pulled her into his lap. His hands ran up her back, massaging gently, finding all the tight little muscles and coaxing them to relax. When he finished kneading her neck, his fingers dove into her hair, until he grabbed her head and deepened the kiss.

His orange chakra was on fire for her, resonating to the point it pulsed and throbbed. Hers responded in kind, swelling with growing desire, thrumming as he ran his tongue down her neck.

"Now or never, woman," he murmured against her skin. "If you still want that shower . . ."

"Only if you're in it with me." She yanked his shirt over his head and paused a moment to savor his rippling muscles tightening in response to her. His abs glistened with a developing sheen of sweat—he always sweated when he wanted her, a quirk that delighted her. His biceps tensed as he tightened his grip.

He sucked in a breath before he answered, his voice low and husky. "Shower with you? Yes, please."

They stumbled across the room, unwilling to separate for even the few steps to the bathroom. Kimberly glanced away just long enough to turn the water on, then returned to Sterling, opening her mouth to explore his tongue.

He pulled away and lifted her blouse. Goosebumps erupted on her skin in response to the caress of his fingertips.

"I'm glad you're here," she murmured. "I don't know what I'd do without you."

"I am also glad I'm here." His lopsided smirk played across his lips.

"I'm scared," she confided.

His smirk disappeared, brow furrowing in concern. "Scared? Of me?"

She squeezed closer to him. "No. No not of you. Not even of the relationship. I thought it would be a difficult adjustment. But it hasn't been."

He pushed a loose wisp of hair behind her ear. "What's scaring you then?"

"Something is wrong with me. My psychic abilities are . . . off. I don't even know how to explain it. This has never happened before. Ever. And I don't know what's happening or why or if there's a way to fix it or . . ." She stared at him helplessly. "What will happen to me, to the show, if this doesn't get better?"

He cupped her face in his hands, his dark eyes burning with an entirely different intensity. "Listen to me. Whatever you're experiencing, we will face it together. And if there's a way to fix it, I will make it happen. Whatever it takes."

He kissed her long and hard. And she believed this man would, in fact, do anything for her. She led him into shower, allowing the hot water to sluice over their exhausted muscles. Pressed against the entire length of his body, she reveled in the warmth of his skin and allowed herself to give in completely to his demanding kisses. The taut muscles of his arms held her vertical when her legs wobbled, her breath short. A slight dizziness not entirely attributable to exhaustion muddled her thoughts. He took her breath away, a new sensation, something she'd never experienced before.

His entire body began to quiver. "Maybe we can finish up in here and move to the bed?"

She nodded and swiped cleanser over her face, perfunctorily removing her makeup.

As they toweled dry, Sterling ducked his head and looked at her from hooded eyes.

"What is it?" She'd never see him look so shy.

"Tonight, do you think maybe . . . could you do that thing with the energy?"

She sucked in a breath, not sure she had enough charge to boost their nocturnal activities with a spine-tingling jolt. But she was sure that if she could, even if it was her last drop of energy, she would fulfill his request. "Just tell me when."

CHAPTER THIRTY

THE NEXT DAY, Kimberly sat with Michael and Rosie in a booth at the Tom Sawyer Diner, the waitress far more agreeable than the woman who waited on them when they had dinner here.

"Well, this is like the old days, isn't it?" Michael asked. "When was the last time we sat down at a table just the three of us?"

Kimberly thought for a moment. "It would have been last season. Before Sterling joined us."

"This is much quieter. Of course, the old, old days is even before that. Way back when it was just the two of us." Michael grinned at her. "The Albuquerque Paranormal Society against the world."

"I loved that," she agreed with him. "But I like where we are now."

Michael clutched his chest in exaggerated shock. "What? No more pining away for the good ol' days? What's happened to you?"

"I realized how much I like my crew. And how much I'd miss Sterling."

Rosie heaved a giant sigh.

"Yeah," Kimberly agreed. Sterling had left earlier to drop

Lorenzo at the airport. Lorenzo needed to get back to his home and job and ghost tours in Eureka Springs. "I miss him already."

"At least he's coming right back. Lorenzo is flying home and who knows when I'll see him again."

Kimberly grabbed Rosie's hand and squeezed. "I'm sorry. Look at us. What happened? We used to be two single ladies, footloose and fancy free—"

"Well, one of you was looser than the other," Michael said.

"Hey!" Rosie punched his arm. "You're not wrong. But that was still rude."

"Someone needs to be the voice of reason in Sterling's absence," Michael said. "And I'd like to point out you weren't happy single either. I was forced to listen to your whining about not being able to hold onto a guy, wondering what was wrong with you, bemoaning your persistent single status. Now you have Lorenzo and I have to listen to you complain about having a guy. What's the deal?"

"I'm not complaining about Lorenzo," Rosie said. "How could I? He's an Italian god."

"Mmmm, would we really call him a god?" Michael asked.

"He's a tall, dark, and handsome scoop of yumminess. And he's so good to me."

Michael shrugged. "He is good to you. And beauty is in the eye of the beholder, so . . ."

"But the distance thing is gonna kill me." Rosie heaved another sigh. "How long can we maintain it? He has a life in Eureka Springs. We don't know how long the show will last. I mean, it could be another ten or fifteen years, God willing. And Lorenzo is gonna just wait around all that time?"

She pulled Rosie into a hug. "If it's meant to be—"

"Yeah, yeah. If it's meant to be, it'll work out. But what guy will be satisfied with a long-distance relationship that long? Phone calls and the occasional weekend here and there? For years? I'm not all that."

Kimberly and Michael spoke over one another in their rush to disagree.

"You *are* all that!"

"Any guy would be lucky to have you!"

"You guys are the best friends in the world, and I love ya. But I know better. I'm just a basic hairstylist who got lucky and happened to cut Kimberly Wantland's hair before she got her own show and got famous."

"You do so much more than cut my hair," she reminded her best friend. "You keep me looking good and manage my psychic health. I'm lucky to have you!"

Rosie could not be cheered. "Every show gets canceled eventually. And then what? I want to go back to Albuquerque, and Lorenzo wants to stay in Eureka Springs. It's hopeless."

"I thought you were thinking about retiring to Eureka Springs with Lorenzo." A rush of relief shot through her. Perhaps her best friend had second thoughts about uprooting her life.

"That was infatuated Rosie talking. You know how I get with a new guy."

"I do. What was the name of that guy you were going to move to Alaska with? That was not long after I met you."

"Ugh. Robert. Gross."

"You hate snow!"

"And cold! What was I thinking?" Rosie shook her head. "No crazy schemes since you brought me on this show though. You guys keep me grounded."

"Ehhhh." Kimberly wobbled a hand in front of her best friend.

Michael curled his lip and wrinkled his nose. "*This* is grounded?"

"Grounded for me. And you know it, Kimberly, so stop giving me that. You heard all about my former flames and the fiascos that ensued. Glad this show lasted longer than *Spook-Busters*, that's for sure."

"What about *SpookBusters*?" Sterling slid into the booth beside her.

"We're glad we lasted longer," Rosie said, then quickly added, "We're sorry you got cancelled though!"

"I'm not." He picked up Kimberly's fork and helped himself to a bite of fruit from her plate. "Otherwise I wouldn't be here." He swallowed and pecked her with a quick kiss.

She looked at him hopefully. He caught the look, his face clouded, and he shook his head.

Damn. She'd really hoped for good news.

"What was that look?" Michael demanded.

Kimberly blew out a breath. "I'll tell you later."

Rosie lifted an eyebrow at Michael. "What about you? You the lone holdout single or are you and Ian . . ."

She rarely saw Michael blush, but he fought a grin and his cheeks turned crimson. He quivered with excitement.

"Tell us already before your head explodes!" Rosie said.

"I think we're a thing. I mean, I know he's a little younger than me, but it's not too much, is it?"

"It's not the age that'll get you," Rosie espoused. "It's the distance."

"I told him he could use my place in New York anytime he wants, if he wanted to go see a show or maybe even audition for something. But he said he wouldn't want to be there if I wasn't."

"Awww." Kimberly delighted in seeing Michael swoon. About time. While his relationships never got as crazy as Rosie's, somehow they never seemed to last long. Maybe he'd found someone he could get serious with.

Michael looked to her for approval. "That's sweet, right?"

"So sweet."

"You barely know this guy!" Rosie seemed like the wrong person for relationship advice, but Kimberly bit her tongue. "You never offered to let me use your place in New York!"

"Well, I didn't know you'd want to! How would I know that?"

"Hello! I grew up in the Bronx!"

Sterling frowned. "I thought you were from Albuquerque."

"Long story." Rosie waved a hand. "Actually not that long. My mom is from the Bronx, Puerto Rican descent. My dad is from New Mexico, Native American and Hispanic roots. They met in New York, where I was born and grew up. Where'd you think I got this accent from? As soon as I finished cosmetology certification, I moved to Los Angeles thinking I'd work on movies. Meanwhile my parents missed family and relocated to New Mexico to be near Dad's family and closer to me in LA. When my film career didn't pan out and I got sick of waiting tables, I moved to Albuquerque to be close to family again. Got a job at a salon there. And one day some lady named Kimberly Wantland booked an appointment with me, nervous but excited as heck about helping some college girl with a ghost in her apartment. She needed to look good for the camera of course, and we started visiting, and I was absolutely fascinated by the—"

Michael held his watch in front of Rosie's face. "I thought you said this wasn't a long story."

"And the rest is history," Rosie finished.

"I like that story," Kimberly said, remembering her early days as a paranormal investigator. "I don't mind hearing it. But seriously, Michael. Ian. You're sure? What about long term?" She wasn't sure she could handle both of her best friends dealing with one crisis after another related to relationships. She stood by her belief that they were messy and complicated and difficult. Then she squeezed Sterling's hand, realizing how lucky she was to have someone who traveled with her.

"He says he's willing to go wherever I am. No strong ties anywhere. His parents . . . Well, he's not close to his parents."

Rosie sighed wistfully, staring into her coffee mug. "I wonder if Lorenzo would be willing to move to New Mexico with me someday."

Kimberly glanced at Sterling.

"Actually, Kimberly had me offer him a job on the show when I drove him to the airport."

Rosie's jaw dropped. "Are you kidding me?"

"Hang on. Don't hug me yet." Her heart broke for her friend. "Apparently he turned it down."

"What?"

"He's happy where he is," Sterling said. "He really likes you, but—"

"But not enough," Rosie finished.

"He's set in his ways, that's all. It's him, not you."

Rosie laughed, a short, sad sound. "Ha. It's always him, not me. Except I'm starting to think it's really me."

"He didn't break it off," Sterling pointed out.

"But what future do we have if we want lives in different places? Why didn't I listen to my mom and join an order of nuns? I could be in a convent right now."

"Come on," Kimberly said. "You know you'd hate that."

Rosie's head dropped and Kimberly knew she was fighting tears. She'd consoled Rosie after disastrous relationships went down in flames for years. But this one hurt, she knew. She'd really thought maybe this could've been the one.

She looked to Michael, who shrugged and shook his head. "What time are we meeting Jillian at the bank? I think Rosie and I need to—"

"No. I'm fine." Rosie wiped her cheeks. "We need to get you ready for the shoot, not waste time on me and my latest failure."

"You're not a failure! I won't let you run yourself down. You are amazing, and you don't need a guy to validate that."

Michael watched the dejected Rosie and appeared unsure what to do. His features twisted into his "eww face" and he looked at her for suggestions. When she shook her head, he tried another approach. "So, Kimmy, thoughts on the show? What's the deal this week? You've been out of sorts."

Oh great. His diversion tactic might help with Rosie but now she had to figure out what to say. "I don't really know what exactly . . ." She looked to Sterling.

He took her hand and held it between both of his. "Go ahead and tell them."

Michael's eyes widened. "Oh my God what? Tell me what?"

Rosie's head snapped up and her hands covered her mouth. "Oh my God, are you actually pregnant?"

She held her hands up and waved them as though erasing all their concerns. "Nothing like that. No. At least, I'm pretty sure that's a no." *Breathe in. Breathe out. They can handle this. Maybe they can even help.* "Something is wrong with my psychic senses." There. She'd said it.

Michael cocked his head. "What do you mean wrong with? You mentioned being tired and not feeling well, but—"

"It's worse than that."

"Why didn't you say something?" Rosie asked.

"Because I don't even know what's wrong, much less how to fix it. I thought maybe it would fix itself. But I've been sliding in and out of the spirit realm and I have no control over it at the moment."

"That's . . . not good," Michael said. "What do you mean spirit realm?"

"I think I might be getting pulled into the Nightshade."

"Without even trying?" Rosie asked.

"Right." The looks on their faces told her clearly that they understood the gravity of the situation.

"The place you brought Faith back from last episode?" Sterling asked. "You know, I need to follow up on the analysis of that goo Faith was covered with when you came back with her."

"Ectoplasm," Kimberly said. "If you want to sound more science-y than goo."

He sighed. "Except of course that ectoplasm has no basis in science. I'd like to know where the lab is in that analysis."

"You haven't been covered in ectoplasm," Michael pointed out.

"I've only been sliding in and out. And only my spirit, not my body. No way for a coating to form."

"A coating?" Sterling asked.

"Like an oyster covers a grain of sand. The human body is a foreign object in the Nightshade. We don't belong there."

"Then why do you travel to it?" Sterling asked.

"I only traveled there once intentionally and that was to bring back Faith. I open portals into it when I assist in spiritual translocation. But I normally don't cross over. This week, I've been pulled into it spiritually without realizing it. In fact, I only just started to suspect that's what was happening last night."

"What would cause that, Kimmy?"

"I have no idea. But it's scaring me. What if I get pulled in but then can't come back?"

Sterling curled an arm around her and held her close. "We won't let that happen. I'm your anchor, right? I keep you here."

"That's the idea." She smiled her gratitude. "But something is happening that I don't understand and have no control over. What if I drift over during my sleep and never wake up? No one would know what happened to me."

Michael glanced at his watch. "And on that terrifying note, we need to leave to meet Jillian."

The waitress returned with a waffle, heaped with fruit and whipped cream and placed it on the table.

"Umm, we didn't order that," Michael said. "And I need the check."

"Compliments of the gentleman," the waitress said, nodding across the diner. "For the lovely lady."

Sterling scowled and shot a look over his shoulder. "The lovely lady is taken. Of all the nerve!"

"No, not for Kimberly. For her." The woman tipped her head at Rosie.

They turned and spotted a gentleman lifting his coffee cup at them, a hopeful grin on his face.

Rosie wiggled her fingers in return. "Well, hello, Tall, Dark, and Handsome. Being single does have its perks."

"Well, that was a quick recovery." Michael accepted the check and shook his head. "Don't dally."

Kimberly snagged a whipped-cream-covered strawberry from the plate and gave Rosie the look. "Keep it quick. Main focus is the investigation. We need to see what that key unlocks."

CHAPTER THIRTY-ONE

THE POOR TELLER behind the desk looked horrified as the entire *Wantland Files* crew paraded into the bank behind Jillian, cameras capturing every moment.

The woman's eyes darted from one person to the next. Apparently the sight of the cameras terrified her. "I'll get my manager," she mumbled.

Jillian shook her head and slapped the key onto the counter. "Not necessary. I just need to know if this key belongs to one of your safe deposit boxes. That's it."

"All these people?" The woman looked again and this time her gaze landed on Kimberly, and she clutched her hands together at her chest. "Kimberly Wantland? And Sterling? Is our building haunted?"

"No," Jillian said. "Mine is. And we're trying to decide if a ghost left this key for me. Well, before he was a ghost."

"Oh. Okay." The young woman looked at the key only a moment. "That's not one of our safe deposit box keys."

Jillian gave them all an I-told-you-so look. "Not a surprise. Thank you."

Kimberly stepped forward and stood at Jillian's elbow. "You're certain?"

Rapid nodding preceded the woman's response. "Yes. I've helped people with their boxes before. Our keys definitely don't look like that."

This was turning out to be a dead end after all. Kimberly turned to Michael, silently asking, *What next?*

"I think I know what it is, though," the woman said. "That could be to a storage unit down the street. I kept some things there when I first moved here."

"That makes sense," Sterling said. "A storage unit could be easier to access than a safe deposit box. Let's try that."

Jillian muttered, "Yeah, and you were so sure it went to a bank box." But she left with them and seemed willing to try again.

They drove to the storage facility, as it was too far to easily walk, particularly in a short amount of time. Kimberly hopped into the i8 with Sterling.

He pulled into traffic and cleared his throat. "You know, I had an idea to share with you."

She nudged him when he didn't continue. "Normally you just tell me what it is. Go ahead."

"Don't laugh."

"When have I ever laughed at you? It's normally the other way around."

"Everyone has been talking about what will happen when the show ends—"

"I don't like to even think about that."

"It's inevitable though. And I've been thinking . . . Have you thought about opening a school for gifted children?"

She turned and gave him a once-over, searching for the smirk or other tell that would tip her off this was a joke. He appeared utterly sincere. "A school? What's brought this change about? You're admitting you think I have psychic abilities?"

His head wobbled as he seemed to weigh his words carefully. "I think there is more to this universe than meets the eye. Not unlike an excellent illusion. But I'm trying to keep an open mind.

And in the time I've known you, you've encountered at least two children who seemed to have different abilities."

"That's true."

"And maybe instead of growing up in the mainstream schools, misunderstood and ridiculed, maybe they'd thrive in an environment with other children like them, surrounded by adults who would understand and help them."

"Like Professor X's school for the gifted?" She kept it light, teasing him, so overwhelmed by his suggestion she didn't know how else to react. It wasn't that long ago he scoffed at her at every turn, determined to prove her a fake.

He laughed with her. "Well, we won't suggest our students are mutants, that's for sure."

"*Our* students?"

"Well, yeah. I thought we could open it together. In Albuquerque, so you'd be home."

"What about you?" She remembered him sharing that his parents were gone, but she'd never brought it up or asked about it. "Your . . . your parents are gone?"

His brow furrowed and he nodded. "They were on the older side when they had me. Waited to have kids but then had trouble, I guess. I was all they got. Dad's health took a turn, then Mom's a couple years later."

"I'm so sorry."

"I wasn't as young as you when you lost your mom. That had to be worse. At least I was an adult. Never easy to be orphaned though."

"No, of course not. Rosie told me . . . they gave you a trust fund?"

"Yes. And then of course I inherited everything when Mom passed. I'd gladly give it all away if it meant I could have them back." He squeezed his eyes tight for a moment.

She rested a hand on his. "It's just not fair."

"No. But no one ever told me life was fair."

"True." Why was she born with this gift? What was she

supposed to do with it? Why did her mother die so young, leaving her to figure everything out alone? Nothing was fair. She waited a moment, watching historic old homes pass by her window. "I guess you're not worried about living close to family?" She glanced sideways, waiting for his reaction.

"Don't have any to live close to. Think I might give Albuquerque a try." He smiled at her, his eyes burning for her. "It holds a pretty strong appeal for me."

She never was witty or quick with a comeback. Before she could think of anything clever, he'd pulled into the parking lot of the storage facility. She left that comment hanging and circled back to the original topic. "Well, a school sounds very complicated. But I like the idea of offering an option to kids who could benefit from it. Maybe we could offer a summer camp and see how that goes. I'll think about it."

The assembled crew once again startled the person behind the counter, this time a young man who appeared barely out of high school, if he even was.

Jillian presented the key and her ID and said nothing else.

The boy typed the keyboard of his computer. "How can I help you, Ms. Olson? Are you closing the account?"

"She has a storage unit here?" Michael asked.

The boy frowned. "Yes?"

Jillian blinked. "Can you remind me of the number?"

"It's a small unit. But it's only paid for a couple more weeks. You'll need to extend the agreement or close it."

"I'll check to see what's left inside and then decide."

"Cool." The boy gave them the unit number and directions to find it.

As they wound through the facility, Jillian commented, "Okay, I'm actually intrigued. What in the world could Donny have left? He put the account in my name so he must have meant for me to have it."

When they found the correct unit, Kimberly stood in front of the locked door and spoke into Stan's camera. "Donny left a key for his sister Jillian to find. Has he been speaking to her from beyond, trying to ensure she discover the key and lead her here? We're about to find out."

Stan and TJ swung their cameras to face Jillian, capturing the moment.

Jillian hesitated. "This could be a bunch of junk. Or nothing at all."

"We'll never know until you open it," Michael said, gesturing to the lock.

Jillian took a deep breath, inserted the key into the lock, and twisted it. Sterling helped her raise the door.

The small space echoed, empty but for a table smack in the center of the room. An envelope lay on the table.

Jillian lifted the envelope and withdrew a piece of paper. After staring at it, she dropped it, a scowl clouding her face. "I told you this would be a waste of time!"

"What is it?" Kimberly asked, pressing forward.

"Garbage! It's a piece of wrinkled-up paper with an X on it."

Kimberly picked up the paper, noting the grit it left on her fingers. "Why is it so filthy?"

Sterling examined it. "The paper isn't that old. But it looks like someone intentionally distressed it to make it seem old."

"There's an X on it?" Michael asked. "Is it a map?"

"It's not anything but Donny's sick idea of a joke or . . . No, that's it. I can't think of anything else it could be. The bastard is laughing in his grave right now, I'm sure."

"It does have something else on it." Sterling shone his cell phone flashlight on the paper. "Correct me if I'm wrong, but I think this is a map of the cave system."

Kimberly picked up the envelope and peered inside. Another, smaller slip of paper had escaped Jillian's attention. She extracted it and read, "It's got to be done or there ain't no style about it. Blame it. Where's the fun in a thing if it's got no style?" She looked at Jillian. "What does he mean?"

"I think it means he was losing his mind. What else would it mean?"

Elise flipped pages in her notebook. "Hold on. Ian said Donny was a big Mark Twain fan. That he performed as a Mark Twain impersonator and loved his writing. I recognize those lines. He's referencing Tom Sawyer, paraphrasing from *The Adventures of Tom Sawyer*."

"Why?"

Elise took the paper and scrutinized it. "Sterling is right. This is meant to resemble a map, I believe."

"But . . . why?"

"I think we're meant . . . to go on a treasure hunt."

"I don't remember a treasure map from *Tom Sawyer*. The boys just went around digging."

"But Donny apparently wants to do this 'with style.' Hence he left a map."

Sterling looked at her, concern in his eyes. "Looks like we're going back in the caves."

CHAPTER THIRTY-TWO

DESPITE BRINGING a jacket to the caves this time, Kimberly shivered. The idea of going back inside terrified her. She knew her crew would do everything they possibly could to keep her safe. But if she lost control of her abilities, or worse if a spirit took over and pulled her into the Nightshade as she feared was happening, every one of them would be helpless to stop it. And no one could bring her back if she got lost.

Her gift had always branded her as different, left her an outcast. Other kids in school considered her too weird to befriend. Not anymore. Loneliness no longer plagued her. She spent her days surrounded by crew and often by more strangers than she'd like on the street. But this was something else entirely. She'd never felt so alone. She didn't belong anywhere, couldn't connect to others like herself. Her friends would listen and commiserate. But they couldn't understand. No one else understood what she went through. Even the people close to her who believed in her abilities had no true understanding of what it meant or the weight she carried. She had no one to turn to or guide her. She was completely on her own as she struggled to figure out what was happening to her.

What if she couldn't figure it out?

Sterling had spoken with the owners of the cave system. Either the thrill of being on television or Sterling's inherent charm—or both—had convinced them to allow the crew and their cameras into the caves after hours. They would be accompanied by a guide, of course, to ensure they inflicted no damage. And she'd had no problem agreeing to that. She didn't want to cause any problems or damage the iconic caverns. She wanted to follow Donny's map, determine if it actually led to anything or was a final joke as Jillian continued to insist, and get the heck out of there.

Something in this cave had exerted control over her before, and once was enough as far as she was concerned.

Standing in front of the cave entrance as they prepared to delve inside, she stood still as Rosie touched up her face.

"You're a little shiny, girl. Makes you look nervous."

She *was* nervous. She couldn't show fear though and smiled through the anxiety as Rosie tucked an errant lock of hair behind her ear.

Michael counted her in, and she began. "We're following what could be a wild goose chase according to Jillian, who believes her brother intended one final joke at her expense. Will we find anything? Does X mark the spot? Or perhaps playing out this final prank will allow Donny the resolution he seeks and enable him to move on and rest in peace. Let's see what we find."

Jillian rolled her eyes. "If he moves on, maybe *I* can finally have some peace."

Stan and TJ recorded as they moved into the dim light of the cave. Elise carried her digital recorder. Michael held the KII, monitoring the temperature of the environment, which unsurprisingly dropped inside the dank, enclosed space.

Kimberly swore she heard the faint sound of water dripping, slow but methodic, in the distance. Without the benefit of a noisy group of excited tourists, the space seemed smaller and tighter. Eerier. Their steps echoed in the silence.

Their guide held the map, Elise close at his elbow as if she didn't trust him to read it correctly. The crew followed along, equipment ready just in case but mostly to record what happened.

Normally, Kimberly took the lead in an investigation and following didn't sit well with her, underscoring the gnawing worry she was losing her psychic prowess. A coil of anxiety, tightened by general helplessness, twisted in the pit of her stomach, ready to spring at the slightest provocation.

They retraced their steps from the tour. When the group reached Jesse James' Hideout, their guide stopped. He scrutinized the map, turning it a few times, then looked about as if to get his bearings. Finally, he nodded. "This is it."

Michael looked around. "This is what? I don't see anything. This is on the tour. We could have found this ourselves."

Elise took the map. "Let me see that." Their researcher traced the landmarks, nodding as she verified each, then came to the X herself. "He's right. Jesse James' hideout is the X."

All heads turned in Kimberly's direction.

"Don't look at me. He did this while he was alive. Nothing paranormal about it. My part was to connect and help find the key he left behind."

Everyone shifted to stare at Sterling.

"Oh. Wasn't expecting this to fall to me." He scrubbed at the back of his neck.

"Ms. Wantland is right though," TJ said. "No ghost left this. He was alive when he—"

"I get it," Sterling said. "Let me think."

"If he really wanted us to find something, he could've left a better map," Michael grumbled.

Sterling stared over Elise's shoulder. "Anything more specific on there or . . ."

Elise tipped the map so he could see it easily. "No. Just . . . here." She waved a hand in the vicinity.

Sterling tipped his head at a cavernous space labeled as the gunman's hideout. "May I veer off the path?"

"I will have to come with you, but yes," the guide said. "Don't touch the walls and watch your step."

Kimberly watched them pick their path gingerly. No sooner did they turn a corner out of sight than Sterling called, "We found something!"

She and her crew clustered around the opening.

"What is it?" Michael called.

"Another envelope!" Sterling said.

Over his shoulder Michael asked, "Stan, TJ, you have the shot to catch his return?"

"I'll focus on him and zoom on the envelope," Stan said. "Teej, can you get some wide shots and also focus on Kimberly's reaction?"

"On it," TJ answered.

"The guide is inspecting it," Sterling said. "He's verifying no historical value before we move it."

"It's not old," the guide called, his loud voice echoing through the cavern. "Whatever it is, someone snuck it in recently without being seen. Somehow." The guide sounded like he held himself personally accountable for the assault on the cave.

"I can't believe they actually found something," Jillian said. "Although sneaking around and hiding things and breaking rules sounds completely on brand for Donny."

The two men turned the corner, Sterling holding the envelope aloft for everyone to see, huge smile across his face. "Who wants it?"

Michael accepted the paper and inspected the writing on the front. "It's labeled 'Jillian.' Clearly intended for you."

Jillian accepted the envelope and stared at it. "I don't know what to do with this."

Kimberly thought tears misted the woman's eyes but couldn't be certain in the low light.

"Open it!" Michael said, immediately echoed by every member of the crew.

Jillian flipped it over but hesitated, finger poised above the sealed edge.

Kimberly rested a hand on the woman's shoulder and felt the conflict churning within her. "I know. I understand. But it will be okay."

With a nod, Jillian ripped the envelope open and extracted the paper within it. "Dear Jillian, If you're reading this, I'm gone. I know I've been a terrible brother. You've always been there for me and it's my turn to be there for you, albeit only returning a fraction of what I owe you. This is the login information for my CryptoBase account. I hid money there before I left New York, but rest assured all my debts were settled before I fled. The balance is yours, whatever it may be. I only hope you can accept this and find it in your heart to forgive me. As Mark Twain said, 'Forgiveness is the fragrance that the violet sheds on the heel that has crushed it.' Be well, Jillian, and be happy."

Remorse spun off of Jillian in great waves. Kimberly squeezed her arm. "He wanted you to find peace."

Jillian swiped at her cheek and nodded. "I didn't need his money. I wanted . . . If only he'd talked to me while he was still here. This sounds like he knew his days were limited."

"Admitting fault and saying sorry can be some of the most difficult things to say."

"He didn't technically say he's sorry," Jillian pointed out.

"He is," Kimberly assured her. "That's the entire reason he stayed behind. He needs your forgiveness before he can rest easy."

"He left a lot of years of anguish in his wake." Jillian shook her head. "I'm not sure this erases all of that."

"Crypto, huh?" Michael said. "That's a pretty volatile investment. It's been all over the place lately."

"Depends where he invested it and how much he invested," Sterling said. "Will be interesting to see what exactly the balance is."

Elise adjusted her glasses. "That isn't actually a Mark Twain quote. Commonly misattributed to him, but not—"

"Elise," Michael said. "He made his point. Let it go."

Sterling drifted to Kimberly's side and whispered in her ear. "There we go. Another mystery unraveled. And we kept your concerns mostly secret. For once I got to play a role in the big ending. No psychic powers required."

"I did connect long enough to find the key," she reminded him. She'd still been integral to the investigation, even if the ending wasn't what she would have scripted. And he was right. This allowed her to keep her concerns to herself a bit longer while she attempted to sort out what exactly was causing them. And hopefully fix it.

A tremor of anxiety quivered through her stomach, sending her pulse hammering. As anxiety thrummed through her nervous system, a pulling sensation tugged at her, coaxing her farther into the caves. Her feet propelled her as if she had no control over them.

Oh no. It was happening again.

CHAPTER THIRTY-THREE

THE PULLING SENSATION INTENSIFIED. Kimberly's stomach fell and flipped upside down as if she dropped suddenly on a park ride that simulated weightlessness. Her feet remained on the ground yet part of her seemed to float away.

A spirit demanded her attention and tugged her psyche in tow whether she wanted to oblige or not. In her current, weakened state, she did not.

The world around her glitched, staticky blue lines fizzing in bursts, obscuring the cave walls. Her feet plodded along as a feeling of dread consumed her. *The Nightshade.*

It was happening again, this dim, hazy otherworld seeping in, attempting to replace her real world. She heard her crew call to her, felt hands attempt to stop her mindless trek forward. But the sounds were distorted and grainy, the touch distant as though a wall of gelatin separated them, obscured by the crackling and shifting. The world appeared to be breaking apart around her. Nothing mattered anymore.

The single thought, *This is my last chance*, obliterated all else, buzzing like a brilliant neon sign in a landscape of sheer nothing.

Last chance.

Last chance.

This did not, however, refer to a last stop for fuel or snacks on a lonesome highway. This was a last-ditch effort by a desperate soul to escape an eternity of oblivion.

Realizing this insistent tug equated to an SOS beacon sent out by a lost spirit did not assuage Kimberly's all-consuming anxiety. She threw her hands to the sides like a newborn thrust into a cold, foreign world and groped the clammy cave walls, rough and bumpy yet somehow worn smooth too.

Must get out.

Complete darkness consumed her. Her oil lamp had long ago burned out. Kimberly shook her head, knowing full well she'd never carried an oil lamp in her life, and tried to synchronize this with her current absolute certainty that she had been carrying a lamp moments ago. The candle pieces she'd carried as an emergency backup had dripped rivulets of melted wax over her hands until they'd burned out completely. Her fingers still hurt where each dribble had seared her skin with a jolt of pain, then dried quickly, as though sealing her doom.

She was living the last moments of the spirit's life, retracing its steps. Though she'd extended no invitation, a spirit had grabbed her and connected. Why was this happening?

Hoarse from screaming for help, her throat burned, shredded vocal cords no longer able to produce a sound. She wept silent tears.

The realization no one would hear her and that she was going to die here produced fresh tears, which washed tracks down her dusty cheeks. So much dust. No water.

A cough wracked her frame, every muscle on fire.

Mama would be inconsolable. Gone were the imagined scenes of showering Mama and Papa with gold pieces and solving their money problems, imagined fancy new frocks for Mama and her sisters replaced with black mourning and deep wailing.

Why had she thought she could do this? She should have stayed with the other children.

She stumbled and fell and crawled. The walls scraped against her arms as the passageway grew narrower. Until she could go no farther. Her cracked lips opened to gasp ragged breaths into her lungs, dry as parchment, aching for air. She couldn't breathe. She clawed at her throat.

Her necklace. Mama gave it to her. She groped the floor. Where had it fallen? Where was it?

Kimberly's fingers raked at the stones and debris beside her —and looped around a delicate chain. She lifted it and held it in front of her, straining to see in the pitch black. This was important. She was meant to find it. She knew that without knowing why.

Disoriented, she blinked hard and tried to turn around in the narrow passageway she'd wedged herself into.

How did I get here?

The utter darkness left her panicky and breathless until she forced herself to calm down. *Breathe in. Breathe out. They won't leave you behind.*

Certain she spotted a light in the distance, and hoping against hope it wasn't wishful thinking, she relaxed a bit. All she needed to do was go toward the light and she'd find her friends and get the heck out of this creepy cave.

But something tugged again at her psyche. She couldn't leave yet. The necklace.

She fished her cellphone out of a pocket and activated the flashlight.

A tiny gold cross graced the delicate necklace.

The same small cross she'd seen in a vision at the Old Catholic Church.

Someone needed her help, and this cross was the key. As badly as she wanted to leave, she couldn't go just yet.

Last chance, echoed through her mind.

She closed her eyes and tightened her fist around the pendant.

Who are you? How can I help?

She waited for an answer from beyond. Nothing happened. Her energy felt low again, drained, though she hadn't needed to tap into her reserves for any reason up to this point. Why couldn't she send out her usual beacon, her guiding light to draw spirits toward her? And how could she share energy if she was depleted? Something was wrong.

The hairs on her arms stood on end. Her skin crackled with ozone, an electric charge sizzling through the air around her. She detected a whiff of sulfur drifting by on a current.

A current? The air here was still. Stagnant even. Where would a current come from?

She opened her eyes. Hazy blue tinted her surroundings, emanating from a fissure, a crack not in the rock of the walls but directly in front of her, in the air.

A fracture in the membrane separating the living world from the Nightshade, neither here nor there, a limbo of lost souls.

The figure of a young girl stood in the crack, arm outstretched toward her. The girl's eyes seemed to plead for help.

Without thinking, Kimberly reached through the opening to take the girl's hand and gasped at the cold, electric pulse that shot through her. A whooshing filled her ears and time seemed to slow, almost as if she found herself underwater. Though no water surrounded her, she didn't know how else to describe the odd sensation that overtook her, muting all of her senses and pressing in on her.

She jerked, retracting her arm from the opening, holding fast to the girl's hand, yanking her through.

The crack snapped shut behind the ephemeral girl. Kimberly's ears popped, as though a sudden change in pressure had released her. The girl hovered in front of her, reaching for the necklace. When Kimberly held it toward the figure, the girl closed her hand around the cross pendant. The necklace glowed blue and seemed to absorb the light cast off the ghostly figure.

The girl faded, the necklace pulsed with bright light, then everything went dark again.

Left alone, unsure what had happened, and completely enervated, Kimberly leaned against the cavern wall. She slumped down the wall until she sat, propping herself up with a hand.

Whatever her hand connected with moved, shifted and clattered at her touch. She lit up her cell phone again and shone a light—

A skeleton. A pile of bones curled on the ground beside her, the small hands still tucked under the little skull. The skeleton of a child. Most likely a little girl.

Find her bones. May she rest in peace.

When she heard faint voices calling her name, she rallied her last reserves to push on, retracing her steps back toward the main pathway. She picked up her pace when the light in the distance grew stronger, the voices louder.

"I'm here!" she rasped, her voice rattling in her oddly sore throat.

Beams of light sliced through the darkness, blinding her as they slammed into her retinas. She continued to crawl forward until hands reached into the gap, grabbed her by the arms, and pulled her free. She fell against Sterling, allowing his strong arms to envelope and warm her.

"What happened? I turned around and you were gone."

Rosie and Michael clutched her hands and fussed over her. Everyone spoke at once. She couldn't understand a word. She sought the tour guide and motioned him close. The chatter quieted as she spoke to him, her voice barely a whisper. "I found bones. A skeleton. Remains of a lost soul, most likely a child."

Her crew gaped at her. "A skeleton?"

"I think it's Hannah."

Sterling lifted her arm, staring at the hand clutching the necklace. "What did you manage to get into? Your hand is covered with goo. But the rest of you is filthy, smudged with dust. This almost looks like—"

"I know. It is." She knew what it was but had no idea how to explain it. Her body shook with repressed tears.

"What is it?" Sterling asked. "What's wrong?"

She let go and sobbed openly. "I don't know what's happening to me. I'm scared."

CHAPTER THIRTY-FOUR

Kimberly held out the gold cross necklace for her crew to examine. Her hand shook slightly, causing the little pendant to quiver.

"So you low-key stole this from the cave?" Michael asked. "You know it's a crime to remove anything from a national monument, right?"

"I didn't chisel out a piece of rock from the cave," she said. Michael always exaggerated. "Or deface it in any way. This wasn't part of the cave."

She had brought them back to the cemetery, to Hannah's empty grave. The cave tour guide had alerted the authorities and the skeleton would be removed and analyzed. Eventually the skeletal remains could reside in the empty grave. But Kimberly knew Hannah's necklace now held her spirit, which wanted to return to her mother's side.

Stan focused his camera on her. She spoke to the camera lens. "Though we came to Hannibal to investigate the Old Catholic Church for Jillian, we discovered another spirit in need of our help. I repeatedly saw the manifestation of a nun, who urged me to find Hannah. Elise, can you remind us what you found out about the girl?"

Her researcher pushed her glasses up her nose and referred to her notebook. "Hannah Atkinson disappeared from the group of youngsters picnicking before their First Communion. Her body was never found, her mysterious disappearance never solved."

Kimberly filled in the missing pieces. "I discovered Hannah's remains in the caves when her spirit called to me and led me to them. Through our spiritual connection, I learned Hannah entered the cave system alone, hoping to find a fabled lost treasure the other children talked about around the group's campfire. Shortly before she left this world, Hannah discovered she'd lost this necklace given to her by her mother. Distraught, her spirit has wandered in the Nightshade, unable to translocate to the next world until she resolved this. Finally, we can lay Hannah to rest."

Standing over the grave, she cupped the necklace in her hands. "Hannah, you've roamed alone too long. It's time for you to rest at your mother's side."

Sterling dug a hole beside the rudimentary tombstone.

As Kimberly settled the piece of jewelry into the indentation, wind soughed through the surrounding trees, rippling the leaves, as if nature applauded the repair of the spiritual world. A breeze lifted Kimberly's hair and brushed against her cheek.

Hannah. The name sighed past her ear, content relief releasing nearly two centuries of pent-up grief. The wind shifted. *Thank you.*

Kimberly swore she heard a giggle and brushed a tear from her cheek. This, this was what it was all about. The long sleepless nights, the constant travel that kept her from home, from a normal life. These moments made it all worth it.

She wasn't normal, though, and she knew that. And in this moment, she'd never been more thankful to be unusual. Her psychic gift enabled her to help lost souls. She was meant to do this.

What would become of her if she lost her abilities? Nonbelievers would think nothing of it, arguing she didn't have anything special to lose. But her sixth sense made up a large piece of her identity. Show or no show, celebrity or not, she'd been connecting to spirits nearly as long as she could remember. She'd helped spirits find their way to peace since well before her show cemented her in popular culture. And she would keep right on assisting lost spirits until her dying day.

Unless she lost her sixth sense. Which to her would be similar to another person losing their sight or hearing. If she couldn't see and hear spirits, she didn't know what to do with herself. She needed help. She needed to figure out what was happening to her and how to stop it from getting worse.

And if she couldn't . . . She couldn't even consider that.

"Kimmy?" Michael broke her train of thought. "You okay?"

Sterling curved an arm around her shoulders. "Go ahead and tell them."

"Tell us what?" Michael asked.

She took a deep breath. "I brought Hannah back from the Nightshade. She was stuck in the in-between, and I brought her back here before she passed on."

"How is that possible?" Michael asked. "Are you sure?"

"I don't know. She was stuck in the caves but also in the Nightshade. She couldn't cross alone."

"That's never happened before. You're sure?"

"Very sure."

Sterling squeezed her. "The sample of the gelatinous compound I took from Kimberly's hand after she got lost in the cave appears to match the material we took from Faith at the last investigation. I'm waiting for formal lab results, but they appear identical at first observation."

Michael's eyes widened. "Ectoplasm?"

Rosie stepped closer. "How did you travel to the Nightshade with no support?"

"I've been sensing the spirit realm around me, like I'm getting pulled in and not able to control it. But this time a portal opened. I saw Hannah's spirit. She wanted me to bring her back from the Nightshade, I could feel it. I reached in and—"

Rosie grabbed her by the shoulders. "You reached into a portal? You crossed the spirit barrier? You shouldn't be able to do that. Why would you risk it?"

"I didn't think. I saw her there, alone and just . . . reached for her. I don't know how it opened. I didn't do anything to create the rift. It simply opened."

"What if you'd been pulled in instead of the other way around?" Rosie demanded. "What if you got lost and couldn't find your way back? You'd wander the spirit world forever."

Sterling frowned. "I thought you said the Nightshade was a spirit realm, not for living people. And you said you need an anchor anytime you open a portal to make sure you don't get pulled in."

"Yes, I know. None of this was intentional. That's why I said I feel like I'm losing control. My psychic energy feels weakened, and yet I keep getting pulled into the spirit realm and somehow this portal opened."

Rosie clicked her tongue. "And you reached into it. That was risky."

Sterling shook his head. "I don't know what to think about any of this. It's too much for me. But I do know you had an unrecognizable viscous substance on your hand again. And your coworkers seem to think you're putting yourself in danger. I don't like it."

Michael frowned. "Kimmy, maybe you need to step away—"

"No. Absolutely not. I can't stop the investigations. This is exactly why I didn't want to tell anyone what was happening."

Rosie rested a hand on her shoulder. "But you're not well. If you were sick, we'd make sure you saw a doctor and got the care you needed."

"This isn't the same," she insisted.

"Isn't it?" Rosie lifted her eyebrows.

"No doctor will know how to begin to approach this. They'll assume I have a mental psychosis."

"Not your primary care physician," Rosie said, "but maybe we can find a specialist who can help. We do have an investigation in New Orleans coming up."

"What does that have to do with anything?" Sterling asked. "Maybe she needs to rest."

"You think exhaustion caused me to excrete ooze from my pores?" She nudged Sterling with an elbow. "I love ya, but psychic problems aren't exactly in your wheelhouse."

"No, but your health means everything to me. Maybe we should at least consider a pregnancy test. We can't put you at risk in any way if you're expecting a little one."

Rosie's eyes glazed over, her voice dreamy. "A little Kimberly or Sterling. How adorable would that be?"

Kimberly looked at Sterling. "And what would you do the first time your little girl told you she'd seen a ghost? Heard a voice no one else could hear?"

His forehead wrinkled. "If that happened, I'd learn to deal with it, just like I have with you. Whoever our daughter turns out to be, I would love her."

Well. She hadn't expected that response and fought tears. Why hadn't her father taken that approach? How different could life have been if he had? But she wasn't pregnant, she reminded herself, surprised at the twinge of disappointment she felt. "I maintain that I'm not pregnant, so you don't need to worry about it."

"If you're not, I still have no choice but to worry about you. Whatever might be causing it."

Elise scratched her pencil across the notebook she always carried. "I'll start looking into possible avenues to pursue in New Orleans. Maybe we can find—"

"A witch doctor?" Sterling asked. "No quacks. I won't let some con man anywhere near her."

"I was thinking more along the lines of alternative medicine,"

Elise said. "Can you trust us that we want the best for Ms. Want-land too?"

Rosie hugged her. "I'm sorry, girl. I feel like I've done something wrong. It's my job to keep you well and your sixth sense honed. I've failed somehow."

"Using your illness analogy, you can't keep me from catching a cold."

"But I can help you get well again. Anything you need. Tea. Elderberry. Elise can help me research the best healing herbs for the psyche."

"On it!" Elise scribbled more notes.

Michael blew out a long breath. "Didn't see this coming. But we will figure it out together. We're all here for you, Kimmy."

"Thank you. You're all the best." What would she do without them?

Michael glanced at this watch. "We better head back to the theatre or we'll miss the matinee. And considering we're guests of honor, that would be in poor taste."

She turned to traipse back to Sterling's i8 but caught sight of the man in overalls near a tree. "Sterling? Can you see that man?"

He turned and looked where she pointed. "What man?"

"There at the edge of the cemetery. In overalls."

Concern filled his eyes as he answered. "No one's there."

"I keep seeing him, but I don't know what he wants. He seems threatening but he comes no closer. And then he simply vanishes."

"Keep seeing him? He doesn't stay here at the graveyard?"

"He was in the church parking lot during Trunk or Treat."

"This spirit can move locations?"

"He seems to, yes." She shuddered. Everything she thought she understood was yanked out from under her. Who was this spirit and what was he trying to tell her? Was he threatening her? Or warning her? An omen of something coming for her?

Whatever this spirit represented, she couldn't get out of this town fast enough. And she hoped they left him behind.

CHAPTER THIRTY-FIVE

KIMBERLY AND STERLING stood beside Jillian, greeting each person as they entered the auditorium. Tickets to this matinee had sold out in moments, even at a premium cost to watch *Blithe Spirit* with *The Wantland Files* crew. The fundraiser would help Jillian keep the theatre operational for now.

And apparently the money Donny left her in his crypto account would save the building. He'd invested well, and the cryptocurrency he'd backed had skyrocketed. Jillian had shared she intended to cash out a chunk for the needed building renovations and would leave the rest in hopes it continued to climb.

"But why did he send us into the caves?" Jillian had demanded. "He could have left that information in the storage unit!"

"But that wouldn't have had *style*," TJ reminded her.

They entered the auditorium and took their seats. Michael rested a hand on hers as the lights dimmed. "Good work on this one."

She shook her head. "I didn't resolve the haunting. Donny has been quiet, but I know he isn't gone. That bothers me. I hate to leave him here, restless."

"You can't make him go. And you saved Hannah. That's not nothing. Maybe Donny wants to stay with his sister a bit longer."

"Maybe."

The play began. Sterling twined his fingers with hers and squeezed.

The players moved on stage. The other audience members watched, laughing at the on-stage antics. But Kimberly noticed a figure at the back of the set. No longer the grotesque, decaying manifestation she'd seen before, Donny was now a younger, healthier spirit. He moved forward and lifted props, levitating them around the stage. The audience went wild with applause, assuming the floating pieces were somehow part of the show. She saw the delighted smile on Donny's face. He finally got the applause he'd been wanting all his life.

Jillian beamed at the audience enjoying her play. Leaning close, she whispered, "Donny is still here? I thought you got rid of him."

"I can't force a translocation," Kimberly whispered back. Well, she could and had, but it was a terrible and difficult process she knew she couldn't handle in her current state.

Donny moved front stage center and stared out into the audience. The speakers crackled with static.

Jillian whispered, "New wiring will top the list of renovations."

"It's Donny," Kimberly told her. "He looks like he wants to say something."

Donny's spirit stared down, clutched his hands together, then looked directly toward Jillian. "I'm . . . sorry."

Kimberly sucked in a breath. "He says he's sorry."

Jillian leaned forward. "I think . . . I think I heard him."

The play continued, but Kimberly couldn't focus on that with the real drama unfolding. "You did?"

Tears escaped Jillian's eyes as she nodded. "I wish I could see him like you do. Oh, Donny. I forgive you. Can you tell him I forgive him?"

Donny seemed to sigh in relief.

"He heard you," she said.

Donny held his hands over his heart and delivered his final line. "'Let us endeavor to live that when we come to die, even the undertaker will be sorry.'"

Kimberly brushed a tear from her cheek. "He says to live well and be happy."

A blue shaft of light, so brilliant it glowed nearly white, opened and shone down beside him. He smiled. "There's my spotlight."

This light was "the light." Not a passage to the Nightshade but the real deal—the door to the next existence. Kimberly grabbed Jillian's arm. "He's going to cross over now."

Donny lifted a hand, waved, and stepped into the light.

On that note, she could end the investigation satisfied, knowing she'd accomplished her goal.

She didn't know what would come next. But she knew she wasn't alone. And now, neither were Hannah and Donny. She squeezed Sterling's hand.

He stared at her with his vivid dark eyes. "You okay?"

"Yes," she answered honestly. "Yes, I am."

And she was ready to take on the next investigation.

SIGN UP FOR MORE

Did you enjoy *Halloween in Hannibal?* If so, please leave a review wherever you purchase books.

Sign up for my newsletter to be the first to know of upcoming releases, chances for contests, and to receive previews and insider information http://www.larabernhardt.com/contact

I'd love to hear about YOUR supernatural encounters! Feel free to reach out and share!

PREVIEW OF CHRISTMAS SPIRIT

PROLOGUE

Macy didn't care what her boss thought, she loved Christmas. He could bah-humbug all he wanted but she wouldn't let him ruin the happy season for her. She sang along to "Winter Wonderland" as she opened the storage closet door. She ran a hand down the boxes, foot tapping in time to the tune playing through the hotel. Finally, she caught sight of the scrawled label she searched for: *Christmas decorations*. She yanked the box loose and noticed another one with the same label. She'd have to make another trip. Hoisting one onto her hip and pushing the door to, she headed for the lobby.

A new employee, Cristal, worked the front desk, singing along with "Baby, It's Cold Outside." Macy smiled, then realized she would need to give the young woman some pointers on how to navigate Christmas around their boss. She dropped the box by the desk. "Oof. That's heavier than it looks." She pointed to a corner by the front door. "I always set up the tree there, so it's visible through the windows."

Cristal clasped her hands and squealed. "Working on Thanksgiving is worth it to start decorating for Christmas."

Macy thought about her daughter home alone and silently begged to differ. "Isn't your family missing you?"

The girl rolled her eyes. "Nah. When I left for college, they were like, good riddance. Besides, I'm a vegetarian, and they refuse to accommodate."

Parents who didn't care if they spent holidays with their children? Macy shuddered at the thought. Too many holidays went by with her working and dreaming about being able to spend more time with her daughter, Abby, who was growing up entirely too fast. Macy felt like she was missing it all. But she had bills to pay—a lot of bills—and what could she do? "You're welcome to join my daughter and me this evening. It'll be a late dinner but better than nothing."

"Awww, thanks, Ms. Crawford. I have plans with some friends though. It's cool."

Macy heard a low moaning sound and spun toward the hallway. Cristal turned with a frown.

"Sick guest?" she wondered. *Great.* A hotel guest probably overdid it on Bourbon Street. Last thing she wanted to do was clean up vomit. "I'll go check. You listen for the phone." Even though no one ever called on Thanksgiving.

Her business casual heels, second-hand from a consignment shop, clicked rapid steps on the tile floor.

The hallway was empty. Strange.

She returned to the storage closet to wrestle the tree from the back as the musical track switched to *Sleigh Ride.*

The closet door stood open.

I know I closed that. She approached slowly, watching for movement, and peeked inside, heart hammering.

Nothing. No sign anything had been moved. *Huh. Someone must have...*

But who? She and Cristal were the only two employees on the clock today. Mr. Flint complained bitterly as it was about being forced to pay time and a half on holidays. He wasn't about to schedule more employees than the bare minimum.

Weird. Maybe she hadn't closed the door all the way and it blew open.

She grappled with the boxes, playing Tetris until she finally managed to extricate the tree box with a huge heave and a grunt.

This time she made certain the door closed all the way, then shuffled back to the lobby, the box banging against her with each step.

Cristal waited anxiously, phone in hand, and waved her over. "Was someone sick?"

She shook her head. "I didn't see anyone. Don't know what that noise was."

"Thank goodness! I have a guy on hold."

"Really? Someone actually called today?"

"It's a guest. He says the WiFi isn't working. What do I do?"

Macy took the phone and pressed the HOLD button. "Good afternoon. Trouble connecting to the WiFi? Go ahead and type in the passcode for me again. That got it? Good! Yes, probably fat-fingered a key. No problem. Glad it was an easy fix."

She hung up and opened the box, lifting pieces of the tree and trying to remember how it went together.

"I should have thought of that!" Cristal said.

"You'll learn. No one knows everything when they start."

"You know how to handle everything. Mr. Flint is so lucky to have you."

"Wish he felt that way."

"He must! He trusted you with his hotel today so he could be home with his family on the holiday."

"He doesn't have a family. Well, one nephew. But I guarantee he's not spending the day with him."

"Oh."

"Yeah. Here, you work on figuring out the tree while I go grab the other box of decorations. We want everything done today so it'll be finished when he comes back tomorrow. That way it would be too much work to take back down, and he will leave it all up."

"Take it down? Why would he take down the Christmas decorations?"

"Technically, he wouldn't. He'd demand we take it back down. He's not really—"

Another moan, longer and louder, filled the hallway.

Cristal jumped. "What *is* that?"

Macy hurried down the hall and rounded the corner—

The storage closet door hung open. And this time a pasty, bloodless face peered out at her.

She opened her mouth to scream but only gaped, incredulous.

This cannot be happening. This cannot be happening.

Chalk-white fingers curled around the edge of the door and widened the gap.

The black pit of a mouth opened, and another agonized moan ensued.

The figure of a man emerged from the closet, chains rattling with each step.

He moaned again, then stared at her with empty eyes that seemed to offer a view of the depths of the universe.

She couldn't move, couldn't even back away as the rattling, wheezing, dusty bones clanked toward her. He leaned low and moaned one word.

"Flint."

MORE BY ADMISSION PRESS

Looking for your next great read?
Visit www.admissionpress.com

A NOTE FROM THE AUTHOR

Hannibal, Missouri is a fantastic place to visit. As always, I incorporated local history and lore into my story while taking liberal creative liberties. References in this book to people from history or myths are made in a fictitious way. No actual living people are depicted in the story.

ABOUT THE AUTHOR

Lara Bernhardt is a Pushcart-nominated writer, editor, and audiobook narrator. She is Editor-in-Chief of Balkan Press and also publishes a literary magazine, *Conclave*. Twice a finalist for the Oklahoma Book Award for Best Fiction, she writes supernatural suspense and women's fiction. You can follow her on Amazon and on all the socials @larawells1 on Twitter and @larabern10 on Facebook, BookBub, and Instagram.

ALSO BY LARA BERNHARDT

The Wantland Files Series
The Wantland Files
The Haunting of Crescent Hotel
Ghosts of Guthrie

Women's Fiction
Shadow of the Taj

www.ingramcontent.com/pod-product-compliance
Lightning Source LLC
Chambersburg PA
CBHW031936110726
47902CB00001B/205